"GIVE HONOR

to the Masters of the Hunt!

"Give honor to the Hunters! In the nine-hundred-and-sixty-fourth Hunt in our illustrious history, forty-seven individuals hunted gallantly from Eclipse to Eclipse and nineteen have gone to join their illustrious ancestors!

"Give honor to the Sacred Prey! Seventy-four fought us valiantly and provided us with a splendid Hunt, and for the three-hundred-and-ninety-eighth time, there was at lest one survivor, who has been brought here so that you may see the rewards which await a successful Prey!

"Honorable and Sacred Prey, we welcome you to the nine-hundred-and-sixty-fifth cycle of hunting of this recorded era. The Hunt will commence at dawn!"

G. Barr

HUNTERS OF THE RED MOON

Marion Zimmer Bradley

D A W   B o o k s ,   I n c .
Donald A. Wollheim, Publisher
1633 Broadway, New York, N.Y. 10019

PUBLISHED BY
THE NEW AMERICAN LIBRARY
OF CANADA LIMITED

Cover art by Carl Lundgren

DEDICATION

Grateful thanks and acknowledgments are due to

PAUL EDWIN ZIMMER

Marshal and Weapons Consultant of the
Society for Creative Anachronism

who kindly supplied me with information about the nature
and use of all the weapons used in the Hunt, and provided
continuity for all the fighting scenes. However, the reader
is urgently requested not to blame him for any feckless
mistakes which I may have made in using the material
which he supplied. Whatever is good or accurate in what
I say of weapons is my good brother's; whatever is wrong
or misinformed is certainly my own.

—M.Z.B.

First Printing, September 1973

19   18   17   16   15   14   13   12   11

 DAW TRADEMARK REGISTERED
U.S. PAT. OFF. MARCA REGISTRADA.
HECHO EN WINNIPEG, CANADA

PRINTED IN CANADA
COVER PRINTED IN U.S.A.

Chapter One

That speck of light had been hanging in the same part of the sky, it seemed, for a long time.

Dane Marsh lounged on the prow of the *Seadrift*, naked except for trunks and a loose shirt flung over his sunburned shoulders, and watched the unmoving point of light. *Sun on the wing of a plane,* he thought. *Sign of life, the first in days. Human life, that is; plenty of flying fish, dolphins; depends how far you want to go down the scale to call life; billions and billions of shrimp and plankton.*

But we're off the regular jet plane routes, and way off the shipping lanes. The last ship I sighted was that tanker nineteen days ago.

He wondered if it *was* a plane.

He entertained himself briefly with the thought of men in business suits, women in nylons and furs, seated in orderly rows, maybe even watching a movie, eighteen hundred miles from the nearest coast. Out here, where two hundred years ago, Captain Bligh and twenty-two men sailed for weeks and months in an open boat, starving and burned up by the sun; and now Pan American Airlines flew over the same area in a few hours, just time enough for an American first-run movie and a couple of drinks.

I wouldn't mind one of those drinks, right now, with ice in it, Dane thought. *Seadrift* did pretty well, all things considered, in the food and drink department, what with freeze-dried chow mein and beef stroganoff, but he would like a long cool drink with ice in it, served to him by one of those pretty stewardesses. A refrigerator on a thirty-foot boat would be stretching things a little.

Damn it, that plane doesn't seem to be moving. It's just hanging there. One place.

Obviously, then, Dane told himself without moving from his idle vantage point, it couldn't be a plane. Reflection on a cloud, or something.

For miles around, in every direction, the Pacific was quiet, slow ripples moving, almost imperceptibly, out of the east and dying away toward the sunset. *Seadrift* was ghosting along, her vast acreage of spinnaker set to catch the lightest of airs—a light breeze usually sprang up about sundown—but for the moment, even the solitary crew was superfluous. Dane Marsh knew he should get up, check the self-steering, go below and make himself a pot of tea, put out a fishline for any stray overnight catch, but the cumulative effect of sun and sea and silence held him half hypnotized, staring at the distant and unmoving light which looked more and more like the typical circular flash of sunlight on bright metal, the wing of a distant plane. He liked the idea that it was a plane, that there were other human beings within sight, if out of reach. Stewardesses in miniskirts.

It's been two hundred and eighty-four days, by actual count, since I saw a woman who could speak English. Or even one who couldn't. Why the hell did I ever get this notion, anyway? Sailing around the world alone in a small boat—it's not as if I'd be the first. Or even the fastest.

It seemed a good idea at the time, that's all.

So what if he wasn't the first? These days, everything worth doing, in the adventure line, had already been done. Climbing Everest. Sailing around the Horn alone. Reaching the North Pole. Everything except going to the moon, and that took a kind of education and sponsorship he never could manage.

I envy the first guy to hike around it on foot. Now there's an adventure for some lucky bastard, someday. . . .

Reluctantly, Dane Marsh hauled himself up from his lazy perch. Work to be done. The sails were slamming in the first wisps of the oncoming night breeze; he adjusted the jib and the poled-out spinnaker slightly, and set a new tack, then went down to root out some supper. Belowdecks the cabin was stifling in the heat; he had debated taking advantage of the quiet sea to cook something hot, but the steambath effect discouraged him. He opened a packet of rye crackers and a tin of cheese, dumped lemon crystals into drinking water and stirred in sugar, and carried the food and drink on deck, to catch the breeze.

The light lingered long in these latitudes at this time of year, and the sun lingered, low and red on the horizon, making a crimson and scarlet track across the barely moving sea. A tiny crescent of moon, a mere scrap of silver, hung low and dim above the setting sun. High above, a glimmer of the evening star—

No, Dane Marsh thought incredulously, *it's the same damn light!*

He knitted his brows, determined to solve the puzzle. A plane? Hell no; the oldest prop plane would have been miles out of sight-range by now. A jet would have been long gone while he was watching it. Satellite? No; they *move.* Weather balloon? Well, *maybe* one could drift this far off an inhabited coast, possibly with the wind from Australia, but it would be a real freak.

He bit into his crackers and cheese, watching the strange light which hung, seeming to brighten, in the slowly fading red twilight. It seemed self-luminous, and was now the apparent diameter of a golf ball.

Some weather phenomenon, no doubt, but one I've never seen in fifteen years spent mostly at sea.

Oh, well, he told himself, if there was one thing you learned at sea, it was that you've always got more to learn. This old world still had plenty of surprises left for people who kept their eyes and ears open, Dane thought, munching at his crackers.

It was getting bigger. Now it was the apparent size of a small dinnerplate, and had elongated somewhat from round to oval.

I wonder if this is what people are seeing when they report seeing flying saucers—excuse me—Unidentified Flying Objects! This was sure as hell some kind of flying object, and it was about as unidentified as he ever saw!

Now he could see that it was definitely solid, although without any idea as to its actual distance he could not judge its size. He watched, in growing wonder and wild surmise, as it settled slowly down toward the surface of the water, and grew ever greater, greater, more huge and unbelievably contoured.

Flying saucer? Flying skyscraper, more like it!

It was bigger than an ocean liner; bigger than a tanker. No plane ever built was this size. *Not even the Russians . . .*

Fear surged over him. Not yet, the obvious fear of the great vessel, but—to a man of Dane Marsh's type—a deeper, more compelling fear.

Have I freaked out? Loneliness does weird things to people. . . .

He fought for calm, setting his teeth and reaching out to

grip the familiar mast of the *Seadrift*. The smooth white paint he had just renewed two months ago, already specked with the relentless eroding of the salt. His own hand, calloused with handling ropes and spars. His pulse, a little elevated with fright, was still perceptible and pounding steadily away, and his eyes were clear, for when he moved his head and blinked the huge strange *thing* had not moved.

Well, I'm not nuts, anyway. Not dreaming or hallucinating.

Therefore, even if there isn't any such thing, that thing is definitely there. If I'm seeing it, and there's nothing wrong with my eyes, it must exist.

And therefore—his breath caught in his throat at the next, inescapable step of his logic—*if no country on Earth has ever built anything remotely like this, it must somehow come from* outside.

He discovered that his arms and legs were ridged, in the heat of the tropical sunset, with gooseflesh. *Outside.* In one great step, his awareness had transcended the slow steps of scientists toward the stars. *There was something out there.*

And it swept over him, with a shuddering thrill. *Did I think there weren't any adventures left?*

Hard on the heels of that came a suddenly icy fear. All this time, and they had kept their very existence secret; what would happen to him if they happened to notice him watching them? He did not yet believe they were malicious. Why should they be? A spaceship capable of traveling interstellar distances (what strange metal was that hull, pale with a shimmer like a peacock's wing?) would pay no more attention to a little ship like the *Seadrift* than he, Dane Marsh, paid to a flying fish. (But then, what did he do when a flying fish landed on his deck in the morning? Sometimes he threw it back. But if he happened to be hungry, he fried it for breakfast.)

Dane Marsh began, moving swiftly and steadily, to tack his ship to wear around. He was curious, yes, but he'd rather watch from a safer distance. He had no desire to end up in a sort of galactic frying pan.

His arms felt heavy and clumsy as he lifted them to haul on the ropes; then a curious buzzing sound, a tingling, began to ring in his ears. He was possessed with a sense of frantic urgency, but it seemed as if he were wading through a sticky pool of molasses; it was an effort to lift his foot from the deck, and the growing sense of unreality swept him with renewed terror.

Is this all a hallucination, then? A bad dream turning into a nightmare?

With savage effort, he twisted his head around so that he could see the great looming ship. Slowly, slowly, a hatchway was opening, and a blinding light shining from inside, but Dane Marsh hit the deck and lay there, clawing faintly as he struggled to rise.

By the time the deck swayed under the strange alien step, he was unconscious, still struggling in his dreams.

They were off the jet routes and *way* off the shipping lanes, and no other eye on Earth saw the great ship before it winked out of normal space five miles above the central Pacific Ocean. The *Seadrift* was found, empty, drifting, five weeks later by a yacht bound for Hawaii. . . .

Chapter Two

Dane Marsh came up to awareness with a savage pain in his throat, rising up out of confused nightmares of wild beasts clawing at his jugular vein, of spurting blood and smells which somehow roused an atavistic terror (lions, fresh blood, the faint rottenness of something dead), and then, all at once, he was conscious. His eyes, flicking open, took in all at once the white cold surroundings, the two forms (nightmare! Man-tall, but flat-faced, *furred*—a lion's mane!) bending over him. The needles still in his throat. He ripped, tensed swelling muscles, struggled to cry out, but only a tearing numbness lanced with split-second prickles of agony burst his throat.

He was strapped down. Tied, hand and foot, not a muscle to move—

Tortured!

He squeezed his eyes shut again, in spasmodic horror, then, fighting for calm, slowly opened them. His throat was numb, now, without pain; had they tried to remove his vocal cords? The two lion-faced creatures had hands not too unlike human hands, working delicately about his throat, but now he felt no pain at all, only an odd numbness. Well, whatever the hell they were up to, he couldn't have moved an eyebrow to stop them, so they couldn't mean him all *that* much harm if they went to this much trouble to anesthetize him.

He looked around. Odd metallic things hanging from smooth bulkheads; unidentifiable, but they'd have been equally baffling, he supposed, in a really up-to-date hospital. He studied the two lion-faced things. They had hands with, he realized, a double thumb, moving with extreme deft suppleness, and the hands were encased in thin cloth of some sort. They both wore coverall garments of gray-blue fabric. He wished he could see what they were doing with his throat. There was a sudden wrench as one of them twisted and adjusted something there, then he felt the painless prick and tug; they were sewing him up. One of them touched him briefly with a long light-tipped wand, and spoke aloud.

"You'd think sooner or later some of these savages would realize we're not trying to hurt them, but they all fight like fiends," the first one said. "This one's not as bad as most. Is he hooked up yet?"

Dane Marsh blinked. Were they speaking English? No, if he listened carefully he could hear the curious guttural syllables, but they made sense. . . .

"I think so, I'll try him," the second, slightly taller one said, and bent over Dane Marsh. "Please don't struggle, and we will let you go; we don't want you to injure yourself. We have simply equipped you with an implanted translator disk. See, now if you can understand what is said to you. Please tell me if you can hear and understand what I am saying."

Dane Marsh found that the straps holding him to the table were slackened slightly so that he could sit up, although his wrists were still strapped down. He ran his tongue over dry lips. He felt parched. His voice felt hoarse and strange as he said, "Yes, I can hear you all right. What—where am I? How did I get here? What do you want with me?"

"All right," said one to the other. "Successful. I don't like the ones where they never do understand, and we have to treat them like cattle. Nice work."

"Mmm, yes. Not much area for the disk in this one. I was afraid I'd cut a nerve. I haven't had much luck with proto-simians. Okay, take him back to the rest, then."

Dane shouted, "Answer me, damn you! What do you want with me? How did I get here? Who are you people, anyway?"

One of the lion-faced things said, "This is the part that always gets me. When they start asking for answers. It's a lousy job, all things considered." He prodded Dane with the light-tipped wand; Dane flinched with the sharp, painful electric shock.

The other creature said, "No need for that, Ferati, he isn't one of the dangerous kind. Anyway, there's a tangler field up there if we need it." He looked at Dane, warily loosing his wrist straps and said, "It isn't our duty to answer your questions, but they will be answered in due time. You have nothing to lose, and everything to gain, by being patient. In a few minutes someone will come to take you back to your quarters. Now if you will go peacefully, perhaps we can make you a little more comfortable. Is your mouth dry? That's only the aftereffects of the anesthetic and the tangler field they used when they brought you on board. Here, try this." He handed Dane a disposable cup of some liquid; Dane found he could move one hand. He sipped it gingerly and found it was sour but remarkably thirst-quenching.

Over his head one of them said, "I wonder if he's going to be one of the more intelligent and tractable ones."

"Hope so. The Old Man is always talking about getting a couple of real wild ones, but last time—"

A speaker on the wall buzzed and one of the lion-faced creatures said without looking up, "Right away," and, taking the cup from Dane, indicated that he should stand up. "Go over to that door. Someone will be there to take you to your quarters. . . ."

Dane dug in his heels stubbornly. "Not until I get a few questions answered," he said. "I know I'm on board a spaceship. But why? Where do you come from? What are you going to do with me?"

The being who had shocked him with the wand made a threatening gesture. "I already told you; it is no part of our duty to answer your questions. Do as you're told and you won't get hurt."

Dane put his head down and rushed. He actually seized the lion-headed creature with one outstretched hand, giving a sharp judo twist.

And the roof fell in on him and he disappeared.

When Dane Marsh woke again he was in a cage.

That was his first impression; shadows of slanting bars running up and down between him and the light, which was bluish-white and pale. A cage.

He stirred, sat up, dizzily clutching his head.

On second look, more prison than cage. A large barred room, lined on one wall with sleeping bunks, netting criss-crossed in front of them—he supposed, to keep the occupants from falling out during fast maneuvers. In the large room there were about a dozen people.

People; loosely. About half of them were human like himself, or with differences too minor for him to see at once. None were the lion-faced breed he had met in the place where he had awakened before, which he supposed was a sort of ship's hospital. But about half of the occupants of the room where he found himself were very much like himself. The others were—different.

There was a being at least eight feet tall, who reminded him strangely of a spider; gray and fuzzy and with strange large eyes; and he had a confused impression of more arms and legs than there ought to be, although he couldn't quite figure out why. There was one who was squat and powerfully built with leathery skin or leathery clothing and a face-mask of the same. It was too much for Dane Marsh to take in all at once.

My God, am I in a zoo? Just one of the animals?

"Not a zoo," said a woman, standing by his bunk, and Dane realized he had spoken aloud. The words sounded strange but Dane seemed to "hear" them resonating against the disk which the lion-things had implanted in his throat. He supposed it was a mechanical translator of some sort; he couldn't even begin to imagine the technology which had created such a thing. "No, you're not in a zoo. Not quite. You'd probably be better off if you were. This is a Mekhar slave ship."

He started to swing his legs over the bunk; the woman bent and helped unstrap the webbing from the front. He said, "How long was I out?"

"A couple of hours. They must have used a tangler set to stun—they have one in the hospital, and I imagine they captured you with one."

Dane thought back to the last moments on the deck of the *Seadrift*. "Yes. My arms and legs kept moving slower and slower and I finally must have passed out. It was a nightmare."

"It was real enough," the woman said somberly. She was about Dane's age, with red hair waving loosely, uncombed, and wearing a sort of loose shirt and trousers which looked like what a Russian or Israeli girl soldier would wear. "Are you from one of the worlds of the Unity? Slaving is forbidden in any of the Unity star-systems, but the Mekhar ships do it anyway; it pays well enough for them to risk it."

Dane said, "I'm sorry. This is too much for me to take in. You mean your ship really does come from the stars?"

She said, "As nearly as I can figure out, we've covered about thirty star-systems. The slave quarters are almost full; I expect they'll be heading for the Mekhar marts quite soon now. It's rare for them to pick up only one person on a planet; does your world have good guard systems against slave raids?''

"None of us on my world have any idea such things exist," Dane said wryly. "People who talk about ships from the stars are usually locked up—or laughed at, anyway, as lunatics. I was sailing alone in a small boat.''

"Out of sight of land? That explains it, then; they just swooped down and grabbed you up, probably expecting to find eight or ten people aboard," the redheaded woman said. "Somebody in the control room is probably getting a clawing-out right now.''

"The Mekhars? Are they the lion-faced things I saw?'' He hesitated, reflecting that she might not know what a *lion* was, but evidently the mechanical translator provided her with the nearest equivalent, for she said, "Yes, they're proto-felines, and I personally think they're the most savage people in the Galaxy. They've been five times refused membership in the Unity, you know. You—oh, excuse me, if your world is a Closed world, you probably don't even know what the Unity is. Do you have space travel?''

"Only on a small scale. We're exploring our own moon and have had two or three manned expeditions to Mars—our fourth planet," Dane said.

"Well, the Unity is—I suppose you'd say it's a loose Peace-and-Trade Federation. It was the Unity which first formulated the concept of Universal Sapience; before that the proto-felines looked down on us—the proto-simians—and proto-reptilians on both. And so forth and so on. You can catch up on that some other time. Tell me, what's your name?''

He told her. "And yours?'' he asked. "How did you happen to be captured? Doesn't your world believe in starships either?''

She shook her head. "No. I took a calculated risk. I'm an

anthropologist and I was exploring a deserted artificial satellite, under permit, for traces of a prehistoric technology. I was warned that there had been a Mekhar raid in the next star-system but it seemed to me a very small chance they'd make it their next stop. I took the chance—and lost. They killed my brother, and one of my three colleagues. One of the others is over there"—she pointed to where a heavyset man, with a strong ethnic resemblance to the woman, was deep in conversation with a tall frail-looking girl—"and the other was wounded in the raid and he's still in the ship's hospital. Unless they've killed him, too, as damaged merchandise." Her tone was indescribably bitter. Dane didn't blame her. "My name is Rianna. For all the good it does me now."

She fell silent, and Dane looked around. Beyond the cage where he was, there were further cages, equally barred and half open, all filled with people as far as he could see. He said, "How can it possibly pay them to stop on a planet for one person?"

She shrugged. "Normally it doesn't. Slaves are luxury merchandise and they usually take more. Before we were luxury goods, I gather we were not so well-treated, but now they go to great pains to keep us well and happy. They even equip us with translator disks, in spite of the fact that it permits us to talk and possibly even plot against them, because—they say—when we can't communicate with our fellow prisoners it's bad for our morale."

There was a stir down the open corridor between the rows of barred cages, and a loud clanging sound. Rianna said, with a wry grimace, "Feeding time for the animals."

Two of the lion-faced creatures were wheeling a large cart down the hallway. As they drew even with each door, one of them leveled a narrow black tube—evidently a weapon of some sort—at the doorway while the other unloaded several flat packaged trays from the cart, each tray in a different color, and carried them into the cell—or cage. Dane watched the proceeding without moving. When they had finished, the clanging sound came again and Rianna said, "We can go now and get the food. If anyone moves while they're unloading, he gets shot with the nerve-gas. It might not kill you, but it's set to maximum pain-stimulation and it's like being dipped in boiling oil." She shuddered. "I got in the way when we were captured; it was three days before I could move without wanting to scream."

Dane had wondered about that; why all the prisoners in any one cage didn't rush the guards at once. He said, "Doesn't anyone ever try to get loose?"

"Not twice," she said with a wry face. "And if you *did* get loose, where would you go? There are eighty Mekhars, all with nerve-guns, loose on this ship—maybe more." She moved to where the other cell-mates were taking up the food. Rummaging through the stacked trays, she found two color-coded with blue and green stripes. "This is Universal coding for proto-simian food. In a pinch you can eat the plain green or the plain blue. Never touch red-coded or orange-coded stuff; it hasn't the right vitamins. And the yellow-coded stuff will poison you; it's coded for insectivores."

The redheaded man with the strong ethnic resemblance to Rianna came over to them, tray in hand. They dropped on the floor to eat. He said to Dane, "Welcome to the fellowship of the damned," as he tore open his package. "My name is Roxon. I see Rianna has been welcoming you."

"Dane Marsh," Dane said. He slowly opened the package. Heated by some internal mechanism, the food was smoking hot, and, when he began to spoon it up, surprisingly tasty; some kind of mush, slightly sweet, some kind of crisp textured stuff, slightly salty; a soup-like liquid, somewhat bitter, but good. "At least these Mekhars, or whatever you call them, don't mean to starve us."

"Why should they?" The squat creature with the leathery skin—at close range Dane could see that it *was* skin—came and hunkered down beside them. "Welcome, fellow thinker, in the name of Universal Sapience and Peace." His package was coded in yellow and red stripes. Dane caught a whiff of it; it smelled slightly sulphurous and decaying, but the leathery-skinned creature began to eat it with gusto, using his long prehensile fingers with extreme fastidious delicacy, allowing the food to rest only on the tips, and tearing it up with long strong teeth. "Why should they not treat us well? We are their profit. My world is a poor one and I am seldom this well-fed, but what does the Voice of the Egg say? May his wisdom live till the suns burn out. *Surely it is better to hunt flies in a stinking swamp, and live at peace, than to feast on fine foods in a great house torn by war and strife.*"

Dane almost chuckled. To hear calm philosophy spoken by a huge and savage reptile—the giant, squat being turned, his teeth bared.

"Do you laugh at the wisdom of the Divine Egg, stranger?" His voice was very soft and gentle.

"By no means," Dane said, drawing back slightly. "There is a similar proverb in my own—er—my own race's Great Book of Wisdom; it says, 'Better to live in a corner of the housetop than to dwell in a broad house with a brawling woman.' "

"Er, hmmm," rumbled the lizard-man, "Surely all wisdom is one, my proto-simian friend. Even in slavery one may find material for philosophy, then. Yet share your laughter, friend."

Dane said, fumbling for words, "Among my people, it is thought amusing when words of peace are spoken by—by anyone of—of a warlike and fierce aspect, and by my standards you look—er—fierce. No offense meant."

"None taken," he said gently, "although surely it is the large and fierce person who needs to look and speak with peaceful wisdom, in order not to affront others, while the small and weak person proclaims his peaceful nature with his very appearance."

"It doesn't always work that way on my world," Dane said. Not in his wildest dreams had he ever thought of discussing philosophy over a shared meal with a giant reptile—no; he was obviously a man of some sort. But it was mind-boggling, certainly a Mad Tea Party if there ever was one.

"My name is Aratak," the leathery lizard-man said. Dane told the man his name, and he repeated it thoughtfully. "I know not what a Dane may be, but a Marsh is my homeplace name, and we are therefore home-brothers, friend Marsh. Let us be brethren in misfortune, then, since all marshes are one marsh, as all seas are one sea, and all swamps are one swamp within the Cosmic All."

Dane Marsh scratched his head. There was an element of madness about this giant philosopher that he liked. "It suits me," he said.

"We shall explore one another's spiritual philosophy at leisure," Aratak said. "As for me, I have proved what I knew, but never fully believed before; that Universal Sapience is a truth and not only a spiritual philosophy. I have learned in these weeks of slavery that true brotherhood can exist between men and humanoids. I had paid only lip service to it before; it seemed to me that no true intelligence could exist in proto-simians, for they must spend so much of their metabolic cycle enslaved to their reproductive needs. Simians on my planet are only good for pets, and I had never known one in the Fellowship of the Unity before. So to all of you"—Dane and Rianna ducked as his large-clawed gesture took them all in—"my eternal thanks for an enlargement of my spiritual growth."

Roxon said somberly, "Let's hope we live long enough for the spiritual growth to do us some good in what's left of our lives," and they all fell silent again. Dane scraped his tray clean of the last morsel of food and put it aside. He felt better now. He knew where he was, and there was no immediate prospect of death or torture.

Nevertheless the prospect was anything but pleasing. All his life Dane Marsh had been a man of action, in a modern world where that takes some doing. In modern society most men walk an orderly path from the cradle to the grave, not acting so much as being acted upon; Dane had spent his whole life breaking out of that mold, and now the enforced helplessness weighed upon him with an almost personal rage. Caught up without warning, caged, equipped against his will with the damned translator disk which made a thin painless lump against the skin of his neck—it made things easier, but still it was something that had been *done to him* against his will.

Now that the food was restoring his strength, the infuriating sense of helplessness was turning rapidly to anger. These people, these citizens of a great Galactic civilization, might sit in their cages and wait for whatever the Mekhar slave ships did to them; he didn't intend to.

He heard, outside, the clanging sound which he had heard first when the Mekhar came into the corridor to distribute the food. He filed it away for future reference; evidently a single mechanism unlocked all the cage doors when the feeding cycle began and locked them again when it was completed. The Mekhar were evidently pretty confident in their weapons and the terror they inspired in their prisoners, to leave the cages unlocked so long. That knowledge might be useful later, but for the moment Dane decided to bide his time.

The other captives in their cell—the hairy creature who gave the impression of more arms and legs than he should have had (Dane decided it was the curious way the limbs were segmented and joined), a couple of ordinary-looking men and women, a tall narrow-faced creature who seemed covered with dark fur—were finishing their trays of food. One tray had not been touched, and Dane noticed it had the green-and-blue coding that identified human food. He looked around the cell. Yes; on a low bunk beside the wall, a slender form lay motionless, enveloped in a long white robe, the face turned away from them.

Dane said, "What's the matter with that one? Hurt, sick, dead?"

"Dying," Rianna said quietly. "She has refused food for ten meal-periods now. She is an empath from Spica Four; they prefer to die, when away from their worlds. It won't be long now. It's all we can do for her now—to let her die in peace."

Dane looked at the redheaded woman with a throb of revulsion. "And you're all just sitting here and *letting* her starve herself to death?"

"Of course," Rianna said indifferently. "I told you, they *always* die, away from their own world and their own people."

"And it doesn't bother you!" Dane burst out passionately.

"Oh, it bothers me." Her voice was quiet. "But why should I interfere with her chosen fate? Sometimes I think she is wiser than we."

Dane's face set in lines of disgust. He scrambled to his feet and picked up the extra packet of food. He said, "Well, *I'm* not going to sit here and watch a woman die, if I can do anything about it." He strode across the room to where the woman lay. He was fuming. *Just sit there and let her starve herself to death!*

She did not move as he approached her, and for a moment he wondered if she was already dead, or too far gone to be within his reach. He stood for a few moments over her bunk, looking down in a sort of wonder at the beauty of the girl who lay there.

Formless thoughts cascaded through his mind: *This is what I seem always to have been seeking, that elusive something I always thought must be just over the next mountain peak . . .*

*beyond the next wave . . . at the end of the rainbow. I didn't
know it could be a woman . . . or take a woman's form. . . .*

*And she's lying here dying, and we're both hopeless and in
prison. Do I see her as all beauty only because it's too late
. . .? Does the impossible dream come within reach only
when it's forever out of reach?*

In a wonder that was beyond pain, he stood motionless, the
food tray forgotten and hanging from his hand; then some
faint, imperceptible movement like a soft breath made him
aware that she was still alive. And at once his formless
thoughts of impossible beauty receded in a wash of hard,
practical sanity. Forget all that! She was just a girl, lying here
slowly dying, but maybe not too far gone yet. The wonder
and awe died away in a surge of purely human pity. He knelt
down beside her and reached out, lightly, to touch her shoulder.

Before his hand actually touched her, as if the very clamor
of his thoughts disturbed her, she stirred and turned slightly
toward him. Her eyes, deep-set beneath feathery dark brows,
opened.

She was so pale that somehow he had expected the eyes to
be blue; instead they were deep russet-brown, the wide eyes
of a forest animal. Her lips moved slightly as if she were
trying to speak, but her voice was too weak to be heard; it
was only a faint murmur of protest, of curiosity.

He said in a gentle voice, "Here, I've brought your food.
Try to eat."

A murmured negative.

"Now listen," Dane said firmly. "This is nonsense. While
you're alive you have a duty to all of us; to keep up your
strength, in case we have a chance for escape or something
like that. Suppose we were rescued, or escaped, and you
were too weak to move, and we had to carry you, and we
were all recaptured because we had to stop and help you
along? Wouldn't that be a dreadful thing to do to all of us?"

Her lips moved again and somehow he had the impression

of a faint smile, although the limp and strengthless features did not actually move. The words were so quiet that Dane had to bend low to hear.

"Why should any of you . . . drink my cup . . .?"

"Because we're all human, and all in this together," he said firmly. But he wondered, were they really? None of them had cared enough to keep the girl alive, and maybe it was that knowledge that had made her want to die. . . .

"Well, anyway, *I* care," he said, and his fingers sought her hand. "Come on. If you're too weak to feed yourself, I'll feed you." He tore open the package, watching the self-heating element gradually permeate it with steaming heat. He spooned up a little of the soupy liquid and put it to her lips. "Come on, swallow," he said. "Start with this, it's easy."

For a moment he thought she would keep her lips obstinately shut; then she relaxed them and let the soup slip inside, and after a moment he saw her throat move and knew she had swallowed it. He felt a vast, wild sense of elation, but he was careful not to show it, only withdrawing the spoon and raising another careful spoonful to her lips. After two or three more reluctant mouthfuls she stirred as if she wanted to raise herself, and Dane put his arm around her and supported her shoulders; he fed her the soup and a little of the mush, then withheld the spoon when she nodded for more.

"Not just now. You shouldn't eat too much right away after such a long fast; wait a little before you take any more," Dane advised, and she smiled faintly in comprehension as he let her slide down on her pillow. "Yes, try to sleep again now, and next time you'll be stronger."

Her eyes were closing with weakness, but she opened them again with effort and whispered, ". . . are you?"

"Just another prisoner," he said. "My name's Dane Marsh. We'll get acquainted when you're stronger. And your name is—"

"Dallith," she whispered, and abruptly dropped into sleep

again, as completely withdrawn from him as if she were dead.

Dane stood for a few more moments watching her, then straightened, reclaiming what was left of the food tray and laying it on a piece of furniture.

Dallith. How lovely, and how it suited her delicate face and wild-creature eyes. For the moment it was enough to know that she lived, that she had *chosen* to live. He turned away, seeing that the other prisoners had broken up into separate groups; but Rianna was still watching him. As he came away she said with a deep bitterness, "You fool! What have you done?"

Dane said, "I think she'll live. It only needed someone to care whether she did or not. Any of you could have done it."

Rianna said with inexpressible wrath, "How could you do that to her? After she had given up, to wake her again to hope—and suffering—oh, you meddlesome *fool!*"

Dane said, "It's not in me, to sit and let anyone die. While there's life, there's hope. *You're* alive, aren't you? And by choice?"

She only sighed and turned away from him. She said, not looking back, "I only hope you never know what you've done."

Chapter Three

There was no way to measure time, in the Mekhar slave ship, except by meal-periods and by the periods when the ship, or at least the slave quarters, were darkened for sleep. Nevertheless Dane Marsh estimated afterward that some three weeks, by his own reckoning, passed without any major incident.

The main event of this time, by his own awareness, was the slow return of Dallith from willful death to life. She slept, that time, for some hours, and when she woke Dane fed her again. The next time he encouraged her to sit up for a few minutes and, when she was able to stand and move around, he asked Rianna to help her to the bathing quarters set apart for the females in their section. He had made the request with some qualms—after all, Rianna had expected, almost wanted the girl to lie there and die, and he had halfway forseen that she would refuse to involve herself at all—but to his surprise she agreed and thereafter she took over a good part of Dallith's daily care, with an almost motherly concern. Dane didn't try to understand it, but he accepted it gratefully.

For a long time Dallith was not strong enough to talk much, and he did not press her. He was content to sit by her side and let her hold his hand . . . almost, he thought, as if in some way he could give her some of his own strength and vitality. But she was growing in strength daily, and one day she smiled at him and asked about him.

"And you're from a world none of us have ever heard of. Strange, that they should risk so much to come there. Or perhaps not, if all your people are as strong as yourself."

He shrugged. "I've spent most of my life hunting new adventures. This is just a little more bizarre than most, that's all. I got hooked early on the idea that nobody would willingly pass up any kind of experience that was—what do they say—neither illegal, immoral, nor fattening."

She laughed a little. Her laugh was enchanting, as if all the gaiety in the world dwelt within her voice. "Are all your people like that?"

"No, I guess not. A lot of them settle down early and never do anything. But the adventurer strain keeps coming back. I guess it's a pretty durable part of our makeup." He remembered then that Rianna had told him that Dallith's people invariably died, away from their home world, and bit his lip to keep from asking questions about that. But as if she followed his thoughts, a shadow passed over her face. Her sadness seemed as all-pervasive as her gaiety, as if her small slight body held room for only one emotion at a time and it wholly possessed her. She said, "I only hope your strength and bravery don't mean that the Mekhars have some especially fearful fate planned for you."

"All I can do is wait and see what happens," he said, "but like I told you, while there's life, there's hope."

The shadow lay deep on her. She said, "I could not imagine, could not even dream, of hope or anything good ahead, away from my world and my people." Her voice was desolate. "Oh, others have left our world, but with some purpose, and never—never alone."

Dane said, "It's like a miracle that you came back. But it's a miracle I still can't completely understand."

She said simply, "You reached me. I felt your strength, and your will to live, so that I could believe in life again. It was that which fed me . . . your own hope and your belief in life ahead as well as behind. And with so much will to live, there was no room in me for death, and so death took his hand away from me and I began to live again. The rest was"—a small disinterested shrug—"only mechanics. The important thing was that you still believed in life, and you could share your belief with me."

He clasped her small hand in his. The fingers were as soft as if they were boneless, completely pliant, molded to his. "Come, Dallith, are you trying to tell me that you read my mind, or my emotions, or something?"

"Of course," she said, surprised. "What else?"

Well, how can I say it isn't true? It seems to have happened, and anyway she believes it. Dane thought, but he still felt a little disquieted; uncanny. Still, he was content, for as her strength grew, Dallith clung to him more and more. Sometimes it almost frightened him, that she should be so completely dependent on his will—what would she do if they were separated? he thought—but mostly it did not trouble him, for she was not obtrusive or demanding. Most of the time she was content to sit quietly at his side, without speaking, almost like a shadow, while, during the next days and weeks, he took the measure of his fellow prisoners.

He seemed to be the only one—at least in their separate cell—from an isolated world. All of the others were, more or less, from the same interstellar civilization as Rianna. They were a mixed crew. The spider-thing was from a hot, wet world where his race was in a minority, and his name was an incomprehensible mangle of sibilants. And even the enormous lizard-man, Aratak, found his mental processes inaccessible, although he tried. He told Dane kindly, "He is very bewildered. I do not think he is sure what has happened; his mental processes have been shocked." Dane was less charitable; privately he didn't believe the spidery alien *had* any mental processes worth noticing. All he seemed able to do was huddle in a corner, hissing at anyone who came near, and when food was brought sidle out in a rush, take it, and retreat with it. Dane wrote him off as probably being of no use in their present trouble.

Rianna and Roxon, the two sturdy red-headed anthropologists, were far more congenial. Dane kept forgetting that they were not Earthmen like himself, unless one of them happened to allude to some commonplace of their lives which to him, was straight out of a science fiction movie . . . Rianna offhandedly saying that she had served a four-year apprenticeship in alien technology surveying an asteroid belt for fragments of the civilization on the exploded world; Roxon complaining that the main axis of the civilization was interested only in proto-feline technologies and tended to ignore the proto-simians (or humans) as being superficial. "Just because the damned proto-felines invented the extra-light drives, they think they own the Universe," he grumbled more than once.

As for Aratak, the lizard-man quickly became a companion, then, surprisingly, a friend. The immense alien seemed quickly more human than any of the others. His gray, rugose skin, his huge claws and teeth, were quickly forgotten; his mind worked, Dane swiftly found out, very much like Dane's own. His philosophy reminded Dane very much of the Hawaiians and Filipinos he had met on his first voyage to the Pacific; a calm acceptance of life, a willingness to take whatever came, not exactly submitting to it, but going along with it until something better came along, and incidentally getting what was good out of it. He never left a crumb of his food, he slept long and well, and he tended to fill every lull in the conversation with some excerpt from the Wisdom of the Divine Eggs—who had been, Dane gradually gathered, the Confucius, Lao-Tzu, Hillel, and Hiawatha of his race. On the surface he seemed content and even complacent in their captivity, enough so as to be infuriating.

But Dane was sure it was not quite what it seemed. At first this was only a suspicion; on the eighth or ninth "day" of their captivity, the suspicion ripened into certainty.

That was the day when a man in the next cage, or cell, went mad. Dane saw him crouch, when the clanging sound came which meant that the Mekhars were on the way with food, tense and huddled within himself and all one purpose which could almost be seen. And the instant that the food-cart came into sight around the curve of the corridor he rushed the door, flung it open, and threw himself against the edge of the cart, sending it careening back and knocking the Mekhar who pushed it off his feet.

For an instant Dane tensed, thinking, *Now! Now, if they all rush him at once, at once, he couldn't kill more than one or two of them—*

He actually began to spring; and then the man at the cart began to yell, incoherently, a hoarse half scream.

"Come on, you bastards! Kill me all at once, not by inches! Come on, everybody get them, better to die fighting than sit here waiting—" He grabbed the end of the food-cart and ran it over the prostrate body of the Mekhar, by now howling gibberish and screaming. Dallith shrieked and hid her face in her hands. Aratak gripped his claws on the bars, and as Dane tautened his muscles for a rush the lizard-man reached out one hand and grabbed him. His claws dug into Dane's shoulder, tearing his shirt.

"Not now," he said. "Don't throw your life away like this. *Not now!*"

The loose prisoner was still howling and raging, charging

up and down with the runaway food-cart. The other Mekhar raised his weapon and gestured; the madman did not seem to see him. He ran right up against him and in the instant before the food-cart ran him down the Mekhar with the weapon raised it—almost, it seemed to Dane, reluctantly—and shot him.

The man screamed, a terrible tearing sound. He dropped to the floor, writhing, convulsing, froth coming from his mouth as his muscles went into spasm after spasm of shuddering. He screamed and screamed, fainter and fainter, and at last he lay still, twitching and still convulsing. The Mekhar bent and dragged him into his cell, gesturing at his cell-mates with the drawn weapon. They all edged back before it, with horrified gasps and murmurs.

The feeding went on without further incident; but Dane could not eat, until Dallith, white as her own loose robe, refused food and faltered into the women's area to vomit; then, with hard self-discipline, Dane forced himself to pick up his food and chew it, doggedly. He should have known. Dallith was so much a reflection of his own moods. . . .

With the new knowledge of this, he ate, refusing to think about the would-be escapee; when Dallith, gray and shaking, came back, he pulled her down beside him and gently fed her little pieces from his own tray until the color began to come back into her cheeks, then sat by her until she slept. The wounded man in the next cell moaned and twitched and foamed and screamed more and more faintly, although his cell-mates tended him, until some time that night he died. The next morning at feeding-time the Mekhars hauled his body away.

The rows of cells were very quiet as the man's body was taken away. But when the Mekhars disappeared again and the clanging sound of the cell-block lock assured them all that the Mekhars were gone, the quiet tension of horror broke and everyone began talking at once.

Dane found Aratak by his side; the lizard-man's great scaled paws, claws flicking in and our, rested lightly on his shoulder. He said to Dane, "For a moment, yesterday, I thought you were going to throw your life after his."

"For a moment I thought of it. But it isn't in me to commit suicide, and I realized in time that was what he was doing. If everyone had joined him, of course, we probably could have done it."

"Yes," Aratak said. "This has been on my mind. But it must be carefully planned and decided. A mad rush, even with the wild hope that the others will join us, is not the way to begin such an effort. The Divine Egg has said that a man is a fool who holds his life too dear—but twice a fool is he who holds it cheap enough to throw away."

Dane glanced guardedly around. Dallith was sleeping, and he was glad; already the fear of frightening her was a daylong preoccupation with him. (He asked himself then: was it love? Certainly not in a sexual sense, at least not yet. But a constant, living preoccupation, so that her welfare was more to him than his own, so that she lived somewhere in the innermost core of his being . . . yes; call it love.) Then he said, "I take it you go along with me—that it ought to be possible to escape, with care and cooperation. I thnk these Mekhars underrate us. They probably think no one but themselves is clever enough to think it out. But have you noticed that the doors are unlocked, and virtually unguarded, for the best part of half an hour, twice a day?"

"I've noticed," Aratak said. "For a time I thought it seemed almost too easy. As if they were trying to tempt us to escape, for some unknown reason of their own. But why would they do that? Sheer blood-lust? They could have one of us up to kill every day, if that were their pleasure. So I have come around to the conclusion you seem to have reached; that it is their arrogance. They simply do not believe that anyone except themselves could take advantage of such an opportunity;

they believe we simply fear them and their weapons too much.''

He stopped; his normally placid voice was fierce.

''Would you like to teach those damned cat-things their mistake?''

Dane thrust out his hand in a spontaneous gesture of camaraderie. ''I'm with you.'' Only when the scaly paw, claws carefully retracted, closed gingerly over his hand, did he recall that his new comrade was not what most people would call a man.

Agreed, they sat down in a corner of the cell to make their plans. ''We can't do it alone, just the two of us. And it's going to need time—and planning.''

''True. The Divinely Wise Egg has told us that an act of folly can be successful only if it is planned twice as wisely as an act of wisdom.''

The basis of the plan was simplicity itself and hardly more complex than that of the man who had died; to take advantage of the early unlocking and late closing of the cell to slip out, rally other prisoners to join them, knock the weapon from the hands of the Mekhar guard and force their way out of the slave quarters. The Mekhar might kill one or two of them before they were disarmed—Dane faced the possibility that he might be one of the first ones killed, probably, in fact, *would* be—but certainly the Mekhar couldn't kill them all, and the rest would escape.

Once they were out of the slave quarters, what then? They would have to face the rest of the crew; in the hospital area there were tangler fields, and perhaps in other areas of the ship too.

''We can't do it alone,'' he said to Aratak.

''I never thought we could.''

''But we can't even *plan* it alone. I don't know enough about the Mekhars; I don't know enough about your spaceships; I don't know enough about your civilization or weapons or even your Unity. We need help, and quickly, even to make sensible plans.''

"I think you are right,'' the great lizard-man said. "We must decide which of our colleagues we can approach for help, and which of us would go mad like that poor creature and give us away with rashness or panic, or even betray us to the Mekhars in return for some small advantage—oh, yes, some of us in here, even, might do that.'' The edges of his leathery gray jaws began to glow slightly, luminous. "I will consult the wisdom of the Egg. And I suppose you will break it first to Dallith.''

Dane felt his throat close with a spasm of sudden fear; not for himself, but for the girl. He had tried so hard to keep all upsetting thoughts away from her; and the man who had gone berserk had upset her so greatly that he had been afraid, for a moment, that she would drop back into that deathly, death-seeking lassitude. "I think not,'' he said hoarsely. "First I will speak to Rianna.'' Perhaps Dallith could be kept free of this, protected until all the danger was over. . . .

He was beginning, now, to be able to distinguish subtle changes of expression on Aratak's leathery countenance; but he did not, yet, know what emotions ridged the rugose forehead and made the small wattles around the amphibian's gill-slits glow luminous. Aratak was moved; but whether by sympathy, disagreement, or annoyance Dane Marsh could not yet tell. His voice was as flat as ever when he said, "Well, you proto-simians know one another as I never could, so perhaps you are right. I will inquire carefully and seek wisdom; speak to Rianna if you will.''

Dane waited until the next meal period, and when all the inmates of their particular cell had seized their coded food trays and were seeking places to eat, he laid a hand on Rianna's arm.

"I want to talk to you,'' he said in an undertone. "Sit here beside me, in this corner, and eat.'' As they tore open the strips of their trays, he outlined what he had noticed about the locking and unlocking of the cell doors, and saw her dark eyes light up fiercely.

"I've wondered if anyone else saw that! It seems that everyone else here is either a coward, or insanely rash! You're right, something could be done, but what could I, a woman, do alone? I'm with you, Dane, even if I'm the first one shot down!"

He grinned a little sourly. "I thought you were the one preaching the virtues of resignation. You were feeling hopeless enough to let Dallith die."

"I was doing what seemed best on the basis of what I knew of her people," Rianna said stiffly. "Anyone can act in ignorance. I'm enough of a scientist, I hope, to change my theories as I acquire more facts. After observing the Mekhars for a few periods—and the quality of our fellow prisoners—I feel a little more optimistic."

"You do know," Dane said slowly, "that if we take the lead, you and I may very well be the first ones to be shot down? It's not a pleasant death."

"But at least when it's over, I won't have to worry about what happens next, would I? But just in case we should survive long enough to have that particular worry, what happens after that? I take it you don't mean to stop at letting us out of the cages. What next?"

"I don't know," Dane said frankly. "That's why I came to you. I'm no good as the leader of this enterprise. I might be able to help us bust out of the cages. But once we're out, I'm about as much use as sails on a spaceship. I'm the one from the backward world, remember. What I know about spaceships could be painlessly engraved on my thumbnail in large block letters. I'd kind of thought that we might hold the Mekhar guards hostages for our own freedom; arrogant races usually hold the lives of their own kind very precious, even if they treat other races as expendable. But I don't know the

Mekhars. And even if we could manage to kill off or subdue every damned lion-face on the ship, we'd still be out of my element. I wouldn't know how to get us to a safe port, or even how to hit the distress button and yell for help if we started to crash-land or fall into a sun.''

"Oh, as far as that goes, Roxon has a pilot's certificate," Rianna said. "I don't think he's ever handled anything this *size*—he certainly isn't licensed to—but the ultralight drives are standard all through the known Galaxy. Once the Mekhars are out of the way, he could land us somewhere inside the Unity."

Dane reflected that this wouldn't help *him* much, but after all, that was a small point. He couldn't help being better off inside a civilized government—no matter how strange or alien—than outside it. The Unity at least didn't deal in slaves.

"I suppose the next step is to enlist Roxon as part of our plan, then," he said, "if you're sure we can trust him. You know him. I don't."

Rianna said, in disgust, "What do you take him for? He's a civilized citizen."

"Presumably, so is that poor chap who rushed the nerve-guns," Dane said. "I wasn't impugning his standards of decency. I simply don't know him at all. How can I be in a position to judge how brave he is? How likely he is to panic? How well he holds up in a crisis? Or even how well he can hold his tongue and keep from talking to the wrong people? Why in hell do you think I asked you first?"

Her mouth lifted in a small smile and suddenly she looked younger and prettier. "I think I've just had a compliment," she said. "Thank you, Marsh. I'll talk to Roxon. I've known him for a long time, and I'd trust him with my life, my personal fortune, and my scientific reputation, if that's any indication."

"Look. I'm sorry, I didn't mean to offend—"

She shrugged. "Forget it. You have no reason to trust him,

nor has he any reason to trust *you*. He has a prejudice against inhabitants of habitable worlds which haven't joined the Unity.''

"How in—how could I join your what's-it, Unity, when nobody on our world was ever given any inkling that it even *existed?*''

"I didn't say Roxon's prejudice was rational," Rianna said coldly. "I said he *had* such a prejudice. I was stating a fact, not making a value judgment. But Roxon would probably say there must be some good and sufficient reason why your world has never been offered the Unity.''

That sobered Dane a minute; but it was pointless to get involved in discussing that right now. As Rianna was turning away he stopped her a moment, and said suddenly, ''Why is it, then, that *you* trust me?''

Another small shrug. ''Who knows? Maybe it's just your pretty blue eyes. Or maybe I'm using Dallith as a barometer. And speaking of Dallith, she's staring at you with that wistful look. Maybe she can't eat unless you hold her hand. You'd better go and cheer her up while I talk to Roxon. None of us ought to behave in any strange ways while we're plotting, or the Mekhars might get wise.''

She went off, and Dane glanced around for Dallith; but she was not looking at him, and Dane did not at once make a move toward Dallith, following Rianna with his eyes. What were her real feelings? Did he know her well enough to judge even the most elementary ones?

Rianna knelt beside Roxon where he sat alone with his empty food tray still on his lap; she put her head close to his and Dane watched anxiously. The one thing that must not happen is that any of them should seem to be plotting or conspiring. Or would the Mekhars even notice? But surely it would be dangerous, for people to begin to gather in groups, talking secretly, whispering, trying to avoid being overbearing—

As he watched, Roxon dropped the food tray, put his arms around Rianna, and drew her down beside him. Dane thought, suddenly a little shocked, *Like this? Right in front of everyone? In a cage?* Then he told himself sternly not to impose his own standards—one little corner of one little planet—on others; even on some parts of Earth this behavior might be quite natural; some South Sea islanders not only made love in public but expected you to join in and got offended if you didn't. He forced himself to look away, as they drew closer together.

Dallith said quietly in his ear, "It is not what you think. Does it matter to you?"

He turned, startled and a little abashed. He said defensively, "Remember, I'm the guy from the backwoods planet who doesn't know the local customs—or rather, knows only his own local customs—"

"It is not the custom of my people either, but you know what I am, I can sense emotions, and I tell you again, there is no desire between them—if that matters to you."

"I don't give a hang what they do," Dane muttered. His ears were red and he was furiously angry at himself because she could read his embarrassment. "Why should it matter to me?"

"My people never ask ourselves *why* other people are as they are," Dallith said coolly, "since we cannot escape the emotions which make them behave as they do, it would be only an added trouble to ask ourselves why. I am embarrassed only because you are, but there is no reason for it. They are pretending it, and if you think a moment you will surely understand the sensible reason for their pretense."

"No. That I can't understand. Why should they—oh. You mean, so the Mekhars won't think they are conspiring?"

"Of course. Rianna is very clever," Dallith said. Her large dark eyes dwelt a moment on the two closely intertwined bodies, half clothed, heads together, whispering, and she smiled. "It is, of course, the one thing they could pretend to do which the Mekhars would never trouble themselves to suspect or to interrupt. It is part of their arrogance, you understand. This, perhaps, you do not know—how proto-felines look down on us proto-simians because—how can I say this? You are embarrassed and I cannot help feeling what you feel—"

She looked at the floor and moved her foot restlessly. "Well, to put it very simply: we proto-simians are supposed to be continual slaves to our sexual appetites. So when you look at Rianna and Roxon, and you think they are talking privately, and perhaps it is suspicious; the Mekhars would look at them and think, oh, yes, just like those ape-people, whatever else they might be doing, how like them to stop and—and fornicate. You see? Rianna is clever."

"She is," Dane said. "I'd never have thought of that." He felt ruffled and on edge. Even Aratak had said something like that, *You proto-simians are involved so much of the time with your reproductive cycle. . . .* It was a little humiliating to be thought of as part of a race which thought of nothing but sex.

Welcome, fellow, to the monkey house at the zoo—female monkeys always in heat. Watch the show. Oh hell, probably other—other races?—couldn't care less. Did he get any charge out of watching a couple of dogs in the street, or a couple of pigeons courting on the windowsill? Dane turned his eyes away from the all-too-realistic spectacle of Rianna and Roxon. No one else seemed to be paying the faintest attention, even among the humans.

Let's hope Rianna's giving him a full run-down on the plan—and that he likes the idea. Because, without it, I'm not going to know where to begin. Aratak and I couldn't do much, alone. And, damn it, I've got plenty on my mind—like an escape attempt—without worrying about somebody else's sex life!

As the thought of the escape crossed his mind again he

remembered, with some unease, that he had been afraid to break this to Dallith. Now, it seemed, she knew—or did she? It was hard to tell whether she read his thoughts, or only mirrored his emotions. Now, as if mirroring his own deep disquiet, her small slender fingers groped for him and clung to them. Her hand felt cold. Dane squeezed it, hard, trying to keep calm and reassuring.

He had always thought of himself as an adventurer. But a solitary one. He knew his own limits, his abilities, what he could trust himself to accomplish and what he couldn't do. He had been accused, once, of taking risks, and had denied it firmly. "I do dangerous things, sure," he'd said, "but unless I get struck by lightning—and that could happen when I'm home in bed—I know so well what I can and can't do that by the time I decide to do it, it isn't taking a risk anymore."

But that was only true when he was relying on his own known abilities. Now he must put all his faith in strangers, some of them not even human. Aratak had a reassuring strength and solidity, and Rianna's bravery and resourcefulness had given him some confidence. But the others? They were all unknown quantities, and the habit of being self-reliant didn't help you at all when it was a question of doing dangerous things with other people. Rather the reverse.

He let go of Dallith's hand, knowing that as she sensed his fear her own would grow, and said, "We'll talk about this later. I want to be sure what I think."

As usual, she did not protest, or challenge him, but accepted his mood quietly as if it were her own, and went away to her own bunk. Rianna and Roxon had moved apart now and Dane wondered what she had said to him, what he had replied. It would be dangerous to go and ask. Of course he could also pretend to be overcome by a lustful mood—he dropped that line of thought, fast. It led nowhere, and could provide a hell of a lot of complications he didn't need. Hadn't Dallith asked, *Why does it matter to you?*

He couldn't answer that one, and didn't want to try.

Chapter Four

Rianna did not approach him until the next meal-period, when as they were taking up their trays she sorted his out for him and said, in an undertone, "Roxon agrees. He cannot pilot this ship alone, but he can handle the communication equipment and the Navigation Central will help him, of course. He will speak to another, in the next cell, who is known to him. You can trust him; he is a good judge of men. He was surprised that it was you who made this plan, but that is his prejudice, and he admits it."

"Damn nice of him," Dane said, a little grumpily. He realized it was unworthy of him. He'd known he couldn't do it all himself. He ought to be grateful that Roxon was willing to take over.

She did not stay near him for more than a moment then—he felt she was being cautious now about the appearance of conspiring—but some time later, as she passed him, she murmured, "Put your arms around me, try to hold me a minute—Dane, have you told Dallith anything yet? I saw you talking together but I didn't have a chance to ask her."

Dane complied. She felt soft and strong in his arms, rounded and feminine, yet firm-muscled and far from passive. He said, "No, I haven't. I was a little afraid to. Anyway, we got off the subject, she was explaining some things to me about—er—Galactic customs and the way the Mekhars—that is, the way all proto-felines—think of us humans."

Is she expecting me to pretend to make love to her?

As if she had caught the thought, Rianna firmly freed herself from his arms and pulled away. She said in an undertone, "Tell her, as quickly as you can. Remember, she's an empath. If you're too indecisive, she'll pick that up from you, and the Mekhars might have enough sense to watch her—to see whether they ought to be suspicious of *us*. It also might be—I don't know all that much about empaths, but it *could* be possible—that she could tune in on the Mekhars and find out how they're reacting to us; when they're off guard, how near we are to where they're taking us, and so on."

"That would be almost too good to be true."

"It would. I've never trusted psi talents, anyhow. But we can't afford to waste any chances, however small," Rianna said. "However small. So you talk to Dallith. And soon."

Dane knew she was right, and he hardened himself to awareness of what he must do. But what if this plunged her, again, into the suicidal fear and hopelessness? What then?

The routine of the slave quarters were familiar to him, now, and he waited on it. About an hour (he estimated, having no timepiece) after the final meal of each "day," the long corridor of cages was darkened, except for dimly glowing night-lights in the long corridors between, and small pale marks at the doors of the toilet areas. Dane went to the bunk now generally regarded as his, at the appointed time. *How quickly,* he thought, *we grow used to almost anything! Already one bunk here is "mine" and I am accustomed to getting into it at a specific and regular time. Are all sapient species such creatures of habit, or is it only us humans—or proto-simians?*

He gave the cell an hour to settle down and for his cell-mates to sleep. Above him, an unknown man, dark-skinned and flat-faced, snuffled and cried out in uneasy dreams. Aratak, in the bunk next to his, made odd snoring noises, and as Dane let himself quietly down from his bunk he noticed that the lizard-man was glowing faintly all over in the darkness. At the far end, surrounded by empty bunks on either side, the long loose-jointed spidery creature hunched, his eyes huge and red and reflecting light; the eyes swiveled to follow Dane, and Dane found himself cringing . . . was it a hungry look? Would the Mekhars, if it came to that, cage a cannibal-istic species with its natural prey?

Dallith lay in the lower bunk, her face turned away as he had first seen her lying her hair scattered and loose. She was sleeping deeply, and when Dane lowered himself gently beside Dallith, to sit on the edge of her bunk, she did not at once waken but made a soft, accepting movement and murmured in her sleep, a drowsy and peaceful sound.

She knew him, even in sleep, and there was no fear now in her. . . . A wave of tenderness went over him; he touched his lips to the back of her cool hand, and she woke and smiled in the dimness. She looked so peaceful that for a moment he forbore to disturb her. She seemed unsurprised and did not question his presence. Putting off what he must say, Dane asked her, for the first time:

"What is your world like, Dallith?"

"How can I answer you, Marsh?" Her voice was only a whisper, accurately tuned to his ear. "It is my home. Can you say anything of your home world, except that it is beautiful? My people rarely leave our world—and almost never of our free will—and so we have no way to compare it with others, except from what we have read. I think it must be the same with you."

A spasm of homesickness, so violent that it was pure pain, passed through Dane Marsh. Never to see Hawaii again, or the great arching span of the Golden Gate Bridge, or the skyline of New York with its thrusting towers, or the blossom of a rhododendron in spring. . . .

Her hands pressed his gently. She said, "I did not mean to make you sad. Dane, why did you come here? You are more than welcome, but I know enough about the kind of person you are to know why you did *not* come. You have something to say to me?"

He nodded silently, and carefully stretched himself out along the edge of her bunk. He told himself that the Mekhar guards passed through the hall once or twice during a night and if they saw him there they would think—what they always thought, damn them. And why not? He told her, in muffled tones with his mouth close to her ear, about the plans for escape. She heard him out in silence, tensing only slightly when he told her that the Mekhars might very well kill some of them, but she made no outcry. At last she said, "I knew it must be something like this. I have seen you and Aratak together, but I was not sure exactly what. But if it is physical force you want, I am probably not strong enough to disarm a Mekhar. What can I do?"

Her voice was so calm that he asked, "Aren't you afraid? I thought you'd panic."

"Why? I faced the worst when they tore me from my home and my people. Now there is nothing worse to fear. Tell me what I can do for you."

"I don't know anything much about empaths," Dane said. He remembered Rianna's words, *I've never trusted psi talents.* . . . "But perhaps you can find out for us how long we have. Are the Mekhars getting ready to land us already? Maybe you can find out what defenses we may have to face. That sort of thing."

A spasm of disgust passed over her face. "I don't know. I

have never tried—to read the minds or emotions of another race. They are so fierce—but I will try. Don't expect too much, but I will try."

"That's all I ask," he said. He stirred as if to return to his own place, but Dallith's arms tightened around him. "No. No. Alone, I'm afraid again. Stay close to me—"

He said, wryly, "You put a considerable strain on human nature, Dallith." But he did not move to go, and after a time, stretched out close to the girl, he fell asleep there, dropping from wakefulness into strange blurring dreams of lions, of curious colors and ambushes lurking behind strange ruined walls, starting awake again to hear Dallith whimpering with fear and protest in unquiet dreams, dropping again into the relentless dreams of hunter and hunted, of ambush and fear and the smells of blood and death.

A day or two later, Dallith joined him, Rianna, Roxon, and Aratak at a mealtime, as the Mekhar moved out of sight down the corridor with the food-cart, and said in an undertone, "We must be quick. We must make our plans quickly. They are hard to read"—her face twisted strangely and she clenched her hands—"and it is hard not to share their—their arrogance. I was afraid—afraid of becoming entangled in their ideas. But we must be very quick."

Aratak asked gently, "Why, child?"

"Because they are going to take us somewhere, unless"—again the look of strain—"unless something happens—I don't know exactly what, but they are expecting something and will be disappointed—oh, I don't know," she burst out, twisting her slim hands and biting her lip. "I don't know, I don't know! I'm afraid to come close enough to know—"

Dane looked at her in deep disquiet. *It's as if they wanted us to attack them. But that's ridiculous.*

He asked Roxon:

"Has the word been passed along? How many can we trust

to join us? We could manage with a dozen, I expect, if we're very well coordinated. But it would help to have more.''

Roxon said, ''The five of us here. Three in the next cell. They tell me that in the area beyond, there are four or five who will join us. After that, it is all a guess. But I am sure we will have enough—and when others see that it is a well-planned, concerted action, they are sure to join.''

Rianna asked, ''What about the tangler fields?''

''Good point,'' Aratak said. ''The guards wear those belts with their nerve-guns. I think there is a control in the belts which makes them able to move inside a tangler field. After we disarm the guards, we must get their belts. Two or three of the strongest of us, physically, must be ready to put them on, until someone can get to the bridge area and cut out the tangler controls. Roxon, can you do that?''

''I'm not sure,'' Roxon said, ''but I can try.''

Marsh said, ''Roxon mustn't be risked. He knows how to pilot a ship. Let me take any risks that have to be taken. That sort of risk, anyway.'' He wished the revolt were today. Now the plans were made, further delay would only let them sit around, worrying, getting nervous. Also, at any moment the Mekhar ship might stop somewhere and take on a new load of slaves who might be dumped in among them, new ones still stunned by sudden captivity, to go mad or impede their plans for escape. He said, ''The sooner the better. Let's make it next mealtime, now we all know what we're going to do.''

He found it hard to swallow; but as he would have put down the rest of his uneaten food, Rianna looked across the circle at him. She said, low and tense, ''Finish up, everybody. We have to act exactly as usual, or they'll know something's going on.''

The interval till the next meal-period seemed to crawl past. Dallith sought Marsh and sat beside him, holding his hand. Roxon went to the bars separating them from the next cage area, and talked in an undertone to his colleague there.

Rianna, disregarding her own directive, prowled nervously until Dallith gave her an angry stare, when she went to her bunk and lay there, pretending to sleep. Only Aratak seemed calm, seated with his huge legs crossed, his closed gill-slits vibrating faintly and glowing blue. But Marsh knew that this was only an outward appearance; he could not tell whether Aratak was as calm as he looked, meditating further on the wisdom of his eternal Divine Egg, or whether the impassiveness of his nonhuman face was due to its form and configuration and inwardly Aratak was as restless, as tightly clamped against revealing anything, as Rianna herself.

Time seemed to crawl, to stretch itself out interminably. It was Dallith, with a quick indrawn breath, who warned them all; her eyes gleamed and she sat abruptly upright, her face drawn and pale. Rianna had evidently been watching her beneath half-closed lids; she sprang off her bunk and took up her place near the bars. Aratak went into a tense crouch. The word, in a whisper, was running up and down through the rows of cages, more than a full minute before the first loud *clang* marked that down in the far end the Mekhar had thrown the switch which controlled all the cage locks.

Dane, moving slowly toward the doors, saw and felt the air of tension in their own area, and thought, *The others, everyone, must know that something's happening. We can't keep them from knowing now, we'll simply have to hope that no one alerts the Mekhars.*

The two Mekhar guards were coming down the corridor now. They shoved the coded food packages into one cage area after another, and withdrew. Now they were about to unload it inside the area where Dane and his friends waited, tensed to the breaking point. The Mekhar with the food-cart, moving exactly as usual, trundled it in through the unlocked door and began to unload the coded trays. Behind him his colleague, with a drawn nerve-gun, covered the cage inhabitants. The Mekhar with the cart finished the unloading, turned to trundle it out again, and at the moment when the cart momentarily blocked the door, Dane and Aratak leaped at his back.

Dane made one vicious karate chop across the lion-thing's neck; he went down, sprawling, roaring an ear-hurting howl, and the Mekhar behind him fired with the drawn nerve-gun; Dane felt the hiss of the bolt behind him, ducked. Someone shrieked, but by that time the Mekhar he had knocked down was coming to his feet again, hissing, roaring, and Dane, taking a fighting stance, was ready for him. He kicked out, a vicious kick that would have thrown any human, paralyzed, to the floor; the Mekhar roared and went for him with claws bared. Behind him, he saw that men from the next cage were pouring out, swarming over the Mekhar with the nerve-gun. They had his gun; they were kicking him; he lay unconscious on the corridor floor. Aratak's huge arms swiped the second Mekhar from behind; he went down, struggling, and Dallith darted in, hauled the nerve-gun from his belt, moving swiftly as a cat herself; the Mekhar made a wild swipe, his claws raking blood from Dallith's arm, and the girl exploded into a biting, kicking fury; she threw the nerve-gun to Rianna and flew at the prone Mekhar, screaming, clawing at his eyes.

Dane hauled her off him with both hands. "No need to kill him," he said. At his touch Dallith quieted and began to tremble. "Unfasten his belt, there. That's right. Aratak, you're the strongest, you put it on; you can do more than the rest of us if we get into a tangler field." He buckled the other Mekhar's belt around his waist, thinking, *It takes two people, skilled in unarmed combat, to disarm one Mekhar. Let's hope they don't throw eighty crew members at us all at once.*

"Come on," he said, between his teeth. "Out, everybody. Out of the cells. We don't know how long we have before somebody notices these two haven't come back from feeding the animals, and comes down to see what's keeping them."

They emerged from the cell area into the corridor and Dane

stood for a moment, confused. He had been brought here unconscious and had no idea which way he should go to the bridge, to the area where the other crewmen were, to the ship's controls. He shot a quick question to Roxon, who was marshaling the captives in the hall and giving them quick low-voiced orders.

"We were all brought in unconscious," Roxon said. "It's their policy. But I think we're at the lower levels; we have to keep going up as far as we can." He led the way along a long ramp, which led upward and upward, curving blindly now and then. The other prisoners swarmed behind him, and Dane thought, apprehensively, *We, who are the ringleaders, should stay together! These others, who've just joined in and don't know what we're doing, may be pretty badly in the way when we start acting!* He pushed and thrust forward through them, toward the lead, Dallith hurrying at his shoulders. Rianna caught Dallith's arm.

"Quick! Which way are the Mekhars? Where?"

Dallith hardly seemed to hear. Her face was set and twisted. Abruptly she cried out in horror, and simultaneously Dane saw Rianna stumble; struggle to rise. The prisoners began to drop, one by one, moving slowly, thickly. *The tangler field,* thought Dane. He himself, thanks to the Mekhar guard's belt, felt nothing, but Dallith clutched at him, struggling to pull herself along.

Dallith shrieked, "They know, they know, they're waiting for us—"

The door at the top of the ramp burst open. Half a dozen Mekhars, armed with nerve-guns, stood there, and at the sight the prisoners stopped, surged forward. Aratak, like Dane unhindered by the tangler field, sprang forward; he knocked one Mekhar sprawling, back broken, laid another out, screaming in a thin high whine, before he went down under a shot. Roxon fell, writhing and convulsing.

Dane fought on, struggling through the prisoners, grimly

determined, before they got him, to kill one or two of the Mekhars; he saw Dallith struggling like a wild thing between a pair of them. Then something struck him a killing blow on the head and he went down into darkness, thinking, *I was right all along; they expected us to attack and they were glad. But why?*

He screamed, "Why?" into the darkness, but the darkness did not answer, and after a million years he stopped listening for the answer. . . .

Chapter Five

His head ached, and his arms felt as if they had been broken off at the wrists. Dane Marsh opened his eyes, and found that he was in a cell he had never seen before. One arm was fastened in a tight cuff to the wall, by a chain about six feet long. Across the cell from him, Aratak was manacled with a similar arrangement. Rianna lay asleep on the floor; Dallith sat hunched over, her arms wrapped around her knees, staring fixedly at him. As he opened his eyes she said, "You're alive!" and her face was suffused with surprise and joy. "I wasn't sure, you were so far away. . . ."

"I'm alive, for what that's worth," Dane said. "I see you are, too. What happened to the others?"

Rianna opened her eyes. "Roxon was the first one they killed," she said. "They killed half a dozen others, too, I think. As for the others, they unloaded them—and I heard them say it was at the Gorbahl slave mart—three days ago. I expect they have something special in mind for us, but as for what it is"—she smiled bitterly—"your guess is as good as

51

mine. My personal notion is that they're saving us for dinner. We killed two of the Mekhars, and that's not something they're going to sit back and accept."

"It isn't bad," Dallith said stubbornly. "There's something hopeful about it. They were *pleased* at what we did."

"How can you tell?" Rianna shouted. "This is all your fault. If Dane hadn't saved your life we'd all have gone to the Gorbahl slave mart, but Roxon would be alive, and there might have been a chance for some of us—"

Aratak said in a commanding rumble, "Quiet, child. None of this is Dallith's fault, any more than yours. You, too, were eager to take part in the escape, and as for Roxon, perhaps he too felt he would rather die than live as a slave. In any case he is dead and beyond your pity or your help, and Dallith is not. The four of us are all together in trouble, and if we begin to quarrel, there is truly no chance."

"There's none anyway," Rianna said bitterly, and rolled over, hiding her face beneath her bright hair.

"Rianna—" Dane said, but she turned her back again and would not look at him.

She blames me for Roxon's death, and the death of the others, he thought.

But there was nothing he could say to that. Perhaps it was true. Perhaps he, having less to lose than the others—whatever happened, his own world was irrevocably lost—had been indifferent to life or death.

Aratak said, "At least you three are of one people, creatures of one blood. None of my kind remain on board this ship. Must I find myself alone?"

Dallith went slowly toward him and slipped her small delicate hand into his huge clawed paw. She said gently, "We are brothers and sisters in misfortune, Aratak, under the Universal Law. I know that. Dane knows it. And Rianna will know it again, sooner or later."

Dane nodded. He felt very close to the huge lizard-man at

whose side he had nearly been killed. "We made a good fight of it, anyway," he said. "Between us, we accounted for a couple of those damned cat-faced things! Whatever happens to us now, it was worth it."

Aratak gave an emphatic nod and his gills glowed blue.

Dane found himself wondering, *What now?* "Do they feed us?"

Rianna sat up, flinging her red hair back. She said, "Who cares? If you do, yes; if anything they feed us better than ever, though they shove our food in through the bars—no one comes near us now."

Dane said, "Then they certainly aren't going to torture us to death, and if they were going to kill us I think they'd have done it. Cats aren't subtle creatures. They'd have torn us to pieces right then, if they were going to."

"That's what I've been trying to tell you," Dallith said. "I don't know what's in store for us—I can't read their minds without going—berserk—as I did then, when I tried—I tried—" She suddenly shuddered. "For a moment, I *was* the Mekhar. I went for him with teeth—and claws—"

She was silent. Then, firmly, dismissing the thought, she said, "But this I know. They are not going to kill us, and we have become even more valuable to them. So it is my turn to say: don't think about dying, Rianna. Keep up your strength and your hopes. We'll find out now, very soon, what is going to happen. We're alive, and we're all together. There's no need to despair."

It was at least evident that their status had changed and that they were now regarded as dangerous. Food was thrust through the bars—from a safe distance—by Mekhars who never spoke to them and seemed wary even of coming close to the bars. Three times a day, the chains on Dane and on Aratak were lengthened—by loosening a staple from outside the cell—so that they could enter a small shower-toilet area. At all other times they were left strictly to themselves to entertain whatever guesses, conjectures, or thoughts they might devise about their eventual fate or fates.

This went on, Dane later surmised, for about two weeks. There was nothing for the captives to do except to exchange life histories, if they chose, to tell each other about their home worlds, and, in general, to get to know one another. Dane told them all he could about the social and political history of Earth, although he suspected part of their interest was wonder and amazement that even a partially civilized world could so far have been missed by the Unity. Only Rianna hazarded a guess as to why this might have been.

"You have a certain degree of scientific and technological advancement," she agreed, "but in other fields you're far behind, probably because you *are* so cut off. For instance, you say that never in your known history have you been visited even by observer or guest teams from other planets."

"Not in our known history, no. Although some scientists have suspected that some of our religious myths may be garbled memories of such visits before written history."

"That seems unlikely," Dallith protested. "Scientist and observer teams from the Unity, at least, are usually very careful to make certain that the planets they visit don't get any such notions!"

"But there's no way of telling that the visitors were from the Unity—if there were any such visitors," Rianna said. "They might have been from anywhere. No, the most likely thing is that they simply overlooked your solar system. There are so very *many* uninhabited worlds that one, or two, or two hundred, could simply be overlooked in cataloguing. Didn't you say that only one world in your system is habitable by ordinary animal life? That's very unusual; the most likely thing is that they visited one or two planets, found them uninhabitable, and gave up on the system. Sloppy scientific work, of course, but it does happen."

Dallith suggested, "Perhaps your Earth was visited at a

time before sapient life had developed. Or while your men were still living in treetops.''

Aratak rumbled, ''That wouldn't stop them. My world entered the Unity before the Divine Egg had gifted us with the wheel!''

This made Dane Marsh remember a favorite theory of science fiction writers. ''People used to suggest that visitors from space had avoided us, or put us under a sort of Cosmic quarantine, because of our atomic wars and such.''

''If total and permanent peace were a qualification,'' Rianna said dryly, ''the Unity might possibly be made up of as many as two dozen worlds, mostly inhabited by empaths. Instead of, as we now have, several hundred. The Unity will do anything possible to help member planets resolve their internal differences—and sometimes even the presence of the Unity helps the people of a planet to develop a feeling of solidarity and internal harmony with one another. But the way the Unity is set up, it simply serves as a total barrier to *interplanetary* or *interstellar* war. Most planets settle the war problem earlier in their history than yours, but then yours seems to have a history torn by climatic changes, natural cataclysms, and the like, which typically cut off small groups of people from other small groups, and exaggerated their ethnic, cultural, social, and linguistic differences. The result would, naturally, be a prolonging of the 'war' period in planetary history. Although I admit it's a *little* freaky for wars to be prolonged past the Industrial Revolution stage of development.''

Dane was glad to get away from discussion of his ''freaky'' culture and to hear about the others. Dallith came from a highly homogeneous world which had, after a long period of ice ages followed by periods of flood and then of tropical growth, placed so high a value on psi powers for survival that ESP and clairvoyance were firmly established in the racial germ plasm. They were a peaceful people, few in number due to rigorous natural selection, with small technology but highly developed sciences of philosophy and cosmology. Rianna's people were more like what Dane had always believed that Earthmen might be someday—a scientific civilization with a highly developed technology and a tradition of endless exploration and scientific curiosity.

Aratak's world couldn't have been more the reverse. Here the dominant race, descended from giant saurians and amphibians, virtually without natural enemies, and vegetarian, had briefly experimented with technology, found that its rewards did not compensate them for its troubles, and peacefully turned their backs on it to live, as a race, a contemplative life in a food-gathering culture. They imported a few—not many—artifacts from their companion world, a highly technological race of people who called themselves by a name which the mechanical translator embedded in Dane's throat rendered as the Salamanders. In return they supplied them with raw minerals, certain foodstuffs, and philosophy, which was evidently regarded as a marketable commodity like any other. In fact, Dane gathered that men of Aratak's lizardlike race traveled all over the known Galaxy as teachers of philosophy, and were highly regarded, and treated with lavish hospitality, in return for the great sacrifice of leaving their beloved and peaceful swamps.

But such stories as they could interchange from their planetary history filled up only part of the time. They had all too much time for brooding, worrying about their eventual fate. It seemed that time dragged endlessly; there were times when it seemed, at least to Dane, that he had been a prisoner for many years.

Abruptly, it came to an end.

One morning—or at least what Dane called morning, for it was the first meal following a period of sleep—their cell was entered by three Mekhars with drawn nerve-guns and a portable tangler field, which they took the precaution of turning up to full force before entering, and unchaining Dane or Aratak.

One of the Mekhars said tersely, "Make no mistake. You will be given—now—no single chance to escape. Even a single unauthorized move, and you will be instantly shocked into total unconsciousness. You will not be killed and you will not be tortured, but you will not be allowed to escape, so you may as well preserve your energies. This is the only warning you will receive, so move carefully. Believe me, you will not be given the benefit of the doubt."

Dane made no sudden moves. He had no desire to try out for himself what a nerve-gun felt like; he still remembered the screams of the man who had died. His curiosity was caught by one unexpected phrase. *You will be given—now—no single chance to escape.* Did that mean that *later*, they would be given some single chance? It was worth thinking about. (The mechanical translator was almost unbelievably literal; on one occasion when Rianna, infuriated by Dallith's calm, had thrown some kind of colloquial insult at her, the translator had rendered it, simply, to imply that Dallith was a bringer of food to children. Which certainly was no insult by Dane's terms, and probably, judging by Dallith's expression, none by hers either—which hadn't made Rianna any calmer!)

Evidently the other three prisoners had reached the same conclusion on their own, for they went peacefully with the Mekhars along the winding corridors and up the ramps, until they reached what looked like a small conference room in which half a dozen of the Mekhars, uniformed like ship's personnel, were waiting; there were what looked like television screens and receivers, various other equipment, and a variety of seats. The Mekhars motioned their four captives into seats in what looked like a jury-box, or musician's gallery, along one side of the room; as soon as they were in their seats, restraints (automatically operated, perhaps by their weight) immediately gripped them around the waist and held them fast.

The jury-box arrangement already had one inhabitant; and he was a Mekhar, but he was held by the same kind of restraints as Dane and his companions. To Dane, all the Mekhars looked quite a bit alike, but it seemed there was something familiar about this one; and no sooner had he come to this conclusion than Dallith, next to him, leaned over and whispered, "It's the Mekhar you disarmed—the guard from the cell. I thought we had killed him."

"No such luck, evidently," Dane whispered back.

"The prisoners will be silent," one of the Mekhars said unemotionally.

Dane looked around the room where he found himself, his attention immediately gripped by what looked like an enormous vision-screen. Reception was wavy and ridden with what, on Earth-type TV, would have been called "ghosts," but it was evidently a live transmission. The picture on the screen was nothing very startling, for none of the other captives gave it even a second glance, far less watching it closely; but to Dane it was an incredible marvel. It was neither more nor less than a planet, seen from out in space, vaguely brick-red, with blue-green areas which looked like oceans and dull brown spots which might have been mountain ranges or deserts. In the sky behind it—or, more properly, in the dark star-flecked *space* behind it—hung a huge moon, or satellite, fully half the size of the parent planet, and partially eclipsed by it.

One of the Mekhars in uniform was seated before a prosaic-looking console and was talking into it, in a low voice, just monotonous background noise, too low for Dane's translator to function. This went on for some time; the planet, and its half-eclipsed satellite, grew larger and more definite in the viewing screen. Evidently they were approaching some planet. Were they going to land on it, Dane wondered, and was it the

Mekhars' home world? And what was going to happen to them there? The extreme caution with which they had been treated seemed like a good sign—they evidently weren't going to be killed out of hand—but were they going to have to stand trial for something or other? For killing a Mekhar, perhaps?

Abruptly the monotonous undertone of the Mekhar speaking into the console stopped—interrupted by a series of soft, but high-pitched beeps, clicks, and mutterings from the console. The Mekhar seated there moved various dials and levers. A speaker on the console came to life, and a curiously low, steady voice—almost, Dane thought, a *mechanical* voice—remarked:

"Central Station, Second Continent, speaking to the Mekhar ship. We acknowledge your message and stand ready to receive your offer."

The Mekhar at the console said—his voice was now amplified, for evidently he had thrown some control which made it come over the speaker as well, "We have five for you, Hunters. They are special prime dangerous ones, and we will not sell them cheaply."

The mechanical voice retorted, with its curious expressionless quality, "You Mekhars have done business with us before, and you know our requirements. Have these been pretested?"

"They have," said the Mekhar. "They are the four survivors of six ringleaders of the usual test escape mechanism—the ones who were intelligent and resourceful enough to see a very small loophole left for escape, brave enough to take it in the face of nerve-guns, and strong enough to keep fighting after we showed them that we were aware of the plot. You will not be disappointed in them. We had hoped to have all six for you, but were forced to kill two others before they could be subdued."

The mechanical voice said, "You spoke of *five* Quarry for us."

"The fifth is one of our own," the Mekhar captain said. "He allowed the prisoners to disarm him and to seize his weapon. The other guard, when given the usual choice, chose to commit suicide rather than face his trial on Mekhar. This one exercised the other option—to sell himself as Quarry to the Hunters. His price will be given to his surviving relatives on Mekhar, so that he is free of obligations and can legally take this single chance of survival."

"We are always glad to accept a Mekhar as Quarry," the mechanical voice said. "We repeat the offer we have made before this, to accept your desperate criminals as Quarry at any time."

"And we repeat," the Mekhar at the console-communicator said, "that our people's honor will not allow us to be represented in the Hunt by criminals; but the guard was bested in an honorable duel, since we deliberately left a chance for the prisoners to escape; he has the legal option to choose his own death, and he has the right to choose to die at your hands if he so wishes, honorably."

"We bow to your rules of honor," said the mechanical voice. "We suggest a bonus of ten percent over our usual price; if this is acceptable to you, you may land the prisoners at once."

"That is acceptable to us," the Mekhar confirmed, but Dane's attention was drawn to Rianna, who had drawn in a great gasping sob.

"The Hunters," she whispered. "Then they're not just a legend! A chance for escape—yes, a chance—but oh, Gods, *what* a chance!"

Dane twisted in his seat, but before he could say another word to her, the Mekhar captain approached them.

"Prisoners," he said quietly. "Your chance of escape, or honorable death, is upon you. You have proven that you are too brave, too courageous, to be sold as slaves; it is, therefore, our honor and our pleasure to provide you this alternative. Do not be afraid. You are about to be given a small dose of mild anesthetic gas, which will have no lasting side effects, so that you need not be harmed by struggling in the transit to the Hunters' World. Let me congratulate you, and wish you all an honorable escape, or a bloody and honorable death.''

Chapter Six

When the mists of the anesthetic gas began to clear from Dane's mind, he found himself lying on a low, soft bed, with a silky-smooth covering. Rianna lay unconscious beside him; Dallith on a similar couch nearby. Aratak was stretched on the floor; as Dane sat up the great grayish lizard-man stretched painfully, yawned, and sat up too. He looked around him and his eyes met Dane's.

"About one thing, at least, our captors told the truth," he said quietly. "We have not been harmed. How is it with the women?"

Dane leaned over Rianna; her breast was rising and falling naturally, as with sleep. Dallith began to stretch sleepily; sat up, looking around in quick panic; saw them and relaxed, smiling.

"So here we all are again," Dane said.

The room in which they lay was very large, with high ceilings and pillars and columns, and had at one time been painted a sort of terra-cotta color; but the paint seemed faded and old, and there were spiderwebs and dust in the high corners, though the place seemed clean enough otherwise. Long windows, unglazed but partially shuttered with narrow bamboo-like slats, admitted a strange reddish sunlight. Outside the arched windows there were voices and sounds of falling water. Dane got up and walked to the windows, peering through the slats.

Outside was a wilderness of garden; flowering bushes, long stony paths, low trees with golden-colored cones or long red seed-pods; everywhere the pervasive green, although no single tree looked familiar to him.

Unearthly, he thought, *and that is a very exact description.* The sky was lowering and reddish, with great grayish masses of sunset cloud, and in the sky the huge moon he had seen from space hung low, glowing reddish and seeming to cast its own fiery-red light over the trees, the paths, the flowers, and the fountains of falling water which seemed to flow and gurgle everywhere in the enormous garden.

There were people on the paths. People, as Dane had begun to think of them from his days on the Mekhar slave ship; not a mixture of people and strange animals, just different kinds of people. They were all dressed in tunics of the same terra-cotta red as the walls of the room; human and nonhuman alike. There were people who seemed to Dane all but human, human as he was himself; there were some who reminded him vaguely of the Mekhars; there was at least one covered with fine woolly hair who looked like a taller, more alert gibbon or ape; there were too many to see and classify all at once. Another slave mart? No, the Mekhar had said, at last, that they were "too brave and courageous for slaves," whatever that meant. But the uniform brick-red tunics, and the close enclosure of the garden, told him that they had not yet reached freedom.

The variety of beings in the garden reminded him that when they left the ship their number had been five; and he looked about for the Mekhar who had, at the last, been imprisoned with them. He found him curled up, his head hidden between his hands. on another of the soft silken couches, evidently still sleeping.

"The gas wears off quickest on my kind," said Aratak from where he squatted before the window. "I was conscious again even before the small shuttle-ship landed us here. I repaid them by not resisting; I did not want to be separated from you, my companions. Now you are waking; and the Mekhar still sleeps. Evidently their metabolism differs from ours in some way. I hope he is not dead. Perhaps we should examine him and see—"

"I don't care if he's dead or not," Rianna said, "but probably no such luck; the Mekhars must know what dosage of anesthetic would work on their own kind."

"Anyway, he's breathing," Dallith said. Dane walked a step or two toward the sleeping cat-form. He was not only sleeping—he was *purring* in his sleep. If it had not been so incongruous, Dane would have laughed; the great fierce Mekhar, purring like a child's pet kitten.

"Well, he'll either wake up or he won't," Dane said. "Let's hope he doesn't start his new day trying to get revenge on us for landing him here! I'm going to keep an eye on him, anyway. Meanwhile, here we are, but where's *here?* Rianna, before we left the ship you acted as if you knew something about the Hunters. Suppose you tell us."

Rianna sat up, swung her bare legs over the edge of the couch, and came toward the window. The reddish light made her flame-tinged hair and sultry skin glow. She said, "Most people think they're a legend. When I was doing research I found out that they weren't. They call themselves by a name which means, simply, Hunters; and they think of themselves, evidently, that way. They've refused to join the Unity—not that the Unity would let them in as they are, of course; but they've preferred staying outside the Unity to changing their ways."

Dallith came straight to the heart of the matter. "Why are they called Hunters? What do they hunt?"

Rianna said bluntly, "Us."

Aratak raised himself to his full height. "I had begun to suspect this. We were sold to them, then, for their hunting pleasure?"

Rianna nodded. "From all I have heard, and seen, in the libraries of the Unity—and it's not a great deal, for they have refused to let any outsiders land—hunting has become their one diversion, their one pleasure—their religion. They never stop seeking for some Prey which can give them a fair fight. For hundreds of years, I understand, they have had no dealings with anyone from off their world except for this—they will buy Quarry for their Hunts."

Dane said, watching the sleeping Mekhar out of the corner of his eye, "I had a funny feeling that it was almost too easy; that for some reason they *wanted* us to try to escape. And evidently that's how they weed out the slaves from the ones they might be able to sell to the Hunters!"

Rianna gave a mirthless little laugh. "Their test doesn't work very well, then. Brave is the one thing I'm not."

Dallith said quietly, "Perhaps what they want is not so much the *brave* as the *desperate*."

"This explains why they spoke of a chance for escape, then," Dane said. "But what chance is that?"

The sleeping Mekhar suddenly stretched, with a great yawn, and sprang instantly upright; when he saw the four gathered near the windows, he came into a wary crouch. Dane tensed for attack. But the Mekhar took a step backward.

"We would not be allowed to fight here." His voice was a deep, purring rumble. "Our skill and strength now belong to the Hunters. Very well; we have been enemies, we may be enemies again. But for the moment I ask a truce."

Dane glanced at Aratak; the giant lizard-man relaxed, with something like a bow. He said, "We are, at least, companions in misfortune; a truce it shall be. If you will, I swear by the Divine Egg that so long as our truce lasts I will not harm you waking or sleeping; will you give the same oath?"

The Mekhar growled, "Oaths are for those who can envision breaking their word; I say I will not harm you without taking my word back, nor any of you who give me a like undertaking. But if there is any who will not give me that word, I will fight him—or her—here and now, with or without weapons, to death or to surrender."

Rianna and Dallith glanced at Dane. He said, "I'll speak for all of us. We're all in too much trouble to fight among ourselves. I have no quarrel with you. Your people had no right to steal any of us from our home worlds, but fighting you won't put that right. Your own people seem to have played you a dirty trick, anyway—putting you in the same category with us!"

"Don't dare to say that," the Mekhar said. "I chose to redeem my honor this way of my own free will!" His long curved fingernails, like claws, contracted and retracted with rage.

Dane said hastily, "Well, be that as it may, I won't debate points of honor with you, since you and I probably use different meanings for the word." He thought to himself that anyone whose code of honor permitted the stealing of slaves probably couldn't have a meaningful discussion with him on the subject anyway, translator or no translator. "Anyway, if you let us alone, we'll let you alone; and I speak for the women too."

The Mekhar eyed them warily, his yellow eyes narrowed to slits; then he relaxed and dropped on the floor. "Be it so; while our word runs we hold a truce. Since you are no longer slaves but have proven your courage, I accept your word as good."

Rianna said, "I know very little about the Hunters; your race evidently deals with them. Can you tell us what they're like?"

The Mekhar stretched his lips in what could have been anger or irony. "You know as much as I; they do not let themselves be seen by outsiders," he said. "The Hunter is seen only by the Quarry he is about to kill."

Rianna shivered. Dallith came close to Dane and slipped her hand into his. Even Aratak seemed momentarily taken aback. "Does that mean they're *invisible?*"

"Visible or invisible, I know not," said the Mekhar. "I know only that no one I know of has seen one, and lived to tell."

He fell silent for a moment, and Dane thought about frying pans and fires. He was off the Mekhar slave ship, but it seemed he had escaped slavery only for what sounded like certain death at the hands of terrible, unknown Hunters. He thought, even the man who said, "Give me Liberty or give me Death," had had the kindness to preface it by saying that he knew not what course others might take. Besides, Dane hadn't been given the choice between liberty and death, but between slavery and what sounded like certain death anyway.

Dallith, her now-familiar trick of reading his mood, said angrily, "Why, then, did the Mekhar captain speak of honorable escape as an alternate to honorable and bloody death?"

The Mekhar looked startled. "I thought you knew," he said. "Surely you did not think we would condemn any brave creatures to a certain death! The Hunt—as all those who know of the Hunters should know—runs from Eclipse to Eclpise of the Red Moon. Those who still live when the Eclipse comes again—go free. Free, and with a great prize, and great honor. Why else would I be here?"

The Mekhar turned his back on them, whiskers twitching, and Dane stood watching him, trying to take this in.

A chance for escape—but from fierce people, so fierce that

they had no other name than Hunters, feared even by the Mekhars. An enemy no one had seen except in the moment of being killed by them. So that they must fight, or flee, or somehow escape them, for the period of Eclipse—however long that was—never knowing what form their enemy would take, or if he might come, invisible, out of the air.

For a moment, ignobly, he wished he were back on the slave ship. He'd been looking for adventure all his life, but a journey across the Galaxy, even as a slave, was enough adventure for one lifetime!

Then, for no good reason at all, he found himself more cheerful. If the Hunters made a quasi-religious ritual out of the Hunt, part of their fun would probably be in the risk involved. Hunters on Earth didn't get all excited about going out to shoot rabbits. Fox-hunters made a big thing about not shooting the fox. The real mystique about hunting, for those who got involved in it, even on Earth, seemed to be the stalk, the danger, the thrill of running a risk. Therefore, the humans involved—or whatever races their Quarry might be—would somehow be given something like a fair chance.

I've gone soft, Dane thought, I'm out of condition. I used to be in fair fighting trim—those lessons in Japan in aikido and karate, the strenuous night-and-day hard work of solo sailing—but three weeks of complete inactivity have softened me up. Aratak might make it; he's huge and tough. The women—well, if it was physical strength that counted, Dallith at least would have to be protected—although she'd been fierce enough, fighting the Mekhar, to scare him! But the Mekhars hadn't tested them for physical strength, Dane realized. The Mekhars had tested them for desperation, courage, willingness to take risks, and the ability to think out the loophole left for escape. So these must be the qualities the Hunters wanted in their Quarry, to give them a good fight. He said aloud, "Maybe we've got a chance, after all. Not a good one. But a chance."

Dallith gasped and clutched his arm, for the door at the far end of the long room was sliding open; Dane turned, wondering if they were to see the first of the mysterious Hunters. Instead what he saw was a tall, narrow metal column, which seemed to glide forward as if on invisible wheels. It had small slits covered with metal mesh, and small blinking lights or lenses, and after a moment Dane decided that it must be some sort of robot, even before it began to speak in the same sort of mechanical voice he had heard from the Mekhar ship's console.

"Welcome to this House of the Sacred Prey," it said, in that flat, metallic voice. "Food will be brought to you of whatever kind you desire, if you will state your preferred nutritional requirements. We have also for you"—the metal column whirred, turned slightly, and extruded a long metal arm—" garments suitable to the sacredness of your condition. Please to bathe in one of the pools or fountains, as you desire and as your custom suggests to your mind, and clothe yourselves in them." The clothing extended on the metal arm was of the same brick-red color that Dane had seen on the others in the great garden. Then they, too, were among the—what was that word the robot had used—the Sacred Prey? *All of them?* Dane suddenly wondered if the Hunters would hunt them down singly, or all together?

The Mekhar turned on the robot and snarled, "You metal nothing, it is not the custom of my people to wear any garments other than our own!"

The robot said passionately, "It is impossible to insult a creature constructed of metal by describing him as such, but we deduce that this was your intention, and the intended insult is registered and acknowledged as such."

The Mekhar scowled and said, "You mean if I insult you, your masters the Hunters will regard it as an insult to them?"

"Oh, no." The robot's inflection did not change. "However, we have been informed that it is frustrating for a sapient

being to insult another creature if the one insulted is not
aware of the intended insult. We wish deeply to avoid giving
cause for frustration to any of the Sacred Prey, so we were
only reassuring you that we are aware of the intention of
insult. Pray do not be frustrated.''

Dane burst into a gurgle of laughter. He couldn't help it.
The robot glided toward him and inquired anxiously, ''Are
you in distress?''

Dane, managing to get his face and voice straight, reas-
sured the featureless robot that he was quite all right. The
robot returned to the Mekhar who turned his back and the
robot calmly glided around to face him again. The Mekhar,
with a long sigh, remained still; and as if he had never been
interrupted the robot continued. ''As for your unwillingness to
assume the garments of the Sacred Prey, it is customary that
they shall be worn. Clad in the color assigned to the Sacred
Prey, you will be admitted to any portion of the Hunting
Preserves, and you will not be killed by accident or for any
disciplinary action.''

''You can't win, old fellow,'' said Dane to the Mekhar,
trying hard to control his laughter. ''Customs of the country,
and all that. Here, you—'' He turned to the robot, and the
inexpressive voice said, ''You may address me as Server.''

''Give me your customary garments, or whatever; I'll wear
them.''

Aratak said in an undertone to Dane, ''If I am going to be
hunted, I want to be in decent condition. Let's see if this—
Ahem! I have a problem. Server—'' he said hesitantly.

The robot who called himself Server wheeled noiselessly
toward him. ''We are here to serve you.''

''Server, your presence proposes a problem to me,'' Aratak
said. ''Are you a sapient being?''

Server was motionless before the huge lizard-man. ''The
question neither interests us nor makes sense to us,'' he said.

Aratak said, ''Then let me rephrase your question. Do you

partake of Universal Sapience? Shall I regard you as an independently intelligent being? It is obvious that your answers are reponsive to unforeseen and unprogrammed happenings. Therefore, how shall I regard you?''

"It is not necessary to regard us as anything in particular,'' said Server. "You are Sacred Prey, therefore transient, and we represent a permanence. But if you will forgive a suggestion, Honored Prey, we would prefer to delay any possible discussions or disputations or philosophical questions as to the nature of our being until your material wants have been met. Have you a material request which we may honor, or have we leave to wait upon your companions?''

"I have a material request,'' Aratak said. "You spoke of bathing. In traveling one bathes as one can or must, in whatever way will serve the needs of sanitation, but can you provide me, for the repair of my integuments, with a bath of warm mud?''

Server's answer was instantaneous. "If you will proceed through that door beside the archway and travel along the path in the direction of the shadows, you will find a pool of mud for bathing. If the temperature proves unsuited to your integuments, report this to us tonight and we will duplicate whatever conditions are most suitable to you.'' He wheeled to the others and said, "There are water baths both hot and cold, ice baths, steam baths, and dry sand baths, as you prefer; make yourselves free of them. Now, if you would state your food requirements—''

He happened to be standing beside Rianna at that moment, and after a moment of thought she said, "I require a diet suitable for proto-simians, and am accustomed to a mixture comprising roughly a third of protein, a half of mixed carbohydrate and vegetable bulk, and the remainder of fat. My preferred flavors are either sweet or salty, with no objection to mild sournesses; I dislike great sourness or bitterness. Is this stated adequately?''

"We applaud your explicitness," said Server, "and will do our best to comply. Will this combination adequately nourish your other proto-simian companions?"

Dane said, "That's fine by me." After Rianna's scientific analysis of the human diet he'd have felt foolish asking for a steak dinner, although he did wonder how Server would have reacted to such a request.

Dallith said, "It is suitable for me also, with the reservation that I dislike salty flavors, but have no objection to mildly bitter ones. Also, it isn't customary for my race to feed on animal flesh."

Server acknowledged this with a little blink of lights, and turned to the Mekhar, who said harshly, "I'm a meat-eater."

"You prefer to consume a diet almost exclusively of animal protein or analogues thereof?" Server said. "It shall be provided for you. As for you, Honored Philosopher—"

Aratak's gill-ruffs glowed faintly blue as he bowed to the metal creature. He said politely, "The philosophical man consumes what nature sends his way. Fortunately our metabolism has adapted to the point where I can digest nearly anything, provided there is enough of it. An advantage to a harsh world where survival depends upon flexibility."

"We will attempt to please not only your digestion but your palate," Server said, and rolled away, while Dane stood marveling at a metal robot which could—almost—match Aratak in courteous philosophizing!

Aratak was evidently troubled. "I must speculate upon the place in Universal Sapience occupied by intelligent beings who are nevertheless constructed, rather than evolved by the grace of the Divine Egg. If you will forgive me, I will assume the customary garments and go to repair my integument in a pool of hot mud."

He stumped away toward the door which Server had indicated.

Rianna said to Dallith, "A hot bath sounds marvelous. Shall we go and look for one?"

Dallith turned to Dane, hesitantly. "Shouldn't we stay together?"

"I guess we're pretty safe here. Go and get your bath before supper." He didn't know if mixed bathing was customary in either of the women's worlds, but it wasn't anything he cared to bring up just now. Left alone with the Mekhar, he asked, "What sort of bath do you generally use? You—I can't just keep calling you 'you'; what is your name?"

The Mekhar growled, "I am known as Cliff-Climber; you may call me Cliff for the sake of brevity. And I prefer a bath of cool water, preferably in a stationary pool where swimming is possible."

Well, Dane thought, *there's that one touch of nature that makes the whole world kin. I never imagined I'd find anything in common with a giant sapient cat.* He said aloud, "I could do with a swim myself. Let's go look for one out there."

Chapter Seven

Outdoors, the Hunter's World was cold; the great red moon, obscuring much of the sky, cast down a fiery light which seemed to suggest warmth, but Dane was glad of the woolly-textured tunic, and Cliff-Climber was shivering before they had gone a hundred yards from the building. Cats liked heat, Dane thought; they were all jungle creatures originally. The Mekhar ship had been steamy hot.

The path led away between green lawns and gardens; it was apparently a vast park, garden, or forest preserve. Before they had gone very far they passed a vast pool which looked like yellow mud and smelled to high heaven of sulfur; little plops and gurgles all over its surface proclaimed volcanic action beneath, and small wisps of odoriferous steam escaped in gusts from them. A long, reptilian snout emerged from the mud, surmounted by two oddly familiar eyes; then the creature heaved itself up, and Dane recognized Aratak.

"Most comfortable," he rumbled. "Will you join me?"

Dane pantomimed clothespin-on-nose. "If that's your idea

of a comfortable bath, old fellow, I wish you joy of it, but I'm going to find something that smells a little better!''

"Suit your own tastes, of course," Aratak said, settling himself comfortably back in the stinking yellow mud, neck-deep. "But I cannot imagine how this delightful fragrance can displease you. Well, I rejoice with you in the infinite diversity of Creation.''

Dane looked at Cliff-Climber. "Feel free to join him, if you'd rather!''

The Mekhar grimaced expressive disgust, and they moved on. They passed a bubbling spring whose waters were so icy that Dane shuddered when he stuck a careful toe into them, moved on to an area where a natural hot spring had been diverted so that the water flowed into a large bathing pool surrounded by a variety of small stone-circled round pools or tubs. In one of these Rianna lay at length, naked, her red hair curling with the steam and surrounding her body with floating rings. She lifted a hand in greeting to Dane, quite unabashed.

Why, she's beautiful. I didn't realize it; I've never thought of it. But she's a beautiful woman.

In the central hot pool, a variety of men and women were bathing or swimming; seven or eight who seemed as human as himself, with five or six others of varying alien species. Dane had grown used to this on the Mekhar slave ship, and no longer stared with goggle-eyed wonder at their strangeness.

Yeah, quite the blasé sophisticated Galactic traveler . . . he told himself sourly. *Just another spider-man, another proto-canine or proto-feline species—*

Wonder what the hell the Hunters are like!

At the far end of the pool he spotted, close together, two beings who closely resembled the Mekhar at his side. Cliff-Climber saw them at almost the same instant, and his claws contracted and relaxed.

"I must go and see if they are people of my own world,"

he said, and moved away, circling the pool with his quick, bounding run.

Dane was not sorry to see him go. The close proximity of the Mekhar—word or no word—had been disconcerting. The hot water looked good, and it was too cold for a swim, so he decided to enter the pool himself.

He hesitated a moment before dropping his garment, but evidently there were no modesty taboos here. *When in Rome, do as the Romans do*, he told himself, stripping off the warm tunic and dropping it on the stone rim. He stuck in one foot, found that the water was as pleasantly warm as a heated swimming pool at home, and deepened toward the center for swimming, although at the edges it was no more than ankle-deep. He struck out toward the center and swam around for a few moments, enjoying the warmth after the chilly air.

The warm water seemed to ease the kinks from his muscles, aching and sore from the long confinements. *I'm out of condition*, he thought. *I hope I get a chance to limber up before the Hunt!*

He turned on his back to float, and someone beside him spoke his name.

"Dane?"

He turned to see Dallith floating beside him.

"I thought you were probably soaking in a hot tub like Rianna."

"I was, for a time," she said. "The water in the smaller pools is much hotter than this, and very"—she sought for a word—"very comforting. Then I felt you coming and swam out to speak to you."

They floated side by side for a moment, Dane looking up at the enormous red moon in the sky.

"Calling it a moon is really not quite right," Dallith said. "It must be another planet, and almost the twin of this one."

"It looks larger than this planet's sun," Dane agreed. The sun was an undistinguished yellow-orange ball, the apparent size of a dinner plate; the moon covered almost a sixth of the visible sky. "The man in the moon is a giant here," he said humorously, looking at the strange markings on the full red face.

Dallith said soberly, "We will soon be the men in the moon."

"What do you mean, Dallith?"

"There are two men here from a world in the Unity," she said. "They know my world and know of my people, although they have never been there. They were, of course, surprised to see one of my race away from our home world— when we must travel we do so in groups, for we cannot be alone, as you know—and they asked me many questions, and in return they told me what they knew of the Hunt." She gestured with one hand at the great red disk above. "The Hunt takes place on the moon."

She explained. The planet of the Hunters, and the Red Moon, revolved around one another in a stable path, so that eclipses of the sun were frequent on the Hunters' world, and eclipses of the moon almost as common. During the next eclipse of the sun—as seen from the moon—the Prey would be taken to the moon, and there, as the light returned, would be hunted. The Prey's only task was to survive until the darkness of the next eclipse—at which time the Hunt would end. The Hunters who had been victorious, and successfully killed their Prey, would bring the bodies back to the Hunters' World for ceremonial feasting, and great ceremony; the Prey who had managed to survive would be honored, rewarded, and given safe passage back to wherever they wished to go.

Dane asked, "Do they know what the Hunters are like?"

Dallith said, "No. I'm told no one knows that. They quoted the same thing Cliff-Climber said: 'The Hunter is seen only by the Prey he kills.' "

"That's ridiculous," Dane said. "Some people must have fought a Hunter and lived to tell about it."

"Maybe they're unkillable," suggested Dallith, in all seriousness. "Some races are said to be. When wounded, they simply regenerate their own parts."

"I don't think so," Dane said slowly. "If the Hunt is virtually a religious ritual for these people, Hunters, it must be associated with some genuine danger and risk for them. Most religions emphasize, one way or another, a conquest over death. A people who made a religion out of hunting, and went to such lengths to secure really dangerous prey, must be vulnerable. If they just wanted the fun of killing things, they could pick and choose among all the slave races, but they pay enormous sums and go to enormous amounts of trouble to get brave and desperate people for their Prey. So it hardly stands to reason that they'd make it a massacre. We must have some chance—maybe not a good chance, but a chance of some sort—at killing them right back."

Dallith did not reply. She struck out for the shore; Dane followed her. Near the edge of the pool he overtook her. She was standing knee-deep in the water, and for the first time he saw her wholly naked, without the all-enveloping loose white robe of her home planet.

She is beautiful too, he thought. *When I first saw her she seemed all beauty to me, incomparable*. Yet he did not react to her nakedness with the immediate sensual response as he had felt for Rianna. *Is it only the habit of protecting her, caring for her, sparing her all trouble and fear?* He quickly stifled the automatic response, knowing she would—with that eerie empathic sensitivity—pick it up from his mind and emotions.

I love her. And yet she doesn't appeal to me—sexually— half as much as Rianna. I look at Rianna lying naked in her bath, and I revert to the barbarian—I could jump on her right there, the way all proto-simians are supposed to do. And I don't even particularly like her!

The air struck icy and chill after the hot water, and Dane

made haste to get into his warm tunic, belting it around him. He looked down at his bare legs and thought, *It's funny how much we depend for our self-image on our clothes. If you'd asked me, say a year ago, I'd have said I didn't give a hang about clothes, they were just something to keep off the cold, and keep the cops from running me in for indecent exposure. But being without pants does funny things to Western man. We even define our masculinity that way—we talk about a man wearing the pants in his family.*

He joined Dallith at the edge of the pool. The light was dimming, and the other swimmers were leaving the baths. In the long, loose terra-cotta tunic, her light straight hair falling like a curtain over her shoulders and nearly to her waist, Dallith looked shy and lovely.

"It is strange—to feel that people are looking at me."

"Me too," Dane said. "Nude bathing isn't done in the part of the world I come from, though of course I've traveled where it *is* customary and it doesn't bother me. We have a proverb, though, 'When in Rome'—Rome is a city on my world, a big one—'do as the Romans do.' "

Dallith smiled. "We have a similar saying. 'When travelling on Lughar, eat fish.' "

"Probably Aratak could find a proverb from the Wisdom of the Divine Egg to match it," Dane said wryly. "Human nature seems to run in the same channels. . . . Human nature?"

"Universal Sapience," Dallith corrected him gently. "But you're right; most sapient beings do discover the same truths and put them down in their proverbs. . . ."

Dane's mouth twisted. "Where do the Mekhars fit into that?" he asked, and Dallith said slowly, "They are surely sapient beings. They seem to have their own strict codes of ethics. But they have not yet accepted the Unity. . . ."

Her words fell, as if of their own weight, and trailed into silence. Then she said, "Before we began talking of proverbs and sapience—I was saying, it feels strange to think people are looking at me.''

"Nude bathing is *not* customary for you, then?''

"Oh, no. It *is* customary—in fact, we seldom wear clothes at all on our own world, unless it is snowing, or we have to travel in very wet and thorny woods—but we seldom *look* at one another. It's easier to react to other people of my own kind by the way they feel to our minds. It was so strange to feel people thinking about my body, my outside image, rather than what I was like inside—am I very ugly, Dane?'' It sounded rather pathetic, and Dane, taken aback, said simply, "No. No. To me you seem beautiful.''

"And do—do men of your world judge women by their beauty?''

"I'm afraid so. Sometimes. The more sensible ones, of course, try to judge women by their other qualities—their intelligence, their good manners, kindness, gentleness, good nature—but I'm afraid too many men *do* judge women by whether or not they're good-looking.''

"And women judge men that way too?'' Suddenly Dallith blushed, turning away, but Dane could see that she was almost as red as her tunic. She said, still not looking at him, "Let's go and find Rianna. See, the others are all coming out of the water.''

Dane went with her, feeling oddly confused, wondering how much of his own indecision and sexual awareness she had picked up. Rianna joined them in a minute or two, her hair drying in a frizzy copper-colored cloud around her head, her tunic tucked up to her knees. She said, "Aratak has gone to wash off that damnable yellow slime; I gather he considers it a precious perfume and meant to wear it to supper, but I managed to convince him that probably none of the rest of us could manage to eat much unless he got rid of the sulfur stink. Where's the Mekhar?''

"He found a couple of compatriots, and went off to join them."

"I hope he stays with them," Rianna said emphatically. "I don't trust him. I've never liked any of the proto-feline species—they're stealthy sneaks, and you can't trust any of them, any more than you can a pet mouse-catcher!"

"That's a very prejudiced attitude for a scientist," Dallith said in her grave way. "It's like blaming a proto-simian for being curious; it's a survival mechanism. Proto-felines evolved from hunting carnivores; stealth is a survival mechanism for them, too. Would your house-mouser be any good at hunting if he *didn't* catch his dinner quietly?"

Rianna shrugged. "Anyway, our Mekhar is welcome to the society of his own kind—but no such luck, for here he comes."

Cliff-Climber joined them, Aratak lumbering along behind, as they reached the building in which they had been lodged. The giant saurian said, "I have disposed of the stench which was inimical to your metabolism, Rianna." He managed to sound pitiful. She chuckled.

"Thank you, Aratak. I'm aware of the sacrifices you philosophers have to make when traveling with us hypersensitive simian types!"

Cliff-Climber was sleek and shining under his brick-red tunic, his lionlike mane of hair and beard combed into smooth and elaborate ringlets. Dane said, "I had expected you to remain with your kindred, Cliff."

"My kindred?" Cliff-Climber made a hissing, spitting noise, halfway between derision and annoyance. "Common criminals! Common thieves who escaped from Mekharvin one pounce ahead of the Stalkers, fled here and sold themselves to keep from paying the price of their crimes! These are the folk who give the Mekhars a bad name all over the Galaxy!"

"Of course," Rianna said with heavy irony, "slave stealers aren't in a class with *common* thieves."

Cliff-Climber took her literally. "Of course not. I could not possibly join with such people. In the first place, I have given my word not to harm you, as my companions. In the second, honor will not permit me to associate with such beings. I prefer to keep my wrath and my killing for the Hunters."

Dane asked—not with sarcasm, he was actually interested— "Does honor permit you to associate with proto-simians and slaves?"

"Not usually," Cliff-Climber replied, as they passed into the building which was their temporary quarters, "but you are beings of proven bravery, and furthermore you are to be, it seems, my companions in the Hunt. So it is necessary that I cultivate a feeling of kindliness toward you, so that we may cooperate against our mutual foes."

Dane murmured, "We must hang together or assuredly we will all hang separately."

Cliff-Climber said, "Let us hope no such dishonorable fate awaits us."

Aratak asked, "Did you manage to find out anything about exactly what fate *does* await us—and when?"

"I did," Dallith said, and repeated what she had been told about the eclipses and that the Hunt would take place on this planet's satellite, the Red Moon. Cliff added, "We were brought here too late in the day to join the other Prey in the armory. But, I am told, tomorrow morning we will be taken there."

They were interrupted by the robot, Server, returning through the long door at the end of the hall. His extensible arms—five of them, this time—held a variety of covered trays of food.

"If you will arrange yourselves conveniently for your preferred style of dining," Server's mechanical voice informed them, "it will be our pleasure to serve you."

The Mekhar brought a cushion from his couch, dropped to the floor; after a minute of thought Dane did likewise and the others, except Aratak, followed suit. The great saurian simply stretched out, half reclining.

"It is good to dine in civilized surroundings again," he said.

Server rolled noiselessly to Dallith. "Honored Prey, that it was you who requested food of vegetable origin. It is our pleasure to inform you that the proteins in this meal are entirely of leguminous origin, baked or boiled, and the fats are from the seeds of a tree." He extended a tray to Dallith.

To Dane, and to Rianna, he gave slightly similar trays, whose contents, he informed them, were of mixed animal and vegetable origin. Dane, tasting it, decided it wasn't the steak dinner he had thought about, but it wasn't bad either. There was something like mushrooms, a salad of mixed greens, and a kind of meat loaf. There were also some mixed fruits, very sweet. Dallith had the same kind of fruits and salad but instead of meat loaf she had some kind of dark-red baked grains. The tray given to Cliff-Climber smelled strange and unpleasant, but the Mekhar made a soft purring growl of appreciation and began to tear at it with his claws. Aratak ate delicately, with the tips of his claws; his food looked and smelled almost as bad, to Dane, as the perfumed mud which was his delight, but Aratak positively glowed—blue around the gills, that same luminescence—and said to Server, "You have kept your promise to delight my palate as well as my metabolism. My deepest thanks. I have not been fed so well in a hundred light-years."

Dane muttered, "The condemned man always gets a hearty meal."

Cliff-Climber twitched his muzzle and murmured, "A hearty meal to one creature is garbage to his brother."

Dane laughed, and at Rianna's inquiring glance said, "One man's meat is another man's poison. We were talking earlier of proverbs."

Aratak asked Server, "Are you the same creature who came to serve us before?"

"The question neither interests us nor has meaning."

Dallith—Dane was seated on cushions between her and Rianna—murmured, "He always speaks of himself in the plural."

"I noticed," Dane whispered. "Now, is he using the royal we, the editorial we, or the we of people with tapeworms?"

Dallith giggled. "Could a robot have a tapeworm?"

"Of course," Rianna chuckled, "a parasite that eats computer tapes."

Aratak was cogitating, as Server rolled noiselessly away. "I must think about this. I asked him if he had Universal Sapience, and he did not, or could not, answer. There are many of these Server creatures, for I saw at least four in the confines of the park. Now the question before us at the moment is this." He paused as if he were addressing a seminar in philosophy. "Can a being with no individual sense of identity partake of Universal Sapience?"

Dane was glad to have something to think about besides the impending Hunt. "Does sapience necessarily depend on a sense of identity?"

"It seems to me it does," Aratak said. "For sapience evolves, it seems to me, when a creature begins to regard himself as individual rather than simply following the mass instincts of his species. When, in short, he leaves the general and begins to regard himself as being one of the particular."

"I'm not sure it matters," said Rianna. "If Server is only one of a centralized intelligence, then wouldn't that centralized intelligence, of which Server is part, partake of Universal Sapience? And if he can speak for all of them, or it, isn't any one of Server's parts, or bodies, a part of such sapience?"

Aratak looked troubled. "I have always defined sapience as a sense of one's unique individuality. How do you define it, Rianna?"

"The ability for time-binding," she replied promptly. "When any species reaches the point where it can pass along accumulated knowledge to its progeny, so that each generation does not recapitulate the whole race experience in itself, but can pass along history, I believe at that point a race is sapient."

"Hmmm, possibly," murmured Aratak, picking his enormous teeth. "Cliff-Climber, how does your race define sapience?"

The Mekhar did not hesitate. "A sense of honor—a code of ethics. We regard any race without such a code as animal, and any race which displays it as sapient." He bowed to them and said, "Naturally we so regard you all."

Aratak said, "And you, Dallith? How does your race define sapience?"

"Empathy, I think. I don't mean the developed psi talent, but the ability to think oneself into the other being's place. Maybe I simply mean imagination. No nonsapient animal has it, and every sapient species has it."

"These are all very good answers," Aratak said. "Dane, we have not heard from you, and coming from a planet with only one known sapient species, has your race even evolved a concept of what constitutes sapience?"

Dane said slowly, "It's a common enough point of philosophical speculation. We have two or three species—dolphins, great apes—who appear to have some, if not all, of the earmarks of sapience, and people have thought about it. Some people have suggested that the ability to create art, the aesthetic sense, is a mark of sapience." In his wildest dreams he had never thought he would sit around a dinner with two girls from alien stars, a lion-man and a lizard-man, discussing the possible sapience of a robot. Suddenly he felt ludicrously cheerful. "Probably the mark of sapience," he said, "is nothing more nor less than the ability to ask oneself what it is; in short, the ability to take part in philosophical discussions about sapience. That would cover everything." He raised his glass, full of some kind of faintly bitter and alocholic drink.

"I'll drink to that!"

Once the sun had set the sky darkened quickly, and since there were no artificial lights inside the quarters, only the reddish moonlight, the five captives sought their beds. Dane could not sleep for some time. Once he went noiselessly to the door and tested it, simply to verify a theory he had. It was not locked. But where could they go? In any case, escape now would just mean the Hunters would hunt them down now, rather than later. And later, they would have weapons, or so Cliff-Climber had indicated with his talk of armories.

Returning to his bed, he passed the two sleeping women. Rianna lay flung out on her back, naked and covered only with a thin blanket; Dane hurriedly turned away. *Just like all the rest of the proto-simians. I've got other things on my mind, right now, though.*

Dallith slept quietly, her face half hidden in her long streaming hair, and Dane paused beside her, looking down in an agony of love and regret.

I saved your life, Dallith—but only to bring you here. Rianna was right all along. He turned hastily away and stumbled toward his own bed. But it was a long time before he slept.

Chapter Eight

The next morning, after a meal very like—in quantity—the evening meal, but entirely different in flavors and textures, the five captives were led through the great park, or preserve, by the mechanical Server, at last reaching a great windowless building. It was constructed of the same terra-cotta colored brick as everything else in this part of the planet.

"This is the Armory," Server told them, ushering them over the threshold. "Here you may practice, every day, with the weapons of your personal choice."

The idea brought Dane up short. Weapons. Armory. He realized that despite his brave words last night, he had been thinking more or less in terms of big game, or safari hunting back on Earth, where the game had no defense except to run and hide, or to charge with such natural weapons as claws, teeth or tusks, or sheer size and weight might give him. While the hunters, on the other hand, might be equipped with the most modern and dangerous weapons—guns, darts, special windowed shooting wagons—that science could provide.

When he had spoken about a genuine risk for the Hunters, here, he had been thinking in terms of Earth's own game laws, aimed more at limiting the take, and preserving the breeding powers of the game, rather than giving them a better chance for life. Such things as the laws against shooting underage, or breeding females; laws against jacklighting deer, or using explosive bullets against big game.

But what he had said just might be literally true; in which case the Hunt laws were more analogous to the formalized, quasi-religious sport of the bullfight; a pageant of death, involving a serious combat, a duello of death. . . .

He followed Server into the great building.

Inside, it was evenly lighted, padded underfoot, and divided into huge areas. It reminded Dane, very faintly, of a big gymnasium or practice field on Earth. Four or five Olympic teams could have worked out in it without ever coming close enough to study one another's styles.

And all along the walls, lining them, up and down, for what seemed like acres and acres of space, were weapons.

Weapons. Dane had never seen so many weapons.

There were swords of every make and kind he had ever envisioned, from great two-handed Crusader and Viking swords to short slim rapiers to curved Persian-style sabers. Some were so tiny and slim that they would not have burdened a four-year-old child, and he found himself speculating curiously about the race which could grasp and hold their tiny hilts. Others, on the other hand, were so huge that he doubted if Aratak could have lifted them with both paws.

With the swords there were daggers, and knives, again of every conceivable shape, form or material. There were huge spears and smaller narrow ones. There were shields, great square or round or triangular ones, small light round ones of leather and wicker, oddly-shaped ones evidently meant for no human anatomy since they had at least three handles and could not conveniently be lifted with fewer hands. There were maces, and clubs. There were weapons Dane had never seen before and did not know how to describe.

Aratak asked Server, "What are the rules of the Hunt about these weapons?"

"You may choose what weapons you like, and practice with them from now until the day of the Hunt," Server said. "Then you may take with you whatever weapons you can carry."

Dallith's hand slid into Dane's. She asked the question in his thoughts.

"What sort of weapons do the Hunters carry?"

Server's voice was expressionless, as always; "Some carry one weapon, some another. Each Hunter has his favorite."

Rianna said, "Do they carry any other weapons? Nerve-guns, for instance, or explosive-propulsion weapons?"

"They do not," Server said. "The rules of the Hunt, which are said to be older than their very race itself, prohibit the Hunter from carrying any weapon denied to the Sacred Prey themselves."

That, thought Dane, was a great relief. "Then you mean no weapons will be used against us except those which are displayed here?"

"None whatsoever. The Armory contains a full assortment of every permitted weapon."

He rolled away toward another group of people in terra-cotta tunics who were working out, at the far end of the Armory. Dane thought he recognized a couple of Mekhars among them; he wondered if they were the same with whom Cliff-Climber had arrogantly declined to associate, the day before. They seemed to be working out with something that looked, at this distance, like kendo sticks or short, blunt quarterstaffs.

He went toward the walls of the Armory, looking closely at

the array of weapons displayed there. *A weapons collector would go mad in here,* he thought. *To say nothing of the curator of an arms museum!*

"I wonder if all these weapons were made by the Hunters for their Prey," Rianna said at his elbow, "or whether they were collected from all corners of the Galaxy?"

"The question had crossed my mind also," Aratak rumbled, "but I do not suppose we will ever know."

Dane smiled grimly. "As it happens, I think I can answer it," he said, staring with close attention at one long curved sword on the wall, in a polished black lacquer wooden sheath. "It's likely that some, at least, have been collected or kept in honor of some unusually dangerous or daring Prey." He reached up and took down the sheath.

"Look," he said. "This particular sword, for instance."

"It's not unique," Rianna said. "I can name four planets where this type of sword is used—the same general type, that is; I'm not a weapons specialist."

"But on this, I am," Dane said, sliding the blade from its scabbard with what seemed exaggerated care, and holding it at arm's length. He looked along the bright, highly polished blade. "Note that the curve runs all along the length of the sword—in fact, it's bow-shaped. That may be common enough all over the Galaxy—it probably is, it's an efficient enough design. Curved swords are common even on my planet. But this particular blade—well, look. It's made of two kinds of metal; the core of soft iron which will bend without breaking; the outside of tempered steel. Do you see that wavy line?" Carefully, he pointed to where the metal changed color. "That's where the steel was specially hardened, so it would take a razor edge—although, to be exact, the usual razor is dull by comparison. I've seen an expert cut a silk kimono off a human body, without harming the wearer. Notice the mirror finish—how highly polished it is. And of course, every culture decorates and finishes off their swords in some characteristic way, and this one is unmistakable. Look at the hilt; the grip of sharkskin, wrapped with silk cord in that particular pattern. This sword was made on Earth,'' he concluded. "It can't be coincidence. But if you want absolute proof—'' Carefully he slid a tiny wooden peg out of the handle, and with a few deft movements he removed the grip entirely and stood examining the exposed tang. He turned the blade so they could see the markings. ''This is a Japanese samurai sword, make by Mataguchi in 1572—and probably one of the finest ever made; I've seen other Mataguchi swords, but none this perfect.''

Dallith's breath caught. ''Made on your world?''

''On my world,'' he said grimly, ''four hundred years ago. The samurai were a caste of the fiercest swordsmen who ever existed. And someone—or some *thing*—must have landed on Earth and taken at least one of them back here, to fight against the Hunters.''

He glanced caressingly down the length of the blade before replacing the grip; Rianna reached out as if to touch the blade and he stretched his hand to prevent her. ''Do that and you'll be picking up your finger off the floor,'' he said. ''I told you; a razor is *dull* by comparison. This one's been hanging here a long time, it's a little weathered, but still—those robots, or something, have been taking good care of it.''

He slid it carefully into the lacquered sheath.

''I don't envy any Hunter—and I don't care what kind of creature they are—who runs up against a samurai with this particular sword in hand. He may have been killed—he probably *was* killed—but he certainly didn't give up his life cheaply.''

''Perhaps he was one of those who escaped,'' Rianna suggested, ''and they hung the sword in the Armory to honor him.''

''Not if I know anything about samurai,'' Dane said quietly.

"If he'd lived, he would have taken the sword with him, wherever he went afterward. 'The sword of the samurai is the soul of the samurai.' They'd have had to kill him to get it."

He stood for a moment with the sheath in his hand. The Mataguchi sword—it would have been a priceless museum-piece on Earth, or the cherished heirloom of an old Japanese family—was a little longer and heavier than any he had ever actually practiced with. And it had been years since he had studied the Japanese style of fencing. He should probably test half a dozen swords of the same general type, until he found one of the perfect weight for his arm.

But he felt strangely drawn to the nameless, unknown Japanese swordsman of the sixteenth century who, at some unguessable moment in history, had been kidnapped, like himself, and taken like himself halfway across the known Universe to face unbelievable opponents. "I think I've found my weapon," he said. "Maybe it's a good omen."

He turned to Cliff-Climber and said, "Are there weapons here to suit your people?"

He was growing used to the arrogant curl of the Mekhar's upper lip. "Weapons? I need only these," said the lion-man, flexing his great paws and flicking out long, curved claws razor-sharp and glittering as if—No; they *had* been artificially tipped with gleaming metal.

Like capping a tooth, Dane thought, *but a lot more dangerous*.

"I will meet any creature alive with these. It would be beneath me to use lesser weapons."

Dane raised an eyebrow. "Your motto seems to be, *be prepared*. But I noticed on shipboard you carried a nerve-gun."

"For herding animals," said the Mekhar with contempt. "But I am a member of the fighting caste and I have blooded an enemy in a hundred duels. These"—one sneering nod took in the enormous array of weapons which lined the walls—"are for races ungifted by Nature with weapons of their own. Your weak claws and teeth developed when you abandoned Nature's weapons, and see, your people are paying for it."

Dane shrugged.

"Each to his own weapons."

"As a matter of history," Rianna said tartly, "proto-simians never were, as you put it, gifted with Nature's weapons. We were given brains to make up for the deficiency."

"That, of course, is your own version," Cliff-Climber said, quite unruffled.

"Well, it's none of my business," Dane told him seriously, "but suppose they come at you with a long spear or something of the sort?"

Cliff-Climber thought about that for a moment. He said, "I will trust to their honor—and their wish for sport."

"I wish I had your confidence," Dane muttered. Aratak was studying the long rows of weapons, looking dissatisfied.

"We are a peaceful people," he said. "I know little of weapons. A knife is for peeling fruits or skinning prickle-fishes. I must think about this." He looked down the long room, where the strangers who vaguely resembled the Mekhar had hung up their long sticks and gone away. "Perhaps I will confine myself to the heaviest club I can conveniently lift. With my weight behind it, it should crush almost any attacker within reason. If not, then I suspect I have been designated by the Cosmic Egg as ripe to give up this life and join its own infinite wisdom, and it will be useless for me to struggle to master strange weapons."

Dane suspected he was right. The thought of Aratak wielding "the heaviest club he could lift" was a fearsome one indeed—he imagined the great, powerful lizard-man could crush a rhinoceros with one, if he happened to hit it four-square between the eyebrows—and anything Aratak couldn't kill that way probably couldn't be killed.

Cradling the samurai sword on his arm, Dane turned to the girls. He said, "It doesn't seem real. Swordplay is a sport, a game, on our world. No one expects to have to fight for his life with a sword, these days."

"I thought your world was full of wars," Rianna said.

"There are wars enough. But most of them are fought now, with bombs, or at least with rifles. Even bayonets have gone out of style. And policemen carry guns for when their nightsticks aren't enough to keep the peace." He frowned in dismay. "At that I'm probably better qualified than the average Earthman, who never handled anything more lethal than the *Wall Street Journal*."

Rianna shook her head in dismay. She said, "On my world women never did much fighting, even before we did away with wars for good. I used to carry a knife in case I was attacked out on an archaeological dig—thieves and rapists still turn up now and then in the wilder areas—and once or twice I've had to use it. But usually it was enough to show that I had it; your average rapist is a coward. I wonder if I can find one light enough for me."

Dane grinned a little. "If you can't, it probably doesn't exist. They've got knives up there from six inches long to three feet, and weighing everything from two ounces to ten pounds."

Rianna finally selected a long, thin, leaf-shaped dagger, and a small second blade which could be tucked inside her skirt pocket. She blinked as she belted the longer one around her waist, and said, "It takes some getting used to. The *idea* of having to use this on a—a sapient creature, or having it used on me—" She rubbed her eyes fiercely, but Dane realized that behind her hard courage she was trembling with fear.

He said, "Let's hope it won't come to that, Rianna. I understand that what we have to do is survive—and if we can do it by running, I'm going to run, and hide, the best I can. *I'm* not eager to fight these Hunters, either.''

It was just as well, he thought, that they were being given some time to accustom themselves to the idea of a fight to the death. It wasn't anything a civilized person could readily assimilate. And although some people said that civilization was only a veneer, the veneer was thicker in some people than in others. He'd seen it during his brief Army service—in Vietnam. Some recruits took readily to the idea of killing. Civilization peeled off them in seconds when the drill instructor put a bayonet in their hands and told them to charge. Too many of that kind in one division, and you got a My Lai massacre, where killing erupted and couldn't be stopped until men, women, old people, and little children all lay dead. Other recruits couldn't be taught to kill, went into battle and fired into the air or squeezed their triggers at random, not wanting to die but unable to face the idea of an actual human target.

A friend of his in the police force had told him it was the same there. Some men killed readily—maybe too readily. Others discovered the ability to kill only when their own lives hung in the balance. And some could never bring themselves to shoot at all, and unless they were lucky and got assigned to a desk job or directing traffic in a playground, they were likely to get shot on the job before they could bring themselves to draw their own guns.

He had never knowingly killed anyone. He had studied the martial arts—kendo, karate, aikido—in the same spirit that he had climbed mountains and participated in solo sailing races; for the sport and for the sake of the skills involved. *Could* he kill? He wasn't sure. *But I'll damn well have to make a good stab at it—no pun intended!*

He had a few days to talk himself into it, anyhow. He remembered the time when he had gone—as an alternate, who never got a chance to appear on the field—with the Olympic fencing team. He'd gotten to know one of the distance-running champions, a gold-medal winner from England, who had told him that everything—winning, losing, competing—was all in the mind. "You psych yourself into winning, or into losing," he had said, "into finishing up with the feeling that you're going to drop dead, or into actually dropping dead—some people have."

So you could probably psych yourself into killing.

Cliff-Climber probably didn't need it, he thought. His race seemed to be killers; he had talked about fighting duels. Aratak? A peaceful people, but when angered he could be formidable. He'd seen Aratak in action against the Mekhars. As for Rianna—well, her people were pretty civilized, but if she could use a knife against a thief or would-be rapist, probably when the crunch came she'd be prepared to kill an attacker.

But Dallith?

Her people were peaceful. She was even a vegetarian. She'd come to pieces with terror—

And she'd been fiercer than any of us, against the Mekhars. Aratak had had to pull Dallith off one of them bodily, to prevent her from killing him then and there. . . .

He looked around for her, but she was examining a row of strange-looking, probably nonhuman weapons far down the room, and something in the determined way she had her back turned to him kept him from joining her.

I want to protect her, he thought. *And I can't. I'll have all I can do to keep myself alive.*

Firmly, summoning all the mental discipline he could manage, he put that right out of his mind. His fears could do nothing for Dallith except to rouse her own. Cliff-Climber had gone halfway down the long room and was doing an elaborate, solitary form of shadowboxing against the wall.

He disdains weapons. But those other Mekhars were using something like kendo sticks.

He wondered if the Hunters were like the Mekhars. Cliff-Climber seemed to understand them pretty well.

There were, it seemed, several groups practicing with various weapons. He wondered if it was permitted to watch others, and seeing Server—or another mechanical robot exactly like him—rolling toward their group, he put the question. He was told that the honored Sacred Prey could go wherever he chose within the confines of the Hunting Preserve (he wondered what would happen if he went outside, but he wasn't exactly eager to find out), and that if he had firmly made a choice of weapon, for the duration of the Hunt it would be reserved for him and no one else allowed to use it.

Dane hesitated only a moment before saying that he had. It might be folly, there might be some weapon better suited to his hand, but the lure of a sword from his own world was something he could not resist. If it was pure sentiment, he was prepared to risk his life on it.

He spent the rest of the short day accustoming himself to the feel of the hilt and sword in his hand, to the way it balanced and felt. As the sun was declining, Server came to direct them again to the baths before the evening meal.

Still preoccupied with the discovery of the samurai sword, he separated from the others without exchanging any word, and lay neck-deep in one of the volcanic pools for about half an hour, thinking this over. From time out of mind, stories has circulated—Charles Fort had collected thousands—of mysterious disappearances. "Flying Saucer" contactees told all sorts of tales about ships from outer space. There was the old story of the *Mary Celeste*—the ship found floating in the Atlantic Ocean, all lifeboats intact, the ship in perfect, seaworthy condition, the men's breakfast laid ready in the galley and the coffee still warm—but without a soul on board, living or dead. Now, in his hand, Dane Marsh had held proof of where some of these mysteriously-disappeared men had gone.

Did it matter? No one on Earth would ever know, after all. Even if he survived the Hunt, if these mysterious Hunters honored their promises that survivors would be set free, it was past all belief that he would be, or could be, returned to Earth. And if he did somehow get back, and tried to tell his story—well, no one would believe him. Maybe that chap who claimed he'd been taken to Venus aboard a spaceship hadn't been so wacky, either—and maybe it hadn't been Venus.

Ahead of him, like a great door blocking off all view to the future, lay the Hunt. Lying submerged in the boiling hot pool, looking up at the great Red Moon that covered more than a quarter of the sky today, he realized that until this was over and done he could not begin to imagine what life would be like. *And if I get killed it won't make any difference*, he thought grimly. *Why plan for a future which probably won't come?*

No. That way lay despair and certain death. The only way to insure that there would be any future to plan for lay across the barrier of the Hunt, and he meant to survive it if he could.

The unknown samurai whose sword he bore had probably believed that he had been brought beyond the world's end to fight with demons. But whatever they were, the Hunters were not demons, and they would not meet him with some monstrous unknown weapon. They must be fallible. All the odds might be rigged in their favor—but so was a bullfight rigged in favor of the *torero*, and just the same the bull sometimes killed his man.

The hot water had seeped into every pore of his body and he felt pliant, comfortable, and relaxed. He thumbed his nose at the Red Moon and got out of the hot pool, plunging swiftly, before the air could chill him, into the cooler swimming bath.

He swam around for some time, until his whole body felt alive and tingling, then hauled himself out, dried himself sketchily with the terra-cotta tunic, and, naked on the rim of the pool, began to go through the *kata* exercises.

"You've been doing that all day," Rianna said at his side. "It looks like a sacred dance. I thought you didn't belong to any religion with rituals."

Dane laughed without halting his rhythm, going on with the quick, dancelike movements, which mimicked attack and defense postures; sliding rhythmically from one to the other. "Just getting limbered up," he said. "After today's workout, and a long hot bath, I could easily get stiffened up."

He finished, stopped, bent, and drew on his tunic, aware that Rianna was watching him closely as he fastened it. She said, "You seem to have some unexpected skills you never mentioned."

"I never thought it would do me the slightest good. I studied the martial arts the way a girl might study dancing even if she didn't intend to go on the stage."

"It is beautiful to watch," Rianna said with a smile. "Is it an art in itself?"

Dane shook his head. "No, the exercises are from karate—a form of unarmed combat; you saw me use it on the Mekhar ship." He came closer to her, exhilarated and excited. He was very conscious of the way she was looking up at him, flushed, her eyes dilated, her hair a frothing coppery cloud around her face, the tunic slipping from one shoulder. Without any preliminary, he reached out for her and drew her close into his arms, feeling her respond and melt against him.

He thought, the merest glimmer of thought at the back of his mind. *This isn't love, it isn't caring, it's simple rut. It's instinct, in the face of imminent death . . . to breed, to leave something of the self. . . .* But at that moment Dane could not have cared less for the voice of his mind. He looked quickly around the pool (*Did I notice this subconsciously, before? Was I planning this?*) where small enclosed groves or thickets of trees fell nearly to the ground, screening them from view.

"This way," he said to Rianna, his voice roughened with urgency, and pulled her into the grove. He seized her and bore her with his weight to the grass.

It was wholly instinctive, and so was her response. Sometime, somewhere, he heard himself mutter to her, "I shouldn't—not like this—"

She clasped him closer, murmuring against his mouth. "What does it matter? What have we to lose?"

It seemed a long time afterward, and the light from the Red Moon had intensified considerably, so that she seemed to lie bathed in a crimson glow, that she stirred, chuckling softly deep in her throat.

"As our dear Aratak would say, no doubt quoting his beloved Cosmic Egg—what could you expect of a couple of proto-simians, so deeply in the grip of their instinctive drives?" She bent over and kissed him quickly. "Dane, Dane, don't look so wretchedly apologetic! It's a common reaction—of course it is. Why should you and I be exempt from it?"

He sat up and drew his tunic about him, smiling at the woman.

"I suspect we'd better get back for our supper. Otherwise that damned robot, or one of his computerized brothers, is likely to come looking for us, and I'd hate to have to explain to some blasted servomech what kept us!"

She said serenely, "I'm sure he's used to it."

It was dark enough now so that lights were gleaming from inside the building which was their temporary home and, when Dane and Rianna came inside, the others were already beginning their meal. Cliff-Climber looked up, briefly, with a satirical curl of his whiskered lips, and turned to his food again. Dallith, looking very small and fragile, was bending

over her plate. As they came in, she raised her head and
began to smile at Dane (relief at his return; had she missed
him?), and it hit Dane like a ton of bricks.

*Dallith, oh God. She'll know. I love her, I love her and
here I am fooling around in the bushes with Rianna. . . .
Damn all proto-simian instincts—*

The smile abruptly slid off Dallith's face; she colored deeply
and bent again over her plate, and Rianna's smile went taut,
but she gripped Dane's hand almost painfully, and Dane, for
very shame, could not draw his hand away. Instead, he put
his arm around her waist and drew her reassuringly against
him.

*She deserves nothing but kindness. But oh God, Dallith
. . . have I hurt her?* He looked with deep misery at the bent
head.

Aratak, sensing the tension in the room, looked up in
kindly inquiry, and Rianna said harshly, defensively, "Well,
has the Divine Egg no wisdom for this moment?"

Aratak rumbled, "There are times when wisdom seems
misplaced, child. The only wisdom to which I can lay my
tongue at this moment is that when all else fails, it is well to
give comfort to one's belly. Eat your dinner, Rianna, before
it gets cold."

"Sounds like a damn good idea," Dane said. He started to
go to his usual place beside Dallith, but Rianna was still
clinging to his hand and he could not bring himself to pull
free. He bent and scooped up the tray and slid to the ground
beside Rianna.

As they ate he kept raising his eyes across the circle they
made, trying to catch Dallith's eyes, but every time he looked
at her she was bent over her tray, doggedly eating something
that looked like rice with gravy or peeling a great pale yellow
fruit, her face half hidden between the loose waves of her fair
hair. Before Dane had half finished his meal she laid aside

her tray and went off to her couch, where she turned her back to them all and lay motionless, asleep or pretending it. Once during the evening Rianna went to her side and bent over her as if to speak, but Dallith lay with her eyes closed and did not move or take any notice of her.

They had kept, half unaware, to the sleeping arrangement they had assumed on first being brought there: Dane slept at Rianna's side on a wide bed; Dallith beyond them; Aratak curled in comfort on the stone; the Mekhar coiled like a cat on the softest of the beds. Dane had thought last night of asking the women if they would prefer to share the wide bed and give him the other, but he had been held back by the calmness with which they had accepted the arrangement. It occurred to him now that perhaps to the Hunters, the gender differences between human male and human female were not of any significance.

When they lay down to sleep, Rianna laid her head in the curve of his arm. She said softly, "Dane, Dallith is so unhappy. Can she be jealous?"

Dane had been trying hard to avoid just this conclusion. What right had he to think Dallith cared? "I don't know, Rianna. She may simply be—embarrassed because I was. I told you a little about the—well, the sexual customs of my world. She picked up my embarrassment when you and Roxon—on the Mekhar ship—"

"But then she knew that Roxon and I were pretending," Rianna said shrewdly. "Dane, are you sorry about this?"

"How could I be?" He put his arms around her and held her close. She had been generous in his need—had shared it—and however he felt about her, it created a bond. He had no right to resent it. She drew closer to him, and after a few moments she fell deeply asleep.

But Dane lay wakeful, aware beyond sight or hearing of Dallith's unhappy stillness and withdrawal. It reminded him, all too graphically, of how she had looked, and acted, when she was letting herself die on the Mekhar slave ship.

Does she feel I've withdrawn from her? Does she feel too alone?

Stop flattering yourself, Marsh. There's no girl alive who's going to go off and die because you make love to someone else. Not even Dallith, special as she is.

But she has no one else. And that is why she wanted to die before. Goddamn it, I wish she'd turn over in her sleep or something. . . .

Finally he could bear the quiet no longer. He rose and made his way quietly across the floor. Aratak, glowing blue as always when he slept, stirred, opened one eye, and nodded as if in approval, and Dane felt himself coloring with embarrassment again, but he did not hesitate.

The reddish light made barred colors through the drawn slatted blinds, falling in stripes across Dallith's scattered fair hair. Dane lowered himself to her side, bending over the girl.

"Dallith," he said gently. "Look at me. Please, darling, look at me."

For a moment she was still, and Dane's heart turned over—had she withdrawn again beyond his reach?—but then, as if sensing and answering his fear, she rolled over, her dark eyes wide and unreadable, and lay looking straight up at him.

"Don't flatter yourself," she said quietly, "It isn't that important, is it?"

He felt an unreasonable surge of anger, directed half at Rianna, half at Dallith, and all, by some incomprehensible arithmetic, at himself—his own clumsiness. He said, "Maybe not. I thought you might think so and I wanted to be sure—" His voice suddenly caught. He was the product of a society where men did not weep; but tears suddenly stung his eyes and flooded them, and he knew, in agonized outrage, that he was going to cry. He bent down close to the girl and caught her against him, burying his face in her soft tunic. For a moment she softened and held him close; then she loosened her hands and said, in a tone of gentle scorn, "Me too?"

It was like a dash of cold water. (He did not stop to think that she might be learning at last, painfully, to protect her own vulnerability.) He said clumsily, "Dallith, I—I was afraid—oh, what can I say to you? You seem to know it all. You're so damn sure of yourself now."

"Is *that* what you think?" She lay back, her great wounded fawn eyes dark against the pallor of her cheeks and hair.

He said, stumbling, "I love you. I want you. You know how I feel, you do, you know you do. And yet—what can I say to you? You don't have to blame Rianna, do you? It isn't her fault, and you've frightened her too."

"I'm sorry about Rianna," Dallith said gently. "She was kind to me, too. I behaved very badly. I know that. Dane, it"—for the first time she sounded a little unsure—"it doesn't matter to me—not *that*. I knew. I even—I guess I expected it."

He put his arms around her and said miserably, hiding his face against her, "I—I wish it had been you—"

She tipped his face up so that their eyes met. She said very quietly, "No. It was reflex, Dane. You know that, I know that—Rianna knows it. The difference is, that I felt it too, and I fought it, because with my people— I wouldn't have wanted it like that, a mindless grab at each other in the face of death, blind, instinctive—"

Desolation broke through then, and Dallith began to cry softly.

"But if you couldn't fight it—if you couldn't—I can't bear it that you didn't come to me—"

He held her, helpless against the storm of her grief, knowing that any move he made now must be a mistake. After a long time she quieted. She even laughed and comforted him, telling him it did not matter, and sent him back to Rianna's side. "I don't want to hurt her again; I don't want you to hurt her." She kissed him, before she made him go, warmly and lovingly. But there was still something wrong and they both knew it.

Chapter Nine

"This place," Dane said, only half to the others, "is incredible."

"Credibility is not a concept applicable to any actual event, but only to speculative ones," Aratak rumbled at him. They were standing in the Armory, in the dull reddish light of midmorning; the Red Moon now seemed to obscure a good quarter of the sky. "If an event has actually occurred, it is by its very occurrence credible."

Dane chuckled. He wondered, not for the first time, exactly how his question had come to Aratak through the translator disks. He said, "I take it one would have trouble suggesting to you that one should practice believing six impossible things before breakfast?"

"Surely the essence of an impossible thing is that it is unsuitable for belief," Aratak began, then broke off in rumbling laughter. "What event has taxed your credibility just now, Marsh?"

Dane gestured toward the back of the robot Server, who

was trundling away toward the door of the Armory, and displayed what he held in his hands. "A few minutes ago," he said, "it occurred to me that I ought to have the proper materials for taking care of the edge on this sword. I told Server that I didn't suppose he'd have the exact things I wanted, but if he could approximate them, I'd be grateful; that I needed some finely powdered limestone—only a few ounces—some soft cloth, some loosely woven cloth, a short stick, and a piece of string. I expected he'd come back with some pecular makeshift but he simply rolled off and came back with all of them. Every one." Dane shook his head. "You'd think he heard requests like that every day or two."

"Maybe he does," Cliff-Climber said. "There cannot be more than a few ways of caring for what amounts, in the long run, to a simple piece of steel which happens to have a cutting edge. The savage mind is seldom devious or particularly inventive."

Dane ignored the Mekhar. He was getting good at that. He sat down cross-legged and began tying one of the bits of cloth into what looked like a powder puff on the end of a stick. Cliff-Climber watched him for a moment, then went away and began practicing his shadow-dance exercise before a long strip of mirror. (When asked about it, he had told them that there was a legendary Mekhar duelist who had grown so agile that he could throttle his reflection in a mirror before the reflection could raise an arm.)

"When you have finished," Aratak said, "I would be appreciative if you would show me a little about your skills at unarmed combat. From what you have told me, you are an expert in this field."

"Far from it," Dane said. "I never even reached full Black Belt stage in karate—which is a good long way from being an expert. But I can show you a few of the basics. We won't have time for too much, but I can make a start." *Even a few basics in karate*, he thought, *will make our scaly friend here a formidable opponent.*

"Rianna has taught me something," Aratak said. "I understand that in order to be prepared against would-be thieves and rapists, women on her world are routinely taught something which she calls by a name meaning something like 'The Art of Making an Attacker Defeat Himself.' It is most useful, from what she has shown me, and based upon a philosophy I find thoroughly ethical; that a violent attacker's own strength shall be turned upon himself." He went on to explain the essentials of judo in his own inimitable fashion, while Dane thought, *Of course, it's a normal discovery. But it's damn lucky Rianna has that kind of training. I wish to Heaven that Dallith did.*

Disquieted by the thought, he finished caring for his sword, replaced it on the wall, and went to find Dallith. He found her listlessly examining a wall display of some incomprehensible and probably nonhuman weapons. She took no notice of him, and Dane felt again the mixture of anger and unexplainable guilt.

Something was wrong. Something was deeply wrong between them still. . . .

"Dallith," he said, "have you chosen a weapon? You must have something to protect you—"

She turned on him almost fiercely and said, "Do you think I am expecting *you* to protect me?"

I only wish I thought I'd be able to, Dane thought with a spasm of fear. He said soberly, "Whether you expect it or not, Dallith, I will as much as I can. But I'm not sure. For all I know, they'll come and take us away, one by one, each of us to face the Hunters alone." He did not realize until that very moment how deeply the analogy of the bullfight had penetrated his thoughts; the image of the arena, the mental concept of yelling spectators, egging the combatants on, faceless creatures whose very evolutionary stock he could not even guess. . . .

As if the picture in his mind had reached her, Dallith went pale. "*Are* we to go out alone?"

"I don't know. I hope to God we can stay together," he said. *I could work the four of us—no, the five of us—into a reasonably efficient fighting unit.* "We'll have to hope for the best, but we've also got to be prepared for the worst."

Fools, choosing Dallith for their prey, just because in a mad panic she fought like a tiger. . . . But if she has to fight alone they could tear her to pieces. He looked, in a sort of anguish, at the frail and girlish body, the pale cheeks, the thin wrists, the neck so delicate that her poised head looked like a flower on a narrow stem. How could he protect her? *She looks like one of the Christians ready to be thrown to the lions,* he thought, then firmly controlled his thoughts—they could only exaggerate her defenselessness.

"I know very little about most of these weapons," she said, with a limp gesture at the wall displays, the swords and shields and knives and spears. "My people do not fight with one another, except now and then in sport or trials of strength. And even there we are—careful. You see, the one who killed another—or even inflicted injury in a trial of strength—would share the experience of death, or pain, with his victim. . . ."

The gift, or curse, of empathy would have several side effects and that would be, probably, the most important. It had produced a timid culture, at least where inflicting the slightest pain or distress was concerned, since everyone else's pain would be as important and accessible as one's own. . . .

She took down a sling from the wall and spun it lightly around her head. "I thought," she said hesitantly, "that I might use this. My people use them, sometimes, to drive away pests from the fields and flower gardens. Or, sometimes, to shoot at marks in competition, for prizes. It does not matter, now that my world is gone—'' Her eyes were full of tears.

Dane put his arms around her, and said softly, "What is it, Dallith?"

The sling was loose in her hand. She said, "It is only fair; it is my fate, I suppose—I am here because of a weapon like this—"

He looked at her in startled question.

She said in a stifled voice, "I was reckoned a good shot; twice I had won a silk scarf in the competitions. I was vain of my skill and I did not want to lose my—my name. A few days before, I was practicing with my sling in a distant part of the garden, and I was so intent on my practice that I did not know anyone had entered the garden. Then I heard a cry and felt—oh, such pain—and I saw my best friend among the women lying senseless on the ground." She was shaking and crying. "I knew—I knew the sling could kill; I had not been careful enough. No, she did not die, but she suffered shock and concussion and days of unconsciousness, and we all thought she would die. I loved her. I would rather have killed myself than her. She was my own father's daughter—and so when she was out of danger I was sentenced to a season of exile from the places where people live."

"It seems to me," Dane said, holding her gently against him, "that you'd been punished enough already."

"There is never *enough* punishment for such an offense," Dallith said, rebukingly. "But since she did not die, and spoke for me—she said she too had been careless, not to realize that I was not aware of her presence—I was sent away only for a season and not for a full year. But while I was alone in the place of exile—the Mekhar slave ship came and took me. And the rest you know."

Resolutely, she dried her tears. "And so it seems to me," she said, "that if a sling could nearly kill my dear friend and sister, it should serve against the Hunters. Since I have decided to live, there is no sense in letting them kill me now.''

"It ought to do," Dane said thoughtfully. In the Roman arena, hadn't one of the major spectacles been the sight of a slinger from the Balearic isles, pitted against a man with a net and trident? Of course, the Romans who arranged gladiatorial combats hadn't always been at pains to be fair about it—the important thing seemed to be bloodshed—but most of them hadn't gone in for massacres, either. They were the kind of fighters who would have had more fun in seeing a fight where the contestants were reasonably matched, if only to make the fight last longer, and see more blood shed. There was also the story of David and Goliath. "But how accurately *can* one shoot with a sling? I'm not at all familiar with them.''

Dallith picked up the sling and fitted a small round ball into it. It looked like an ordinary pebble. "Look," she said, pointing to a small pale mark on the Armory wall, a projecting bit of brickwork. It was only three or four inches square and about forty feet away. She spun the sling around her head and let it go; almost simultaneously something struck the pale mark with a sound like a rifle shot and the projecting bit of brick broke away and clattered to the floor.

"If that had been the head of a Mekhar," Dallith said, "I do not think he would have much to purr about.''

Dane knew she was right. She was better protected than he had thought possible. Of course, they did not know what the Hunters were like; if they were huge boneheaded creatures like some of the saurians, her pellet might not be of much use, but that was just one of the chances they all had to take, and Dallith probably knew it as well as he did.

"Just the same," he said grimly, "I think you ought to learn something about using a knife. In case—well, in case you need something at close quarters.''

A grimace of revulsion passed over her features, but she said soberly, "I suppose you're right. Rianna has chosen to use knives, and perhaps her techniques would be more suited to a woman."

"Perhaps. And she has had serious training," Dane said. In any case, teaching Dallith would sharpen up Rianna's own technique, and he would keep a damn close eye on both of them.

If they could all stay together . . .

He spent much of that day watching as Rianna demonstrated to Dallith the kind of training she had had in close-quarter knife play. (Dallith was slightly appalled at the thought of a rapist and Dane reflected that this would be one problem no woman would have on a world of empaths.)

He remembered what Aratak had said about Rianna's skill at unarmed combat; judo had never been his own field of interest—although, like most people who have studied karate, he knew some of it—and he wondered how good she was at it. But when he put the question she gave him her crooked grin and said, "Try, if you want to."

He picked up one of the "kendo sticks"—he had asked Server to bring him one about the same weight as the samurai sword, and Server had taken him so literally that there was probably less than an ounce of difference between its weight and the sword's—and said, "Anyone coming at you will probably be armed, Rianna. You don't think you can take me with a sword, do you?"

"Probably not," she said. "Your big razor there might cut my hand off before I could get my knife out. But with the stick, certainly. Or a club. Or a short knife. Come on. Try."

He said, "I don't want to hurt you. But you asked for it." *Take a little of the conceit out of her now and save her worse trouble later*, he thought and was surprised at his own sense of resentment. He lifted the stick—it was made of some light wood not too unlike bamboo—and rushed at her.

He never knew exactly what happened, but he abruptly found himself shoved backward, the stick thrust into his stomach harshly enough to knock all the breath out of him; he recovered himself in an instant, jerked the stick free, raised it again—and once again found himself wrenching it from Rianna's hands. Her foot kicked his ankle and he nearly went down.

She stepped back quickly and said, "I don't want to hurt *you*, Dane. But as you can see, I'm not really afraid unless they *do* come at me with something like your razor-edge there."

He shook his head ruefully; but the experiment had taught him a great deal in a short lesson, nevertheless: He could not count on the Hunters using any known weapon or technique. It was literally a case of having to be prepared for *anything*. After some thought, he added to the sword a short curved knife. It wasn't much like the dagger a samurai would have had as the normal accompaniment to his sword—briefly he wondered what had happened to the samurai's knife and other gear—but it was going to be damn helpful in close-range fighting.

As he was caring for the sword that night before putting it away—tapping it all along its length gently with his powder puff of powdered limestone, wiping it gently with the cloth—he looked at the blood-etching near the curved end of the blade and wondered. Had it been made on Earth? Or here . . .? And what strange creature's blood had discolored the steel?

During the next few days he concentrated on regaining old skills and reflexes, and spent some time thinking about welding them into a matched group. Of course, until he knew for certain that they would be allowed to go out together, there was not much use in concentrating on that. Each of them should first reach optimum level for individual survival.

The task of teaching Dallith close-quarter fighting was none too easy; she had a horror of hurting any of them and would withdraw at the last split second before making a stroke even with the breakable bamboo stick they had found for teaching her knife skills. But remembering how she had suddenly gone berserk when she faced the Mekhar, he supposed that if someone came at her with murder on his mind, she'd react as she'd done then; by picking up her attacker's murderous rage. And so he concentrated on getting the basics of attack into her head.

I can't teach her vulnerable points, though. We don't know what vulnerable points the Hunters have—or if they have any!

During all this time it struck him as strange that they never came close enough to other groups of the "Sacred Prey" to work out with them. Whether it was an unwritten law of the Hunters that they should not or by sheer coincidence, he wasn't sure. He suspected that the Hunters, though, discouraged any such pooling of survival skills, and this gave him some hope that *their* five would be sent out together, since they had not been separated and forced to wait for the Hunt individually.

He suspected sometimes that Server—or the whole complex of robot mechanisms which went by that collective name—watched over them at a distance and would intervene if they showed any signs of being too curious about the other prisoners. He realized, after five or six days of this unobtrusive surveillance, that he had not even any idea of how many other prisoners dwelt in the huge park-complex; he could still only surmise as he had done the first day, by seeing the others at a distance, or from brief and interrupted encounters in Armory or baths, that there might be between a dozen and thirty humans, and about as many more assorted aliens of other biological types.

It was a few days later, in the Armory, when he noticed

again a pair of proto-felines, very much (at least in the distance, and to him) like the Mekhar, once again working out with a pair of something like kendo sticks. He asked Cliff-Climber about them.

"Are those the two you called common criminals? You seemed to feel that it was beneath the dignity of your kind to use weapons. Do those two use them because they do not share your standards?"

Cliff-Climber looked at them curiously. "They are not the same ones," he said. "I think I will go and see. If some members of my own clan should be here—"

He bounded away, at his curious loping run, but some time later he came back, looking puzzled. To Dane's question he answered, "I did not see them or speak to them." He looked quickly toward the far end of the Armory, with one of those movements that reminded Dane of a caged tiger, and said angrily, "This place maddens me! Mirrors, and reflections, and people who disappear and walk through walls when you try to come near them!" He stalked away, giving Dane the impression that if he had actually had a tail (he didn't) he would have been switching it angrily from side to side.

Not too much later, though, he came to Dane carrying one of the kendo sticks. He said, "I notice you do not use these seriously as weapons. But for footwork and agility they seem a sensible training device." He said no more, and Dane, quite unexpectedly feeling a strange kind of sympathy for the Mekhar's alienation said, "You want to try working out with them?"

"It would seem a sensible precaution," Cliff-Climber said stiffly, "to accustom myself emotionally to the thought that I shall be facing an opponent of some other biological type than my own. For this you are probably the most suitable one against which to test myself."

"Damn right," Dane agreed. "For me, too." For all he

knew, he might be facing something more difficult to guard against than Cliff-Climber with his artificially steel-tipped claws! It was all part of the business of arming himself psychologically, of psyching himself to kill.

He found Cliff-Climber appallingly fast on his feet; but against him, the old karate reflexes began to come back fast. It made him realize, too, that Aratak—or anyone of his proto-saurian species—would be a most formidable opponent, and that night, with Cliff-Climber's concurrence, they persuaded the giant saurian to take turns working out against both of them. At the end of these sessions, Dane had bruises and scrapes which had to be lengthily soaked out in the hot volcanic pools—he even accepted Aratak's offer of the hot sulfur-smelling mud for a poultice, and discovered that in spite of the smell it had remarkable healing qualities—but he felt a lot better prepared to meet his invisible opponents.

They initiated then a regular series of workouts; Rianna welcomed the chance to try her unarmed combat skills against Cliff-Climber, and the ensuing combat reminded Dane of nothing so much as an old *Avengers* TV show on Earth, with the redoubtable Emma Peel fighting against a variety of any kind of antagonist from tiger-cats to robots.

After each of them had come to a gasping draw, Cliff-Climber (looking at her with wonder and respect) apologized to Rianna for the bloody scratch on her arm. "I forgot myself," he said, extending his claws and their razor-steel tips. "But I think you have sprained my foot, so we are equal."

Watching Rianna and Aratak was also something of a revelation; although by sheer weight and size the enormous proto-saurian had the advantage, and eventually demonstrated that when all else failed he could trip Rianna up and sit on her, she was by no means helpless.

Dallith could not be persuaded to take part, and finally

Dane, remembering how she had exploded into instinctive violence, realized that this was what she feared; this, or hurting one of those she now considered friends and allies.

At last he accepted Aratak's advice to leave her alone. "She knows best what is safe for her," he said. Dane was afraid that it might, once again, be a withdrawal into willed death; but if it was there was nothing he could do.

Chapter Ten

Even during the day, the red light of the moon was brighter than the sun; the Red Moon seemed to obscure half the sky now, when, one evening, Rianna said to him near the baths, "There are men here—I mean humans, proto-simians very like us—who do not belong to the Unity."

"Of course. There's me. Why do you think the Hunters would confine themselves to raiding just your group of worlds in the Unity?"

"I don't mean that. I went and greeted them and they did not—or could not—answer. They evidently did not have translator disks."

"Poor bastards," Dane said. "They must be pretty confused."

"If so, they certainly didn't act it. I went to talk to them," Rianna said. "I've been taught nonverbal communication techniques. But they slipped away before I could come near them. I don't know where they went—of course this place is confusing, but still, it was like something done with mirrors."

Cliff-Climber had had an experience something like that.

"I wonder if it ever occurred to you," Dane said soberly, "that they might have been Hunters—or their servants."

"Hardly servants, when Server and all his pack are around. Dane! Do you mean the Hunters might be—human?"

He nodded. "It seems reasonable," he said. "There seem to be as many humans here as all other biological types put together."

"Would men hunt men?"

"They do," he said with a shrug, and explained his theory that possibly the Hunters preferred prey who could give them a good, equal fight. "And it would be a good way to size us up, observe us for the Hunt, decide what weapons we'll be carrying. Maybe even, now and then, take on one of us for a workout, though so far no one's come near enough for that."

Or pick out which of us would make the best trophies. . . . His mind refused to put away a gruesome picture which had come to him, one night, in a nightmare: the head of a Japanese samurai, still in armor and preserved four hundred years by some unguessable technique, hanging on the wall of a Hunter's dwelling. . . .

Involuntarily, Dane shuddered, and Rianna reached for him and held onto him, hard. He clasped her in his arms, feeling her warmth and closeness as the only comfort on this strange, cold, red, mysterious world.

It was a bond. Unwanted. Undesired. But a bond. If he lived, he and Rianna would always belong to one another. . . .

Over their meal that night, looking across at Aratak, Rianna brought that up again.

"If the Hunters are human, would they really want to take on someone the size and—and fierceness of Aratak?"

"Even on my world, big game hunting is regarded as more of a sport than shooting rabbits," Dane said. "A man who kills a tiger is considered braver than one who kills a deer."

Once again he wondered how the words were coming across to the others through their translator disks.

He asked them, curious, and Rianna said with a shrug, "On my world, as on most, there are large fierce predators and small gentle ones regarded mostly as a source of food. If you'd given the scientific name of the creatures probably it would have come through as a strange sound and you'd have had to explain it. But normally the translator gives the nearest equivalent in your own language."

He accepted it at that. He had to; the technology which could evolve such a device was as far beyond Earth's best as a linear computer was beyond a spinning wheel.

Cliff-Climber said roughly, "I don't believe a race could acquire such a legendary reputation for ferocity if they were proto-simian. It is more likely that they are proto-felines, not too unlike the Mekhars. There are also a great many members of my own kind here—or, I should say, of biological types not altogether different from my own."

"That doesn't prove anything," Rianna flared, "except that we're both members of dangerous species!"

Aratak mused, "What you have said is interesting. My own species are of a peaceful habit, and if any of us proto-saurians are renowned for ferocity, I should be surprised, and yet—"

Dane interrupted. "I find that hard to believe. The most terrible predator in my planet's history—*tyrannosaurus rex*—was of saurian origin."

Aratak had no eyebrows but gave the impression of raising them anyhow. "Were they sapient, though?"

"No," Dane confessed, "they had no brain to speak of."

"Oh, well. Animal species of proto-saurian type are often fierce," Aratak said, "And the fierce ones are extinct, which proves the wisdom of the Divine Egg, in that those who seek blood meet only bloody death. But when saurians develop sapience they usually display a peaceful manner of life. I can give you only philosophical reasons why this should be so, but I assure you I know of no exceptions within the Unity, at least.''

"He's right, Dane," Rianna said. "As far as anyone knows, there aren't any, except in old legends.''

Aratak bowed. "To resume. As I said, we are peaceful creatures; I am here almost by accident, as one might say. And Yet, watching as we exercise, I have seen one of my own kind, and when I went to salute him in the name of the Divine Egg, believing him a fellow prisoner, he vanished quite suddenly and I could not find him again. For a moment it occurred to me that I had been the victim of some sort of optical illusion, but now I have another theory.''

"Let's have it," Dane said. He had the highest possible opinion of the giant saurian's intelligence.

"This; that the Hunters are not a single race, but a clan or conglomeration; that they collect to themselves members from the renegades, the outlaws, the outcasts, and fierce mavericks of all peoples. A madman of my people, or an outlaw, might find himself here, one way or another. Most of us are peaceful people, and one who was not might find himself every where an outcast. As I said, I saw at least one, who has been tested presumably as we were tested, for desperation and courage; but if he had been a fellow prisoner he would not have tried to elude me.''

"That doesn't follow," Dallith said unexpectedly. "He might be—ashamed to be found here. A peaceful creature who had—when tested—discovered strange and frightening ferocity in himself. He would hardly want to face someone who knew what he *should* be like. . . .''

Dane realized that Dallith was speaking of herself; it was the first time it had occurred to him that she might deeply regret her outburst of wild fury on the Mekhar ship.

Aratak courteously considered Dallith's theory for a moment before shaking his head. "No," he said, "for he would know that I was in like case and would come to condole with me. So I conclude that he was one of the Hunters watching me, and that the Hunters are not one species but many. That would also explain why they choose Prey of such varying forms.''

It was a valuable theory, Dane thought. It deserved consideration. It would explain why the Hunters had no recognizable form in legend; it would also explain why they did not show themselves to their Prey, but let all contact, even with the slave ships bringing their Quarry, come through the robot Servers. That way they could be certain no hint of their secret escaped.

And yet . . . he wasn't convinced. Could a conglomerate of renegades develop so formalized, so ritualistic an approach to the Hunt? And even more; would not some hint of their recruitment have stolen out into the Galaxy? They argued it far into the night, but went to bed unconvinced.

The shape and form of the Hunters! It obsessed him now, night and day. As the Red Moon grew in the sky toward the full, they took shape after shape in his nightmares, terrifyingly formless. He found a nonsense rhyme from Earth repeating itself again and again at odd moments in his consciousness:

> I engage with the Snark,
>   every night after dark,
> In a dreamy delirious fight. . . .

But instead of hunting the Snark, it was hunting HIM . . . and there was every possibility that he would, indeed, ''Softly and silently vanish away, and never be heard of again.''

At times like this he would draw the samurai sword and look grimly at its edge before putting it away again. *Not so softly and not so silently*, he promised himself.

Later he thought that if this period of uncertainty had been prolonged much more he probably would have gone insane;

as it was, Rianna shook him awake out of nightmare once or twice every night. (But they all suffered from nightmares. Once Dallith woke screaming wildly, rousing them all; and once Cliff-Climber staggered up in his sleep, roaring and fighting, and by the time they managed, by throwing cold water over him, to get him awake, both Aratak and Dane had long bleeding scratches from his razored claws.)

Abruptly the period of waiting ended.

The great Red Moon had grown day by day; when it was all but full it seemed to hang low and suspended over them with a bloody light, cutting away almost all normal sunshine, ghastly and luminous and so large that Dane hated to look up at it; it was like walking under a great floating disk suspended by invisible means. It gave him claustrophobia; knowing it was ridiculous, he still could not banish the image of the moon somehow slipping, plunging down, crushing them all beneath it. . . .

He had wondered what would happen when it was completely full, and on this night, as they were returning from the baths, he looked up, seeing the shadow beginning to creep across the great red disk. Of course, the moon was half the size of the primary planet; when the Hunter's World came between moon and sun, the Red Moon would be wholly eclipsed, darkened. . . .

With startling rapidity the shadow crept over the face, blotting out the red and luminous disk, etching away more and more of the huge red face. Around them the whole color of the landscape changed, growing darker and stranger; there were odd rustlings, and from somewhere a strong rushing wind sprang up.

The five prisoners stood close together, Dane between Rianna and Dallith, knowing they were both clinging to him in the eerie darkness, as the Red Moon slowly faded from crescent to slim fingernail-paring to a pale red glimmer along one edge. And then, for the first time on this world, there was total darkness. Behind the great blot on the sky, dim stars sprang out.

"The Hunt is over," Dallith whispered. "With the moon in eclipse—the Hunt is over."

In the darkness Cliff-Climber's rough voice muttered, "There are dead Hunters there, and dead Prey. And soon it will be our turn."

"But when?" Rianna said into the darkness. No one answered her. They stood there for hours, watching the Red Moon slowly emerge from darkness, the stars fade again into the background of crimson light. Finally, when it was glowing in its accustomed place again, they went silently to their quarters, but none of them ate much, and Dane, at least, slept little.

Was it their turn next?

The next morning, when Server brought their morning meal, he told them, "Last night was the night of the eclipse; last night, the Hunt ended. Today, the Sacred Prey who survived the Hunt—if there were any—will be rewarded and released; and you are bidden to the feast."

None of them had much appetite for breakfast after that. As the sun drew higher in the sky—a strange bright sun with the Red Moon invisible, far away on the other side of the planet—they went briefly to the Armory, and to the baths. But none of them did much in the way of training.

Dane said at one point, "I sometimes wonder. The survivors of the Hunt—we'll see them being feasted and rewarded, so they say, and freed. But I wonder if they are really freed, or if their feasts and rewards aren't for *our* benefit, to encourage us, and if perhaps they'll be quietly put out of the way afterward."

"That's a nice thing to bring up," Rianna said in disgust. "What are you trying to do to us, Dane?"

Aratak said soberly, "The possibility had occurred to me, as well."

Cliff-Climber turned from his shadow-dance before the mirror. He said, "No, they're freed, true enough. There is a man on my world—he is a distant connection to my clan—who returned from the Hunter's World, rich and successful. He founded an Arms Museum with his prize money; I have seen the museum, though the man died when I was still young."

"But he said nothing about the Hunters? He left no word about them?" Rianna said incredulously. "Scientists have been searching for centuries for some reliable knowledge of the Hunters; most people think of them as legends! He should have written up the account of his experiences!"

Cliff-Climber said indifferently, "Why? Why should anyone care?"

Rianna looked indignant, but Dane nodded. He was getting used to Cliff-Climber's lack of what most people would call scientific curiosity. He said to Rianna, "The old proverb on my world says that *curiosity killed the cat,* and Cliff's people seem to have taken it to heart. Let's face it; scientific investigation is a proto-simian characteristic, at least curiosity for its own sake. Even ordinary cats seldom show much curiosity about anything unless they can eat it or play with it, or they think it's a danger to them."

Dallith said peacefully, "The important thing is that survivors *are* freed." She sorted out an assortment of small, round, completely smooth stones for her sling and tied them into a sack at her waist. They were all looking over their weapons, knowing the hour was at hand. Rianna had sharpened one of her knives to a slashing edge and the other point for a thrusting edge; Dane lifted a long spear off the wall and handed it to her. He said, "Carry this. It's not so much that you have to use it, but there should be one long-distance weapon."

She lifted it, balanced it, saying, "This one is too long for me," and chose a shorter one. Dane, watching her completely absorbed in the weapon, had no particular qualms for her. His attempt to work her into a fighting machine had succeeded better than he had hoped.

Briefly, he explained his plan to them, if it turned out that they could stay and fight together instead of singly. Rianna, at the center of a wedge with her long spear, would present a formidable front to an attacker, with her knives and Cliff-Climber's razor-claws for close-quarter attack; Dane and Aratak to either side, Dane with the samurai sword, Aratak with his great club and the short ax he had tied to his belt; and Dallith bringing up the rear with her sling to pick off anyone trying to rush them from behind.

Cliff-Climber frowned, and Dane knew that the Mekhar was the weak link. Cliff-Climber preferred to think of this as a series of duels against individual attackers.

"Can't you see," Dallith said patiently, "that is what the Hunters will be expecting—that we will fight singly. If we remain a unit, and back one another up, we may all have a better chance."

Cliff-Climber frowned again, as if he smelled something bad, and Dane wished Dallith had let Rianna speak to him. Cliff-Climber had come to respect Rianna as a fighter against whom he himself needed to be seriously on guard; Dallith, to him, was a nonentity. The cat-man looked now to Rianna as if expecting that she would back him up, but she said firmly, "Dallith is right," and he shrugged.

"I gave you my word; you have none of you given me cause to break it, so for now I will not withdraw. I warn you, however, that I refuse to compromise my honor."

With that, they had to be content.

Dane held the samurai sword on his knee for some time, thinking about the unknown long-dead Earthman. He did not know how the samurai warrior had died, but he knew he must have done it valiantly. But Dane was a man of another century and another life, and he wanted mainly to live. The samurai would probably have understood Cliff-Climber better than Dane himself. Cliff-Climber was concerned to die with honor; Dane intended, if he must die, to sell his life as dearly as possible, but mostly he intended to stay alive—he intended that all of them should stay alive!

The bright day was shortening toward afternoon, and the sun dropping, when Rianna clutched Dane's arm and said, in a tense undertone, "Look!"

At the far end of the Armory, a small procession was entering, and a strange one. There was a whole small army of the mechanical servomechs of Server's type, surrounding a single living creature. He wore the terra-cotta tunic of the Sacred Prey. He was hung heavily with garlands of green leaves and flowers. Servers bore his weapons—a long spear, a round spiked shield—ceremoniously on trays of precious metal, and as the prisoners looked on, hung the weapons in a prominent place on the Armory wall.

Cliff-Climber said, low-voiced, "He must be the survivor of the Hunt."

"An only survivor," Aratak said grimly, and his gills glowed blue.

Dane said, "A spider-man," in surprise. There had been one of them aboard the Mekhar slave ship, and he had spent all his time huddled, hissing, in a corner. The spider-things were certainly the last race Dane would have thought of as fierce enough to survive a Hunt! And yet one of them had done so, for here he was, being honored. . . .

He said, half to himself, "He met the Hunters, and lived. I'd like to have a word with him. . . ." But, the weapons hung, the victorious survivor was being carefully shepherded out of the Armory again, encircled by his guard of attentive and solicitous robot Servers.

Well, well, thought Dane. *You never know. If that thing could live through eleven days of a Hunt, there's certainly plenty of chance for us.*

"That's by no means certain," Dallith said close to his ear, and Dane realized she was picking up his thoughts again. "Maybe he was lucky, or maybe he managed to spend all eleven days in hiding."

Dane nodded. "Maybe." But that meant it was not an arena, it meant there was some cover and some place to hide if necessary.

It meant that somehow or other he, Dane, must manage to get a word alone with the victor. . . .

The sun was beginning to go down when Server returned to direct them to the baths. He brought fresh clothing for them all—the same terra-cotta color dedicated to the Sacred Prey, but this was definitely fighting gear. The tunics provided for the women were short and could be tucked up even shorter. For Dane, Rianna, and Dallith there were new strong-soled sandals, although neither Cliff-Climber nor Aratak needed any protection for their feet.

"You are to adorn yourselves for the feast of reward and victory, so that you may see what may be in store for you," Server said. "Gird yourselves with your chosen weapons, for you will be taken directly from the feast to the place of the Hunt."

Dane said to the robot, voicing a thought that had come to him as a dim suspicion more than once, "You seem pretty involved in all this, Server. Answer me one question, will you?"

"A dozen, if it is necessary," the servomech said in his flat mechanical voice. "We are here to serve and to instruct and aid you."

"Are you people—you robots—are you yourselves the Hunters?"

It would explain so much. It would explain the fact that they were the only ones who contacted the Mekhar ship. It would explain the way they cared for their Prey. It would explain the way they clustered around to protect and honor the victor.

But the thought of facing a group of abnormally knowing servomechanisms, in duel, was horrifying. . . . These thoughts raced through his brain as he awaited Server's answer. It actually seemed, insofar as a faceless metal mechanism with no features except small metal-mesh apertures could express anything, that Server had expected any question but that one and perhaps, even, that Dane had found at last a question that the robot was not programmed to answer!

At last, however, Server said, in the same flat and inexpressive mechanical tone, "As we have told you, we are Servers. You will meet with the Hunters at the appointed time. May we assist you now to your baths?"

Dane went with him. There was nothing else he could do. *He didn't really answer*, he thought grimly. *He said, We are Servers. He didn't say, We are not Hunters.*

He caught up with Dallith and Rianna as they were separating from Cliff-Climber and Aratak, and said hastily, "Cover for me if that metal monstrosity comes around snooping. I'm going off and see if I can get a line on where they're keeping the victor stashed until this fancy feast. If I could have ten minutes when he's not being surrounded, I estimate our chances for life would be roughly doubled."

Rianna nodded. "If they come looking for you here, I'll tell them you went for a mud bath with Aratak, and, Aratak, if they look for him there, tell them he's swimming."

Dane hurried off across the garden-park. He had observed the direction in which the procession of Servers had taken the garlanded spider-man.

I hope to hell he's got a translator disk; Rianna said some of them didn't, he thought, as he went warily through the gardens and clustered flowering bushes. The sun was sinking fast, and on the horizon was a strange blood-red light which showed where the full Red Moon was rising again.

I'll be up there by morning, he thought. *It's the payoff.* His throat felt tight and he reached in the dusk for the grip of the samurai sword which hung girded at his side.

Near the high wall of shrubbery that marked the outer limits of the game preserve, or park, dedicated to the Sacred Prey, he had noticed once before a smaller building than most, and seeing the survivor garlanded with flowers he now suspected what it was; for the door of this small building was garlanded with similar flowers. Cautiously, Dane slipped up to one of the bamboo-slatted windows and peered in.

The spider-man sat hunched on the floor, looking solitary and dejected. He had been robed in long garments and was still hung about with garlands. Dane whistled softly, hoping to attract his attention. He had to repeat the sound twice before the spider-man tilted his head and looked around.

"Over here," Dane whispered hoarsely. "I'm a prisoner too. Come over by the window; I can't come in."

The spider-man heaved himself to his feet, moving with a quick, scuttling agility. He darted quick glances from side to side, and Dane, watching his fantastic alertness, thought, *It would take some Hunter even to get near him! Maybe it isn't so surprising he survived. . . .*

His voice sounded rusty and hissing. "Who isss it? Who sssspoke there?"

Dane shrank against the shadows of the building.

"I'm up against the Hunters tomorrow, friend. What are they like? What weapons do they carry?"

But before the question had more than left his mouth, he was seized in a firm grip from behind and jerked backward. He gripped at his sword, whipping it partway from the sheath.

His wrist was seized in a steel grip—quite literally; metal clamped over it, and Server's expressionless voice said, "It would be a pity to break your excellent blade. It is forbidden for the Prey to come here. Please permit us to escort you back to the feast, honored Prey; you are awaited there."

As Dane told Rianna and Dallith later, seated between them at one of the long tables while a whole conglomerate of robots—all exactly like Server, and each one of them answering each and every question or request just as if it had been he, individually, who had last spoken to the questioner—passed out the food:

"I halfway expected they wouldn't let me get near the victor. There is something damn funny about these Hunters; damn funny."

"I find it the reverse of amusing," Aratak rumbled.

Dane repeated his theory that the Servers were, in fact, the Hunters.

"In that case," Cliff-Climber said harshly, swiveling his head toward them, "I'm with you, and I remain with you throughout the Hunt! I sold myself to the Hunt, willing to meet in combat any creature of flesh and blood! But I did not volunteer to fight nothing-men who hide behind shielding of metal!"

That's another thought, Dane's mind jumped quickly. *Maybe they're giant amoebas or something hiding behind all that metal; maybe they're not robots at all. I never thought of that.* But at least it had Cliff-Climber with them again.

He looked around, wondering if—as in the Armory—Hunters mingled with Prey. It was hard to tell; the feasting hall was not well lighted.

"Almost," Dallith said, "as if they didn't want us to get too good a look at our fellow Prey."

"Or as if they're afraid we'd gang up on them," Rianna ventured. "I wonder if it's ever happened before and they don't want to take any more chances."

He did see what looked like one or two Mekhars; an enormous ursine creature with a hairy and shaggy pelt; if there were any proto-saurians of Aratak's type they were hidden in the darkness. Again, humans of his own general type—man almost as he might appear on Earth—outnumbered all other races almost two to one. They were badly illuminated, and located at some distance—while the five of them had been seated all at one table—but he noticed that their general types ranged from enormous and fair-skinned to huge and Negroid, while there were a few ethnic stocks he did not recognize as having any counterpart on Earth; two tall men with red skins, not the reddish-brown of the American Indian, but the very color of sunburn; a tiny creature with bluish-gray skin and long white fluffy hair, whose very sex was indeterminate. They bore all kinds of weapons he had ever heard of and some he hadn't.

The food was incredibly good, and there was a very great deal of it. Dane ate well, although not stuffing himself; he didn't know what arrangements had been made for feeding them during the Hunt, nor where his next square meal would come from, but on the other hand he didn't want to be overstuffed and drowsy when it began, which looked as if it might be fairly soon. He encouraged the others to do the same.

They had reached the end of the meal—apparently celebrated with something like a sweet soup and piles of fruits, nuts, and various confections—when one of the various incarnations of Server trundled into the center of the banquet hall and led in the garlanded and robed spider-thing.

"Give honor to the Masters of the Hunt!" Server proclaimed, and for once the metallic voice seemed to quiver with something like emotion.

Dane said nothing. Did they expect him to applaud? The other prisoners—Sacred Prey—around the hall evidently reacted with much the same attitude, for although there was a slight stir and rustle all around, there was no particular reaction.

"Give honor to the Hunters! In the nine-hundred-and-sixty-fourth Hunt in our illustrious history, forty-seven individuals hunted gallantly from Eclipse to Eclipse and nineteen have gone to join their illustrious ancestors!"

"I'd like to applaud to that," Rianna whispered fiercely. Dane held her hand. "The point would probably be missed anyhow."

"Give honor to the Sacred Prey! Seventy-four fought us valiantly and provided us with a splendid Hunt, and for the three-hundred-and-ninety-eighth time, there was at least one survivor, who has been brought here so that you may see the rewards which await a successful Prey!"

The spider-man came forward. He still looked awkward in his long sagging garlands, and his figure was stooped and apprehensive.

How the hell did THAT survive all this? Dane's mind picked at the statistics; seventy-four fought valiantly (and there may have been a few who didn't); one survived. There were forty-seven Hunters; roughly two to a Hunter. And there's one survivor. *What kind of creatures are they anyhow?*

He paid little attention as the Servers loaded down the spider-thing with gems and precious metals and stated that he would be taken off by a Mekhar ship under bond to deliver him wherever, within a hundred light-years, he chose to go.

Rianna said grimly, "That would put him well within the Unity. I happen to know what planet he comes from."

Dallith murmured, "That means—if we live—I can return to my own world. . . ."

She was trembling with emotion; Dane clasped her hand. It was long odds and a big *if*, but the incentive was there. She could go home . . . so could Rianna, Aratak, Cliff-Climber.

Could he? Did he even want to?

He set aside the thought. It was a long road and the way home, if there was one, lay past the Hunt . . . past the Hunt, and the Eclipse, and the Red Moon.

Chapter Eleven

The multitude of Servers had prepared Dane for a high level of technology; therefore he was prepared, as they went out into the night, for the small ship which stood waiting for them, to take them aboard. In any case, even Earth's moon had been reached long ago. However, this moon was evidently no airless hulk, but a planet capable of sustaining the lives of these assorted Prey.

He never saw who was at the controls of the little ship. But he had a strong impression that it was Server—or one of him. He sat between Dallith and Rianna, holding a hand of each, but they didn't talk. It was either too late or too early for that. He tried, at least partly for Dallith's sake, to keep his thoughts calm and confident; she'd pick up his attitude. On the other hand there was no sense in pretending a complete calm he didn't feel; she'd know it was phony.

Aratak put his thoughts into words, as he had a habit of doing sometimes.

"The man who feels fear without cause is a fool; but the

man is twice a fool who does not feel fear when there is cause.''

"That may all be true," Cliff-Climber muttered, "but to speak of fear often gives it form and substance."

Rianna said wryly, "Looks like this one has plenty of form and substance already."

Dane wondered if the Hunters were on this ship; he looked inquiringly at Dallith but she shook her head. "I don't feel anything one way or the other. But then—so many alien presences and most of them hostile to us; it would be hard to tell."

Dane looked around the semidarkened cabin, wondering a little grimly if these were all prisoners or if some of them, mingled among them, were the Hunters, observing the Prey at close quarters; but he did not like to mention the thought again.

It seemed a long time of waiting—although he supposed it was not more than an hour—before the viewscreen flared to life with a picture of the Red Moon, growing and growing and apparently hurtling straight at them. About the same time the speaker at the front of the cabin made a few metallic, premonitory rasping noises. Dallith grasped Dane's hand, painfully hard, in the darkness.

"Honorable and Sacred Prey." The voice was not unlike that of the Servers, but somehow held a different quality . . . the original, perhaps, from which the voice of the Servers had been designed? Dane felt a queer atavistic stirring and knew that the hair along his arms was bristling; Cliff-Climber jerked alert, his whiskers and the elaborately curled topknot he had brushed up for the feast jutting up spikily.

"Honorable and Sacred Prey, we welcome you to the nine-hundred-and-sixty-fifth cycle of hunting of this recorded era," the strange voice said. "Very soon now you will be released upon the Hunting Grounds which have been, since the very beginning of recorded time, sacred to our Hunt. You will have the period of time until the dawn to scatter and find for yourselves the most advantageous stance; you have our word, which has not been broken for seven hundred and thirteen cycles of the Hunt, that you will not be pursued until the sun stands completely clear of the horizon."

Dane whispered, "Wonder what happened seven hundred and thirteen cycles ago?"

Rianna said urgently, *"Hush!"*

"The Hunt will be suspended every evening at dusk in order that Hunters and Hunted may feed and refresh themselves; the areas lighted by yellow lights and patrolled by Servers are neutral areas, and from dusk until midnight no Hunter may approach them closer than four thousand yards." Dane's translator disk evidently had given the closest equivalent; evidently all the others comprehended the measurement. "Other areas are set aside for the Hunters and no Prey will be permitted to enter them on pain of instant and dishonorable death."

That was something. It indicated that the Hunt was formalized and ritualized to the extent where it seemed unlikely that Hunters would wait outside the neutral areas to pick them off as they came out, either.

The voice paused a moment, then continued: "In a few moments, the ship will come to rest. The Hunt will commence at dawn. Until we meet you in mortal combat, then, we salute you, and we honor you, our Sacred Prey. Those who live shall see how generously we reward the valiant among you; we wish you all an honorable survival and reward—or a bloody and honorable death."

The voice crackled into silence; and at that moment there was a slight jar, as if the ship had come completely to rest. There was a short hiss as of pressure chambers, and a deep murmur as the doors glided slowly open.

Dane grasped the hilt of his sword and moved toward the door, following in Aratak's wake. He could see the great proto-ursine, bearlike creature, lumbering toward the doorway. Dallith was grasping his elbow, Rianna and Cliff-Climber moving behind. Dallith said in a wavering voice. "Panic— every single identity going his own way—hang onto me, Dane. I—I want to run, to scatter—"

"Easy." He grasped her hand firmly in his. "It's not yours. You've nothing to panic about. You're picking it up from the others."

"But suppose—suppose I can't free myself from it . . . ?"

They were emerging through a narrow corridor at the top of a flight of steps; Dane paused for a moment before the crush of others at his back forced him down, to look out on the surface of the Red Moon.

He stood a few feet above a dark and ruined landscape, broken and hilly and, in the near-darkness, covered with a thick blackish underbrush. Dark hills rose behind him, and overhead a dark-blue sky lowered, with thinly scattered pale clouds barely perceptible across the face of the huge orb that hung above them: the Hunter's World, glowing brick red in the sky, and more huge, more crimson-lighted, more enormous than the Red Moon itself upon which they stood. In the glowing red world-light, brighter than the brightest Earthly moonlight, Dane saw dark forms, fleeing from one corner to another of the landscape. Dallith made a stumbling step away from the ship and he grabbed her by the hand; he found his other hand grasping Cliff-Climber's hairy forearm. He said tensely:

"Don't run! There's no percentage in *that!* Stop here and think! *Think!* Remember what we decided!"

Aratak was glowing faintly blue all over in the darkness. Calmly, Dane led his group of five until, moving at a slow and steady pace, they were about a quarter of a mile from the Hunters' ship.

"It's a good idea to get well away," he said calmly. "If it takes off again—well, I don't know what kind of fuel their ships use, but breathing it isn't likely to be very healthy. Now let's sit down here and decide what to do. We've got till dawn to work out strategy for the Hunt; judging by the way everybody else is taking off in all directions at once, I'd say we already had a good edge. There are five of us, not one; any Hunter who comes at us is going to find himself in trouble. Dallith—''

Her voice trembled, but she replied quite steadily, ''I'm here, Dane. What can I do?''

''We found out too late, on the Mekhar slave ship, that it was a trap. If I'd listened to you, I might have known; you kept insisting that for some reason they *wanted* us to attack them. I think your main weapon for us is going to have to be your sensitivity. Do you think you'll be able to tell if someone's stalking us, and ready to attack?''

She said, ''I'll try.''

''Tell me. Did you ever sense anything—any kind of emotion or personal awareness—from any of the Servers?'' If they were indeed the Hunters, Dallith should have been able to discover it, it seemed.

She shook her head. ''They felt just about like any other robots. The thought of telepathic or empathic contact with a robot—'' She shook her head. ''I can't even begin to imagine it, so I didn't *try* to pick up anything.''

It was probably too late now in any case, so Dane let it pass, saying, ''All right, then; Dallith is our early warning signal and long-range dispatch. Dallith, if you're aware of anyone definitely beginning an attack, don't wait; pick them off with your sling. Disable, if you can't kill.

''Aratak, you're the heavyweight fighter; anyone who gets past Dallith's warning, try to crush them by sheer weight, and I'll have the sword to cut down anyone who comes closer. Rianna and Cliff-Climber are there for close-in fighting, hand to hand. Among us, we should be able to match damn near anything they throw at us. Did you all stock up with something portable to eat, at the banquéts?'' Dane had put some sweets into the capacious pocket he had found in his tunic; he had advised the others to do likewise.

Suddenly there was a roar and a rush of crimson flame and the small ship which had brought them there rushed upward and was gone, briefly blinding them; but afterward, as their eyes adapted, they studied the brilliantly world-lit landscape. Hills, underbrush, valleys; at the edge of vision, a waterfall, gleaming with light as it rushed downward; and far out on the horizon, some dark and oddly regular structures. Dane wondered if they were buildings and if they were the Hunter areas into which no Prey could come on pain of instant-and-dishonorable death.

Strange that they should have used the Mekhar phrase, he thought. (Or was it entirely the same?) In any case if these Hunters had a concept of honorable death and dishonorable, maybe there was more of a chance than he thought.

Aratak said, ''Are we going to wait here till dawn?''

''I don't know that one place has any advantage over another,'' Dane said slowly. ''I suspect all the *obvious* bits of cover as being the places where the Hunters will wait to pick off their least wary Prey. This is a test too, remember. They probably kill off the easier Prey first, to leave more time and energy for an elaborate duel of strength—or brains—with the more dangerous ones; remember they paid something extra for us because we'd already been pretested and positively *certified* dangerous. Even on Earth, hunters differ in their approach to sport. There are probably a few here who just want to make an easy catch and go home with a trophy.'' He wondered, wildly and absurdly, what the game laws were and if there was some sort of ''bag limit'' for each Hunter. ''Let me think. Aratak, what is your suggestion?''

The big saurian said, ''There is no wisdom in weariness. I suggest that we sleep or rest until an hour or so before dawn, watching in turns so that the light will not take us unawares.

When there is a somewhat stronger light—but well before sunrise,—we can look about intelligently for a kind of cover which is not an obvious stakeout.''

That struck them all as a good idea. Aratak volunteered to take first watch. ''Since,'' he said, ''it is purely formality; the beginning of the Hunt is hours away.''

''And I will watch with him,'' Cliff-Climber said, ''since my species is at least partly nocturnal and I am wakeful now.''

Dane and Rianna and Dallith wrapped themselves in the warm cloaks which had been supplied with the fighting tunics and lay down. The ground beneath them just here was covered with an alternation of rocks and soft moss, rather more rocks than moss, and it took them a while to find comfortable resting places, but at last they stretched out side by side, Dane between the women. Rianna quickly slept, relaxing and breathing deeply, but Dane was too tense to rest. He trusted Aratak entirely—there were times when he forgot that the giant saurian was not a man in every sense of the word—but Cliff-Climber was another matter.

He drifted after a time into a dark and unreal daze, shot with nightmares, but never more than half asleep. It must have been a couple of hours later when, starting awake again (the head of a samurai, fixed in a hideous nightmare grin, looked down from the wall of a Frankenstein laboratory; Hunters, with a thousand shifting shapes flowing into one another like water, saluted it with upraised goblets), he felt Dallith trembling, as if with cold. He drew a fold of his cloak around her, carefully so as not to disturb her sleep, but she turned and murmured, ''I'm not asleep,'' and he drew her protectively against his shoulder.

''You should rest,'' he said softly. ''Tomorrow's likely to be a rough day.'' He was conscious of the ridiculous understatement of the words as he said them and felt from somewhere an idiot laughter bubbling up, which he recognized as hysteria and quickly suppressed.

"I'm glad Rianna can sleep," she said, and they were silent. Dane lay still, racing images moving through his mind, very conscious of the girl's soft body, warm inside the cloak, against his. *I want her. I love her. This is a hell of a time to be thinking about that. What did Rianna say? Blind instinct in the face of death. Why should I be any different than any other proto-simian? Dallith wouldn't want it to be this way, she said so . . . clutching at each other like animals in the face of death.*

Her arms went around him in the darkness, gently and with infinite compassion. "What I want is what you want," she whispered. "I can't help it. Maybe it's not what I would want on my own. But it's real, Dane, it's real."

He strained her close to him, losing himself in her pliant yielding, and for a little while, for the first time in days, he forgot the great brick-red orb of the Hunter's World, forgot the samurai sword and the shadow of death and the Hunters themselves. Later she pillowed his head against her slender breasts and whispered tenderly, "Sleep a little, now, Dane. Sleep while you can," and he tumbled down a dizzying, bottomless abyss of silence and sleep.

The darkness had deepened considerably and the red Hunter's World was low on the horizon when Aratak's hand on his shoulder roused him. "Sorry to disturb you, Dane," he muttered, "but I'm half asleep. Cliff-Climber's been napping for a couple of hours."

He sat up, gently disengaging himself from Dallith, who slept quietly, encircled in his arms, and, covering her with her cloak, nodded to Aratak. "Good. Get some rest."

He took Aratak's place at the highest point on the slope; the great saurian lay down, covering his head with his cloak, and was still. Cliff-Climber was curled up, only a dark snoring ball. After a few minutes a dark form moved in the shadows; Dane was instantly alert but Rianna whispered, "I've slept enough. Let Dallith sleep; I think she was awake most of the night. . . ."

He nodded and the girl lowered herself at his side and sat there, silent. After a time her hand—small and firm and slightly calloused—stole out and clasped his; he returned the pressure, gently, and they sat there in the thinning darkness, watching for the glow on the horizon which would mark the coming dawn. Once Rianna, looking across at Aratak, who had thrown off his cloak and was glowing blue all over in the dimness, said, "That could be dangerous. Before dark tonight, we've got to do something about it," and Dane nodded. But most of the time they sat silently, side by side and watchful.

"It's strange," she said once, into the complete darkness and silence, as the Hunter's World sank below the edge of a faraway hill. "I'm a scientist. I've spent most of my life studying the remnants of other people's lives, and I've been happy doing it. It never occurred to me that I could be so deeply involved in—in a struggle for my very life, I would have been horrified at the thought. I wonder if I'm less civilized than I thought?"

"Someone in my culture said, civilization is only a thin veneer over the primordial ape."

"I'm afraid the layer in my case is pretty thin. I'm not really unhappy about this, Dane. Not—well, not the way Dallith is. She's *really* civilized."

Dallith. The feel of her was still on his skin. He said, "I wonder. She reacts so to what's around her. Perhaps she's civilized because she's with civilized people—"

"Maybe. Dane, how do you feel about this?"

"The Hunt?" He paused to consider. It occurred to him that he hadn't really thought about it. He'd been angry, scared, reluctantly conceding necessity. And yet, down at the bottom, beneath everything else, he became aware that from the very first, there had been a core of deep response. . . .

All his life he had been an adventurer, kicking away from civilizations to immerse himself in one far-out interest after another. The martial arts. Mountain climbing alone. Solo round-the-world sailing. And wasn't this the ultimate adventure, the last risk, a game played in deadly earnest, with his very life as the stake, and an opponent not blind and unaware like the storms at sea or the North Face, but alert, alive, wary, and playing the other side—an opponent worthy of himself?

"I guess," he said slowly, "I'm not very civilized either."

And they were silent again.

It was another hour before the brightening light in the sky—they could see one another's faces clearly, now—made Dane say reluctantly, "We'd better wake the others." In an odd way he was sorry to bring this interval of quiet to an end, not entirely because of the urgent fear of the Hunt, but because, in the last couple of hours, in his own growing awareness of his own feelings, and Rianna's admission of her own deep response to the Hunt, he had realized that they had shared a deeper intimacy than the sexual contact of the last few weeks.

Rianna was right, he thought, *and so was Dallith; it's human in the face of danger, it's natural and even inevitable and therefore nothing to feel guilt about. I was a fool about that. But it isn't all that important either.*

Not now.

Just now, nothing exists except—the Hunt!

Cliff-Climber stretched, with a deep snarl in his throat, and woke. He flexed his claws and sprang up, briefly falling into a fighting stance. Then he relaxed and looked around with a fierce grin.

"There's water there," he said. "I'm for a quick wash and a drink and then—bring on the Hunters!" He bounded off toward the sound of the falling waterfall, and Dane, following slowly, glancing back to see Dallith rise and fasten her tunic and cloak, felt a sharp surge of kinship. Cliff-Climber was also a good one to have on his side.

He thrust his head under the waterfall, feeling the icy sharpness of the water like a pleasant shock, and realized that his system was flooded with adrenalin. *Good, I'll need it.* He looked with positive affection on Aratak as the ten-foot-tall saurian joined them. Everything looked very clear and sharp in the growing light, etched sharply on consciousness and with bright clean new edges, as if everything was new from the hand of Creation, himself included; new and just a little unreal.

Dane looked at all his comrades with something very akin to love before he said briskly, "We've got about an hour before full dawn. Let's start thinking about some kind of cover."

Chapter Twelve

The day broke slowly, light growing on the horizon and the orange sun sliding up from behind a bank of cloud. The increasing light revealed a broken and desolate landscape, sharp treeless hills rising from valleys filled thickly with heavy spiky underbrush; rock-strewn slopes opening here and there in dark cave-mouths. Far away on the horizon were the dark regular shapes which Dane had identified by moonlight as buildings. But now in the light he could see that it was a city in ruins; the tall towers broken, the roofs gaping open to the sky.

It would be easy enough to take cover, Dane thought; what would be hard would be to avoid being trapped in whatever cover they chose. For that reason he vetoed immediately Rianna's suggestion that a cave-mouth would provide shelter in darkness and that the narrow entry could be easily defended. After nine-hundred-and-what-ever-it-was Hunts, he told her grimly, he'd bet even money that the Hunters knew the caves like the very insides of their own pockets. Most caves had more than one entrance—and more than one exit. Maybe they could defend the cave-mouth where they were—but they would be wholly vulnerable to an attack from behind. The same was true of the ruined buildings. They would be no better than traps.

From the waterfall they moved cautiously down through the valley, keeping the defensive pattern Dane had worked out; Aratak going in front with his great knobbed club, and the short ax—*he* called it a short ax, Dane didn't—girded at his belt. Dane thought of it as Paul Bunyan's Boy Scout Ax; the shaft was so thick that Dane could barely have gotten both hands around it, and it was so heavy that all Dane could have done with it was to lift it over his head and drop it. Although anything he dropped it on probably wouldn't get up again.

Dane went warily a few feet away from him, sword loose in its scabbard, and behind them, holding the center, Rianna with her long spear and knives. Just behind her right shoulder, Cliff-Climber moved softly, alert to either side; and at the left, Dallith brought up the rear with her sling. He had warned them all to avoid the thickest of the underbrush; only Rianna and the Mekhar were equipped for really close-in fighting. "Aratak and I need sword-room; and Dallith needs a clear field for a shot. But if they come at us, we've got to be prepared for anything."

So they moved across the deserted land, weapons at the ready, nerves drawn tight, scouting out for a piece of high ground—possibly the top of a steep slope—where nothing could come at them unseen. Dane had half expected that with the rising of the sun the land would explode into violence, battle cries, bloodshed; instead they moved through country that might have never known the print of any living creature, except themselves.

The Hunt lasts eleven days, Dane told himself. *That's the hell of it. We can't relax for a minute.*

Far from it. The longer we go unmolested, the more chance

that they'll spot our defense formation and be prepared to meet it.

Hour after hour moved by. The sun reached its height and began to angle downward; the short day drew near its close and as yet there was no sign of Hunters or of any other Prey. In midafternoon they stopped near a heap of rocks, where water gushed in a spring from a split outcrop of stone, and ate the sweets and confections they had brought with them. Rianna began to step behind the rocks and Dane said, "No. We all stay together."

She lifted her brows and said, "I completely see your point, but what does one do about what one could modestly refer to as a call of nature?"

"Take Dallith with you," Dane said shortly, "and stay within earshot. Until the sun sets, and we find one of the neutral feeding areas, we don't relax—or lay our weapons down—for even five minutes."

Cliff-Climber said with a feral grin, "There's where I have the advantage over you proto-simians. My weapons are always ready to my hands." Nevertheless, as Dane walked away from the group to urinate, he noted that the great cat stayed braced and alert, and kept his eye on where Aratak awaited them with his great club.

The Hunters could be watching us, of course, even now; tracking us. Trying to get some idea of our weapons and fighting style, Dane thought.

Finishing, and fastening his clothes, he looked around and decided to scout a little farther ahead. They were in a long, steep valley, heading in a roughly northerly direction toward the long range of hills at the foot of the ruined city.

We ought to head up the slopes, he thought; *they could hunt us into the tip of the valley and trap us there. Besides, we've got to locate a hilltop near sundown, and look for those areas of yellow lights. For all I know, the Hunters may treat them like salt licks, and station themselves outside to pick us off as we come out, but we can't get along for eleven days without food and sleep.*

He had come a considerable way from the others, although he could still see them below; the women had rejoined Aratak, and were standing on the rock, looking warily around, and Cliff-Climber was coming up the slope to join him. Dane reached a level spot, and awaited the Mekhar, stepping out toward Cliff-Climber.

It wasn't Cliff-Climber, he realized in a split second lurch of awareness. *He's got a sword!*

Almost before the thought had fully reached conscious awareness, his own blade slid free of his scabbard; he stepped back automatically into fighting stance, staring at the Mekhar's throat past the tip of his own blade. The lion-man stopped, raising his weapon to a guard position.

Dane's throat was dry, and the sound of his heart was loud in his own ears. *This was it!*—but his training was paying off, and he could listen to the pounding of his heart with a detached calm.

But was this Hunter or Prey?

Maybe there aren't any real Hunters. Maybe they get their kicks by watching us slaughter each other. . . .

"Who are you?" he shouted, and was surprised that his voice did not waver. "What do you want? Are you after me?"

With a feline scream of rage the Mekhar leaped, and Dane had barely time to catch a vicious cut at his head. The creature's body twisted in midair and Dane's answering cut fell short as the cat-man hit the ground, landing on his feet lightly, and bounded back out of range.

Dane held his ground, studying his opponent.

That stance is almost like a saber stance, he thought; but the Mekhar's blade was long and straight, much lighter than his own. He forced his right hand to relax, to let the left hold most of the weight. *He'll have reach on me,* he thought; *that stance should give him the same extension as a foil-fencer. And those jumps! But of course the gravity here is lighter; the moon is only about half the size of his own world. . . .*

But there was no more time to think. The long straight blade drove in a long lunge toward Dane's chest. He parried and stepped in as the Mekhar's sword glanced harmlessly over his right shoulder, Dane's arms swinging up for the cut.

The lion-man spun away, drawing his sword back over his head, and with a ring of steel the force of Dane's blow drove the back of the straight blade into the Mekhar's scalp.

Then it was Dane's turn to jump back, away from a low sweeping cut at his leg. The Mekhar snarled, a low harsh sound, wordless.

The two faced each other at a distance of about three paces. The cat-man crouched, his blade outstretched before him. Blood was oozing from the slight scalp-wound. But Dane's blade no longer pointed at the Hunter's throat; instead it was fixed skyward, behind him, held firmly over his head with both hands. *Chudan no Kamae, Jodan no Kamae;* technical terms and explanations flowed through his head in a meaningless stream; but his body, unconcerned, was doing its own thing, gracefully shifting into the perfect dancelike posture, carefully turning the sword-edge to the exact angle—

The cat-man slashed at his unguarded belly.

Dane stepped forward, and the old samurai blade caught the Hunter's arm at the elbow. Hand and sword fell to the ground.

The cat-man screamed, a hideous sound neither feline nor human, that turned to a choking gurgle as Dane's point found his throat. But he bent on, down, across the point, toward the severed arm; he snatched it up, and jerked free of Dane's sword-point, and ran, scrabbling up the slope, dodging, shifting from side to side.

Surprise—dismay—prisoned Dane for a second before he could follow. From the arm wound alone, the creature should be bleeding to death! And the stab in the throat—there was no question about it. That would have finished him. That *had* finished him. And yet—and yet—there he was, running up the slope, not even slowed down.

The creature—the Hunter?—dodged behind a rock. Warily, sword still unsheathed in his hand, Dane followed, braced for an ambush.

But there was nothing behind the rock. Nothing. No cat-creature. No severed arm. *Nothing*.

No blood. Not a bloodstain on the ground. Dane walked back to the scene of the fight, his lips pursed, whistling faintly in wonder and astonishment. He'd seen the thing bleed from the scalp. Blood—blood that looked exactly like ordinary blood—had spurted from the severed hand and arm.

There was blood on the ground here, too. But not much. Less that five feet away from the spot where Dane had lopped off the thing's arm, the blood-spots dwindled to a few drops and stopped.

Thoughtfully, Dane sheathed his sword. First blood, he thought. What *was* that thing? It sure as hell wasn't a Mekhar. He'd seen Cliff-Climber bleed. But equally sure as hell, it had looked like a Mekhar.

A variant species of proto-feline?

Was that what the Hunters were, just variant proto-felines?

Yeah, sure. Proto-felines. Sapient cats which could pick up an arm you'd lopped off—after being stabbed right through the jugular veins—and run off with it, and then vanish into thin air.

He began slowly to climb down the slope to where he had left his friends. Aratak and Rianna were running toward him; evidently they had heard the thing's final yell. With a dazed feeling, he realized that he had left them less than five minutes ago.

Rianna demanded, "What was it? A Hunter? I thought for a moment it was Cliff-Climber—"

"So did I, at first," Dane said grimly, "until I saw he had a sword."

"And I saw Cliff-Climber still with us. We began to run—Dane, did you kill him?"

"I should have." Dane told them the story. One by one they came up to look at the blood; but none of them had any explanation. Cliff-Climber was openly scatching; it was evident that he didn't believe a word of Dane's story.

"Your last stroke missed him, obviously," he said, "and he simply ran behind the rock and—"

"And walked straight through the rock wall?"

"Probably he hid behind some of the bushes. There might be a cave-mouth there somewhere, and he worked his way down to it when you weren't watching."

Dane looked grimly at the Mekhar. "Could *you* pick up your arm and run away with it if I lopped it off, Cliff?"

Cliff-Climber shook his head. "Perhaps you only thought you cut off his hand. It was your first fight. Maybe you were overexcited," he said patronizingly. "If you killed him, his body would be there. It's as simple as that."

Dane didn't answer. He couldn't afford to fight with Cliff-Climber, and he knew if he answered this time, he would. In silence, he turned away and gestured to them to come along. "In any case I think we'd better get out of this valley," he said. "If one of the Hunters is here, there are likely to be others."

But they saw no other living thing as they toiled up to the lip of the valley and came up into a long, level, rock-strewn plain. The sun was setting behind the ruins of the city, and the shadowy shapes rose against the light like jagged teeth protruding from a broken skull-bone.

"What's that?" Dallith asked, and pointed to a light against the horizon.

"The moon—excuse me, the Hunter's World—coming up," Rianna said. Dane shook his head.

"No. The light's yellow," he said. "Neutral zone, and the sun's set. The Hunt's off till midnight. We'd better go down there and see what we can get to eat."

Wearily, they turned toward the lights. Dane was very tired, and Rianna was stumbling with weariness; even Aratak dragged his club behind him instead of carrying it jauntily over his shoulder. The lights seemed very far away, and even the knowledge that safety lay beyond those lights hardly kept Dane moving. He wondered if they would reach them before he fell in his tracks.

The great brick-red disk of the Hunter's World was high over the ruined city before they reached the first of the lights. The whole area was brilliantly lighted with great yellow globes raised high on enormous metal poles; within the great circle—three or four acres at least—enclosed by the poles, Servers moved, imperturbable; gliding back and forth as smoothly here amid rocks and moss and underbrush as they did in the Armory itself. There was no other living creature within the circle of the lights except the huge proto-ursine creature, who slept in a furry huddle with the remnants of a large meal beside him.

Of course. There are other neutral areas; other prisoners must have found those. We will, too, if we live long enough, Dane thought.

At the very center of the ring of lights, there was an assortment of food in great bins, color-coded as food had been coded on the Mekhar slave ship.

It was, Dane thought, a symbol of how well this day had welded them together in adversity that they all turned to Dane before touching the food. He said, "Eat what you can, and sleep for a little while. But not too long. I want to be well away from here before midnight—and that's when the Hunt's on again."

"I want sleep even more than food," Dallith said, but dutifully she went and ate some fruit before wrapping herself in her cloak and casting herself down on the thick moss. The others followed her example. Dane said to Aratak, "Get a couple of hours of sleep, and then you stay awake while I do the same."

"You don't think we're safe here? You don't trust the Hunters?"

"I trust them to be Hunters," Dane said. "I think we're safe here. But I don't want to walk out straight into their arms. Get some sleep, Aratak. I'll tell you all about it afterward."

The giant saurian lay down and soon was glowing blue all over as he slept. Dane watched him, moodily thinking over his plans. He let Aratak sleep for a couple of hours, then awoke him and lay down to rest himself.

When he woke, as if his plan had been maturing in his sleep, he knew exactly what he meant to do. Quietly he woke Cliff-Climber and the women.

"Each of you make up a small portable pack with food for two or three days," he directed. "Maybe they *do* call the Hunt off every night at dusk; for all I know they're sleeping the sleep of the unjust— or holding the Hunter equivalent of a campfire and singsong—over in their own rest areas. But remember how the Mekhars *tested* us, on the ship, for thinking ahead? I'm willing to bet this is the same thing here; maybe for the first night, or the first two or three nights, it will be safe to sleep till midnight and then come out, but I'm betting that sooner or later anyone who gets into that nice safe routine, and *trusts* it, will find himself being cut down to make Hunter soup. From now on we camp in the open— standing watches for each other—and go in very briefly, just after dusk, once in two or three days to get food."

"That makes sense," Cliff-Climber agreed. "I was thinking roughly along those lines."

"Good." Dane went and began to select food which would keep—nuts, dried fruits, hard wafers of some dried grain.

When he had seen this laid out among the more perishable food (and, he supposed, its equivalent for non-humans) he had realized that here was another test; if the Hunters intended them to be safe every night for mealtimes, they would have provided only food to be eaten at once. Once again, they were sorting out the more intelligent and wary of their prey, providing them with opportunity—if they were intelligent enough to seize the opportunity—to prolong their lives and even to evade capture until the Hunt ended.

I don't imagine they're doing it for our benefit, Dane thought, *or even out of any exaggerated sense of fair play. They want to prolong the Hunt—stalk us longer. And if we give them a* really *good time, they don't mind letting one or two of us go.*

His mind leaped. *If I could bring all five of us through . . .* No. That was looking too far ahead. Concentrate on surviving through the day—on getting through this night.

He saw Dallith wrapping herself up in her cloak, the sack of dried fruit and nuts tucked inside the front of her tunic; she had knotted her hair into a single long plait. He came up beside her and said quietly, "Do you have a hairpin or something to screw that up on top of your head? Just now, hanging down like that, anyone who came after you would find that braid of yours a damn good thing to grab you by."

She smiled waveringly. "I never thought of that. One doesn't. I'll cut it off if you want me to."

He touched it, a gentle regretful touch, with the tip of his fingers. "It is beautiful hair," he said and on an impulse kissed the fine ends of the braid. "But if we live, it will grow again, and I'd feel safer about you if you didn't have any—handles for easy grabbing."

She drew her knife out of the light leather sheath; with a quick movement she cut through the pale braid and let it fall to the ground. She smiled at him and moved away. Dane stood looking after her for a moment, then bent, on a strange impulse, and lifted the long silky coil in his hands. It clung there, fine and smooth and springy; he coiled it into a roll and thrust it inside his tunic next to his skin. *A favor from my lady*, he thought.

Seeing that the others were girded up and ready, he gestured to them and led his little group into the darkness. Long before the Hunter's World swung at zenith, the yellow lights of the neutral area had receded to a twinkle and then vanished far behind them.

They slept again, in turns, for a few hours, hidden in a fold of the hills; and at dawn moved on up through the foothills, going in the general direction of the ruined city. Once, shortly after the light broke, they heard from far off a sharp clashing as of swords and shields and a high, screaming bellow: a death-cry; but it faded into silence and the landscape was once again as still as death.

As still as death. As still as all the death it's seen. How true these old clichés can be. . . .

It was late afternoon again when they reached a long rock-strewn hill and paused for a break, to eat a few mouthfuls of food and drink from one of the streams of water that flowed from the rocky cliffs.

It was the suspense and tension that was getting him, Dane realized. No one could keep the bowstring at full tension for days on end. So the game was rigged, after all, and rigged in favor of the Hunters, he thought, because they could stalk their Prey, tire them out, come at them at leisure. They could take a break without danger; the Hunted were unlikely to come up on them unawares or take them by surprise, chewing something that looked like strings of dried beef jerky; but probably wasn't. Dallith said to Dane, "If I live through this, I will never hunt for sport again."

Dane felt just the same way. Not that he'd ever been much of a hunter, except with a camera, but he'd always appreciated the mystique of the chase.

He looked at Rianna, who was resting with her head on her arm. Dallith had finished eating and was standing on a rock, her cropped head tilted to one side as if she were listening for some distant sound. He called softly to her, "Did you hear something?"

"No—I don't think so—I'm not sure," she said, and her thin face looked drained and drawn.

If she looks like this on the second day of the Hunt, what's it going to do to her? How long can she keep up?

He let them all rest for another half hour before calling them all together again and starting up the long slope. The top of the hill might be a good place to spend the night, if they were going to spend it in the open. They could sleep fearlessly the first part of the night, and keep watch the rest of the time without worrying about anyone sneaking up on them.

"Be careful at the top of the hill," he warned, as they started upward. "It's about the same time of day that the Hunter attacked us yesterday. Maybe they prefer to attack shortly before sunset."

He began to take his place in line, but Cliff-Climber thrust forward. "I claim the right to lead," he said proudly. "Yesterday you were at the fore, and you took the first blood. This is my turn! Do you want all the glory?"

Glory be damned, friend, Dane thought, but he didn't say the words aloud. He was beginning, slowly, to understand a little about how the Mekhar's mind worked. A human strategist thought in terms of efficiency. But Cliff-Climber wasn't human and he cared no more for efficiency than he did for the advancement of science. He was, in general, cooperating almost incredibly well with them; but if his morale sagged, he wouldn't. If it made him happy to lead and take the risks sometimes, Dane felt he shouldn't fight with him about it.

Cliff-Climber said eagerly, "In any case, my ears are the sharpest. Let me scout ahead."

Dane shrugged. "Lead on, MacDuff. But back him up with the spear, Rianna."

They started up the rocky slope, Cliff-Climber bounding eagerly ahead of them. The path was steep and Rianna fell farther and farther behind; the cat-man leaped nimbly over the same soil which slipped and slithered away under Dane's feet and started little showers of rocks below. Rianna's feet went from under her and she fell, just missing getting her feet tangled in the spear; Dane braced his hand under her elbow. She recovered her feet quickly and said, "Help Dallith," picking her way deftly through the stones.

Dane lingered to give Dallith a hand, noting that Aratak was falling farther and farther behind. *A fine fighting group we make*, he thought, *strung out all over the hillside*. He raised his head to shout at Cliff-Climber to wait.

Dallith gave a strangled gasp; for an instant he wondered if she had picked up his fear, but at that same moment the Mekhar hissed sharply, throwing himself down behind a boulder and gesturing with his arm for the others to take cover.

Dane half pulled Dallith, then Rianna, into the shadow of a huge rock nearby and flattened himself against its side. Aratak had thrown himself flat. There was no cover nearby in which he could hide but, motionless, he blended into the rocky slope like another rock.

Above them Dane saw Cliff-Climber go up the side of his boulder quickly and quietly and crouch, more catlike than ever, at the top. *They certainly gave him the right name*, he thought. At Dane's side Dallith gave a low moan, and above him he saw the lion-man stiffen. *Whatever it is, it's coming*, Dane knew.

He saw it, then. A proto-feline, like the Mekhar. Dane remembered the cat-man he had killed—or failed to kill—and his hand tightened about his sword hilt. He tensed, ready to draw.

There was a sudden peculiar change in Dallith's breathing,

but before he could analyze or understand it, he saw Cliff-Climber leap to his feet, to stand atop the rock, silhouetted against the sky, in plain view of the newcomer.

That crazy Mekhar! He's going to challenge him to single combat!

The other cat-man had not stopped at the sight of Cliff-Climber, but came straight down the slope toward the Mekhar. And then, insanely, Cliff-Climber turned toward them and waved.

"It's all right," he called down to them, and there was joy in his voice. "He wears the topknot of my clan. He is one of my kindred!" He leaped down from the rock and ran toward the other, calling out to him what sounded like a ritual greeting:

"Hearth-sharer and Hunt-helper—"

Dallith came to her feet, screaming. "No! No! Cliff-Climber, no, no, it's—" She gripped Dane's arm, her nails digging painfully into his forearm. "Stop him! Help him! It's a trick, a trap—" Suddenly she bent to the ground and fitted a stone quickly to her sling.

Confused, Dane looked up the hill, to see Cliff-Climber bound up to the other Mekhar with every evidence of joy and trust—and to see the sun glint on the razor-steel of tipped claws that flashed for Cliff-Climber's unguarded throat.

Then Dane was shouting and his sword was out, and dirt and small stones were sliding out from under his feet as he charged recklessly up the hill, expecting any moment to fall and skewer himself on his own sword. Above him he saw Cliff-Climber reel back, blood spurting from a wound in his throat, and then, staggering, close with his attacker.

From below came a deep, rumbling bellow that could only have been Aratak. Dane shouted again, and fought for balance on the treacherous slope.

The two great cats rolled down the hill toward him, locked together in a death-struggle, both covered in blood: red blood streaming from Cliff-Climber's throat, smearing his opponent's claws; Cliff-Climber's own claws raking down for eyes, entrails. But Cliff-Climber was weakening, and as Dane came panting past the boulder where the Mekhar had crouched, Cliff-Climber gave a sudden convulsive shudder and lay still, blood still gurgling from his torn throat.

The other proto-feline crouched over the body, raised his eyes to glare at Dane. One of Cliff-Climber's hands was still entangled in his mane at the throat—*No!* Startled, Dane saw that the dead Mekhar's claws were still sunk deep in his killer's throat, frozen there in a death-grip.

At least he gave as good as he got, Dane thought. *He took the bastard with him!*

And then, incredibly, the cat-man gripped Cliff-Climber's dead arm with both hands, and leaned back. Dane saw the Mekhar's stiffening claws pull *through* the neck of the other. Blood welled out briefly, then stopped. The cat-man rose, apparently unwounded, and stood facing Dane, crouched in a fighting stance, as the Earthman ran toward him.

Something hit the Hunter on the shoulder and spun him around. One of Dallith's sling stones, Dane realized. And from behind came such a crashing and sliding of rock as could only be Aratak forcing his great bulk up the slope.

Another sling stone cracked on the rock behind the Hunter, and for a moment he hesitated, gripping Cliff-Climber's body as if to carry it away. But as Dane came into striking range the creature wheeled and leaped away up the slope, moving at a speed Dane could not match. He paused on the crest, and a great boulder came loose from its bed and clattered down, forcing Aratak to leap out of its way; then he vanished over the brow of the hill.

Dane clambered stolidly on, cresting the hill. But, as he had halfway expected, Cliff-Climber's killer was nowhere in sight.

He vanished just the way the other one did. And he climbed that slope with his throat torn out.

That probably means the one I killed isn't dead either. . . .

He turned back down the slope. Dallith crouched by Cliff-Climber's body. He thought for a moment that she was weeping, but she turned a white tearless face up to him.

"That was a Hunter?"

"That," he said grimly, "was a Hunter, God help us all."

Rianna bent by Cliff-Climber's blood-smeared corpse. Tears were falling on his matted fur as she gently closed the staring yellow eyes.

"His captain wished him an honorable escape, or a bloody and honorable death," she whispered. "Well, he got it. He got it. Rest in peace, friend."

Dane looked down at the body of their dead ally, and his thoughts were grim. "Do you want all the glory?" Cliff-Climber had asked, and instead he'd got all the death, the first to die, running headlong toward death. "It should have been me," Dane said aloud.

But there was no time to mourn, not even time to bury their dead friend.

On this hillside, if that Hunter has any little pals around, we'd be sitting ducks, Dane thought, and grimly gave orders to move on. Rianna protested, sobbing, and he said gently, "We can't do him any good by getting ourselves killed along with him, Rianna. Let's hope that Hunter's caught the bag limit for one day, and doesn't come back for seconds."

Aratak added, taking Rianna gently by the arm and leading her away, "He is one with all wisdom now, Rianna—or else he is dust returning to dust. Either way, your duty now is to us, as ours is to you. Come, my child."

She let the huge saurian lead her away, but she was still shaken with sobs. Dane, too, left saddened. He had not realized how deeply the Mekhar had grown into a part of their group. It was not only the gap he made in their line of defense; it was Cliff-Climber himself he knew he would miss.

His courage, his cheerfulness under pressure—even his insuppressible arrogance, his sharp, offhand insults.

One gone. Four to go, and they were beginning to know what the Hunters were like—and the picture wasn't pretty.

Can those damned things be killed at all?

Chapter Thirteen

The worst of the Hunt, Dane thought, was the way one tended to lose track of time.

He was not sure whether it was the fifth or the sixth day of the Hunt. Time seemed to melt into endless stretches, endlessly braced against attack and kill. They were endlessly alert for the sudden appearance of someone—or some*thing*—on slaughter bent. But since the death of Cliff-Climber—was it three or four or even five days ago?—they had met no other Hunters, or at least had been attacked by none. Once indeed Dallith had brought them all to a halt, with a harsh warning; they had taken cover in the underbrush, and far away they had heard the clash of steel and something, a far-off dying scream somewhere. Crouching there, hidden against the growing red moonlight—or rather, world-light from the gibbous Hunters' World above—they waited for attack; but there was nothing, and after a long time Dallith went limp and let her sling fall to the ground.

"It's gone," she said. "Really gone."

"Dead?" Rianna asked, and Dallith sighed and said, "How do I know?"

Now, by daylight, Dane could see that the Hunt was telling on her, perhaps, worst of all. They were all sunburned and dusty with exposure, but under her tan Dallith looked every day a little more pale and drawn; every day her dark eyes sunk more deeply into her face. Rianna sometimes cried with weariness; Dallith neither wept nor complained, but every day she seemed more wasted and haggard.

She needs rest, Dane thought, *and uninterrupted sleep, and freedom from fear.*

We all do, but Dallith worst of all. She seems able to feel those damned things even in her sleep, and it's probably kept us all alive this long.

They sat resting in the lee of the far range of hills they had seen that first night, beneath the ruins of the city. It stood far up on the top of the bluff, and the worn and eroded cliffsides leading up to it were strewn with dark cave-mouths and long ruined stairs and passageways.

Rianna, looking up at the buildings, said, "I'd like to explore them someday. Under better conditions."

"Not I," Dane said. "If we get off this damned moon alive, I've had enough of it for two or three lifetimes."

"You don't understand," Rianna said. "If the Hunt has taken place here for centuries, the Hunters may even have built this city—"

"Or, more likely, hunted down and killed off whatever *did* build it," Aratak suggested, "and when all their Prey were dead, could not stop hunting. . . ."

"Stranger things have happened," Dane said, thinking of Earth's history and the long insanity of the Crusades.

Aratak seemed the least touched by the days of toil and fear; but Dane could see that even he looked weary. He was smeared with gray mud from head to foot—early in the Hunt they had realized that in the long midnight-to-dawn stretches, when they camped in the open, Aratak's habit of glowing blue while he slept could lead the Hunters down on them; and they had adapted this method of controlling his indiscreet luminescence. Fortunately Aratak enjoyed mud; but he had admitted that there was a big difference between the pleasant warmth of wet mud and the wearing of dried mud. Now he scratched absentmindedly at the grayish smears and said, "I think with pleasure of the bathing pools of the Game Preserve. I hope there will be water somewhere in the ruins. The Voice of the Egg, may his wisdom endure forever, once remarked that a banquet was pleasant in hunger, but that the truly wise man, unless he was starving, would refuse a banquet for a bath. Alas, I have verified all too many of his divinely wise sayings in adversity of late."

"I envy your philosophy, friend," Dane said, and hauled himself wearily to his feet. "I think we'll have to go into the ruins to find water; we have food for a day or so, but we need drinking water and you need a bath."

"I thought you were worried about being trapped there," Rianna said.

"I am. But between sunset and midnight we might risk it. The moon—oh hell, it's a moon to *us* now—the world up there is giving enough light now so that we can probably find our way around well enough for *that*. But we should be well away by midnight. I suspect the Hunters take a great deal of pleasure in playing hide-and-seek in there, if any of the Prey think it might be a good place to hide."

Rianna looked up at the sky. "Near sunset. Thank goodness."

Dallith nodded grimly. "But we're overdue for an attack. I suspect they like to attack just before sunset because then their Prey are tired from a day of running, and are ready to let their guard down."

"I suspect you're right," Dane said, "which means it's the

best time to keep our guard at top pitch. Well—let's go. I'd like to reach the ruins just *after* sunset—and avoid having to fight our way inside.''

Days of traveling, on the alert for attack, had perfected the best lineup; but every time they formed for march Dane still missed Cliff-Climber's alertness. Now, as they crested the brow of a small hill, Dane saw a stirring in the underbrush beneath them, and the flash of brownish-gold. A Mekhar—or one of the catlike things they had fought twice now. He gestured to the others behind him. They halted, falling into their defensive formation; Rianna knelt and planted the butt of her spear against a boulder behind her; Aratak and Dane took up positions to either side. Dallith leaped to the top of the rock, her sling ready.

The lion-man looked out at them for a moment, then turned and ran, melting away into the underbrush. Dane gave a sigh of relief and lowered his blade.

''I don't think that was a Hunter,'' Dallith said, behind him. ''He seemed too frightened. I think he was Prey. Like ourselves.''

''We can't be sure of that,'' Dane said. *Damn near anything,* he thought, *would be frightened at the sight of that five-foot club of Aratak's. Even a Hunter might prefer easier prey.* The knob at the club's end was nearly twice the size of Dane's head.

Dallith jumped down from the rock. ''It didn't *feel* like that thing that killed poor Cliff-Climber,'' she insisted. ''It felt''—she hesitated, groping for words—''a little like Cliff himself. Only not so brave.''

''Probably one of the Mekhars—the ones he called common thieves,'' Dane said, and felt in himself a curious mixed reaction: on the one hand a desire to find the poor scared Mekhar, who was, after all, of Cliff-Climber's kind if not his class; on the other a strange aversion to association with someone Cliff-Climber had evidently felt beneath him. "But we could use a Mekhar's eyes and ears now," he said, "if only to give you a rest, Dallith."

Rianna let her spear drop. "I've no reason to love the Mekhars," she said grimly; "they brought us here. As far as I'm concerned, the Hunters can have them, and welcome. They're all pretty much of a kind, as far as I'm concerned."

Dane said no more. *After all,* he thought, *it could still have been a Hunter. Dallith might have been wrong.*

I'm tired of being Prey, he thought. *I'd like to start hunting them down instead.* But that was foolish and he knew it. For one thing, they didn't even know if the Hunters could be killed. Anything which could run away with its throat torn out was no ordinary proto-feline. *Next time, damn it, I'll cut the head right off and see if the critter's still so frisky!*

"Shall we keep moving?" Aratak suggested. "Even if that feline was Prey, it might have a Hunter after it." Slowly they moved on down the slope and began to follow the valley at the bottom, taking the easiest path to avoid tiring themselves, but alert to the possibilities of the place for ambush.

Dane was thinking over the various encounters they had had. "Even if we may be wronging some of our fellow Prey," he said at last, "we have some idea of what sort of creature we should avoid at all costs. Both of the Hunters we've actually faced have been Mekhars—or at least proto-felines, and near enough to the Mekhar type to fool Cliff-Climber into thinking he was one of his own clan. If we avoid anything that looks even slightly like a Mekhar, we ought to be safe."

"I'm still not convinced," Aratak said stubbornly. "Remember the other proto-saurian at the Armory, which did the same kind of disappearing trick which the imitation Mekhar did. I still believe the Hunters are more than one species."

The sun angled downward. Furtive figures sometimes

watched them from a distance, and once Dallith said she felt sure that one of the stalkers was near, but no one approached.

"The very fact that we're traveling together may be some protection," Aratak said. "Most of the other Prey might feel that any organized group must be Hunters."

"And the Hunters," Dane said, "are probably picking off the easy ones first. Or the ones they can trick—like poor Cliff-Climber."

Aratak said grimly, "If I'm right, and there are more than one species, then if I were you, Dane, I would be very careful of anything that looks like a man and tries to get too near."

"Damn it," Rianna said suddenly. "I have this feeling that I *ought* to know the answer. But I can't put my finger on it. It makes my brain itch."

"Save your breath," Dane said gently. "Tell us later. We're within an hour or so of sunset, and then we can rest."

They moved along for some time in silence; suddenly, as she emerged from the lengthening shadow of a rock, Dallith started as if she had been stung, and called softly for them to wait.

They stood still and tense as deer scenting the wind, until she spoke. "One of *them* is very close, and it's *stalking* . . . it's on some kind of scent . . . but I think it's after someone else. . . . I can feel . . ."

She stopped as there came a shriek from nearby, then sounds as of metal striking metal. "They're fighting—over there, beyond that pass—"

She pointed ahead where two pillars of stone rose, forming a narrow, gate-like cleft. Dane suddenly whipped out his sword.

"To the devil with this! They're just waiting to kill off some of the other poor suckers before coming after us! They want to kill us off one by one, and we're not cooperating, so they're saving us for last. Let's turn the tables on them if we can—and start by helping that poor devil in there!''

"You're crazy," Rianna said flatly, but Aratak shouldered his giant club and started toward the cleft. "There is wisdom in cooperation," he said. "If we can get there in time to help—and if we can tell Hunter from Hunted." He broke into his lumbering run; Dane hurried after him. Dallith stood frozen a moment, than ran after them and Rianna, reluctantly, brought up the rear.

But as he threaded his way through the cleft Dane's rage began to cool. Maybe this *was* crazy! His entire being re-volted at the thought of standing by, not getting involved, while a fellow creature was done to death almost within earshot; but he was risking Aratak's life as well, and the lives of both the women, to help someone they didn't know, couldn't trust, probably couldn't save anyway; and to kill something which might not even be killable in the first place. . . . *We've still got four or five days to go; we should save our strength*, he thought.

He thrust through the cleft and stood looking down into a little round natural amphitheater below. Behind him Rianna cried out softly with dismay.

One of the cat-men lay apparently dead, off to one side. Another, brandishing what looked like a European two-handed sword, stood facing a spider-man—one like the survivor of the last Hunt, like the one they had seen feted and honored in the Game Preserve back on the Hunters' World. And now he could tell how that spindly, frail-looking creature had man-aged to survive, alone, through an entire Hunt.

The spider-thing scuttled in and out on four of its curiously-segmented limbs, deftly avoiding the slashing thrusts of the cat-man, while its other four limbs—Dane stared. One arm was always occupied with holding the small metal shield with which it parried the Mekhar's, or pseudo-Mekhar's, attacks. The other three limbs were *twirling* a long, sharp-bladed lance, the head of which was almost sword-length. And at least once Dane saw the creature shift the shield from one arm to another with incredible swiftness. The creature was *juggling* with its weapons!

And how deadly that style was they saw almost at once; even before they had fully come out of the pass they saw the butt-end of the spear swing down to catch the pseudo-Mekhar behind the leg, tripping him; as he fell, the blade of the spear was already slashing toward his head. The lion-man caught it on his heavy sword, but only barely, and staggered to his feet. Then the butt-end drove in again and this time Dane saw the cat-creature doubled over as the shaft drove into his midsection. The shield bashed against the two-handed sword, pushing it aside, and then the spearhead swept around; and suddenly the lionlike head was rolling on the ground. The body swayed for a moment, blood gushing from its severed neck, and crumpled to the ground, where it convulsed briefly and lay still.

Behind him he heard Dallith gasp with horror and shock, but he could not hold back a moment of wild elation. *He got one of the devils—no! Two of them! Wonder what kind of price the Mekhars get for these spider-things?*

Aloud he said, "If we can get him to join up with us, we ought to be damn near invincible." He looked down and saw the spider-man wiping his weapon. "Let's go down."

"Remember how timid these creatures are," said Aratak. "Let me go down alone, first, and greet him in the name of Universal Sapience. Perhaps he will not fear me." The huge lizard-man lowered his club and began walking down the hill, his hands spread open and empty in front of him. Dane sheathed his sword. Rianna came up behind him, half supporting Dallith, who seemed to be in shock. Of course—she had sensed the death of the Hunter. He turned toward her, concerned, taking her hands in his. They were cold and strengthless and for a minute he thought she would fall over in a faint.

Through his preoccupation with Dallith he heard Aratak's deep rumbling voice, and, glancing quickly over his shoulder, glimpsed the spider-man backing away, his shield raised and his long lance balanced, menacing.

"Do not be afraid. I am no Hunter, but Prey like yourself," they heard Aratak say. Dallith shook her cropped head and seemed to come a little more to herself, listening, alert and tense, to Aratak's words.

"I salute you in the name of Universal Sapience and Peace," Aratak said. "If we can join together against our enemies, our chance for survival will be greatly increased. Can you understand what I say? Can you answer me?"

Dallith stirred. "What's he doing down there?" she asked in a faint voice, and then suddenly her eyes grew very wide; she pulled away from Dane and Rianna, fumbling for her sling.

"Aratak, watch out!" she screamed, *"That's the Hunter!"*

Dane whirled and saw the spider-man scuttling forward, his spear aimed at the saurian's unprotected chest.

Dane shouted encouragement, drawing his sword as he raced down the hill. Aratak's left arm came up in a karate block that Dane had taught him and he knocked the spear to one side, his other hand clutching at the ax in his belt.

One of Dallith's sling stones hissed through the air, and struck the spider-thing's abdomen with an audible thud. The spider-man scuttled back, unhurt but startled; he recovered at once, but Aratak had his ax in hand; he roared, a huge earthshaking bellow, and the monster ax hurtled down, to be blocked unerringly by the shield. Whatever the metal was, it was tough.

But Aratak had to dodge back against a return thrust from the spear, and Dane realized that the shield alone gave the spider-man a major advantage, even without the deadly effectiveness of the three-armed twirling spear. It was like trying to walk into the spinning blades of a helicopter.

*It would be deadly enough, just spinning; it could break
the bones of any ordinary living thing. But it's got that
long-edged blade on the end.* . . . Dane ran on down the hill,
not certain what actual aid he could give his friend except to
die with him.

With his club, Aratak might have had a chance; at least
he'd have reach. As it was, the length of the spear gave all
the advantage to the Hunter; the lizard-man couldn't use his
ax unless he could get within arm's reach of his foe, but
anywhere within fifteen feet he'd be within the range of that
deadly whirling spear. A normal lance technique, depending
on straight thrusts, would have given Aratak the advantage if
he could get inside the spear-range; but with all those hands,
the spider could probably spin the spear down to cut a fly off
his nose if he wanted to.

Another sling stone whirred through the air and struck the
spider-man in the midsection, on the gray and hairy thorax.
The spider staggered, with a wailing sort of scream; only an
instant, but it interrupted the even spin of the spear. It
whirled down, and struck Aratak a blow that sent him
sprawling—and would have crushed the skull of anything but
a proto-saurian—but it had been a glancing blow, and Aratak
managed to roll out of range before the spider-man could
regain complete control of his weapon. Dane was there by
that time, darting to one side to try to come in on the
spider-man's rear.

The Hunter saw him; the lance spun menacingly in his
direction and only the crash of another sling stone against one
of the gray and fuzzy arms kept Dane from being annihilated;
he danced out of the way barely in time. His move had been
pure distraction, of no possible use as an attack; but it worked
this time, for Aratak was climbing painfully to his feet.

But dodging wouldn't work. The thing was too fast.

Another of Dallith's sling stones smashed into the creature's
side; this one must have hurt him, for he jumped away,

startled by the impact, and Dane ran in close and sliced at the fuzzy gray skin of the thing's abdomen.

It was like slicing cheese. The blade sheared through easily, but no blood ran; the only reaction was the sudden spear-thrust that drove into the ground as Dane sprang away, only the lighter gravity saving him. There was something gray and sticky on Dane's blade. Another stone crashed against the creature's side as Dane backed frantically away from a second thrust. He yelled to Aratak, "Now, while he's dazed—before he gets that spear whirling again," but the great saurian was weaving slowly from side to side, trying to haul out his ax but still dizzied by the blow he'd taken.

And suddenly Dane saw Rianna, spear down and extended in bayonet style, running toward them. *Good girl, maybe that's the answer—Oh, God, no, her spear isn't long enough and he's got the shield! She's gone, unless I can distract him—fast!*

He ran in yelling, his blade back against his shoulder in the traditional guard against spear attack. *What good it'll be against that damned airplane propellor I don't know.* And at the same instant Aratak roared again and charged.

The spear whirled into a disklike blur. It drew a red line across Aratak's chest, struck Rianna's spear contemptuously out of her hands to fly, broken, into the darkness, and whipped down toward her leg.

Dane heard her scream of agony through a darkening blur; he jumped at one of the spider-thing's legs and hewed with all his might.

That worked. He should have thought of it before. The great bulk collapsed backward. The thing turned the spear on Dane, thrusting straight back with his two rearmost arms; but a thrust Dane could handle. His sword whipped across his body with the full force of his shoulders behind it, and as the spear slid harmlessly past he swung at the other leg on that side. *Cripple him enough to get away—*

But the leg moved away from his cut with lighting speed. Over the hunched back of the creature he suddenly saw Aratak, his ax lifted for a terrible stroke at the thing's midsection.

The spear snapped back; the butt caught Aratak near the shoulder, knocking him backward; the creature jumped straight up into the air on its three good legs and twisted in midair, landing in a ball at some distance and bringing himself up in a crouched, scuttling heap. Great red eyes swiveled to watch them.

Dane spared a quick glance back to where Rianna lay, moaning, on the ground. She was still alive, but one arm lay crumpled beneath her, and the side of her tunic was dyed red with blood. Aratak seemed unhurt, although he was holding his shoulder where the lance butt had struck at it.

Is it going to run? Or attack again?

From the spider-thing came a high wail—almost like the sound that cat-thing made when Dane got his arm—followed almost at once by Dallith's shriek from the hill.

"Get away quick! He's calling for help—! *Watch out!*"

And the spider-man attacked.

He had dropped one of the "arms" to the ground to serve in place of the severed leg, and had four limbs to walk on; he scurried at them at alarming speed, whirling the spear with two arms while with the third he covered his head and upper body. Aratak and Dane had no time for anything but to draw together, weapons ready. A sling stone struck one of the spider's legs; he caught a second with a deft motion of the shield. *But his head must be vulnerable, or he wouldn't bother with the shield!* Dane thought.

Then he was upon them, and the whirling lance-point forced them to give ground before him. But Dane was counting the strokes, trying to time the spin. If he could jump in fast enough, get the spider's head before the shaft caught him—

Dallith's sling stones were still whizzing around the creature's head, although most of them landed with a crack against his shield.

She's caught on about the head. . . . Oh, good girl, Dane thought.

Suddenly there was a sharp crack! The thing shuddered and one of his arms went limp; the spear-spin slackened, out of control.

Dane leaped.

But the shield thrust out at the end of the long shaggy arm, and suddenly Dane's blade was being forced back against his body, pinned by the pressure on the guard. Hopelessly, he saw the lance-point driving at his throat.

And then the spider-thing's head exploded into a fountain of jetting blood as one of the sling stones crashed directly into his skull; at the same moment Aratak's ax hewed off the arm holding the spear. The thing collapsed, blood still pumping from his shattered head.

Dane staggered back. *Was it really dead?* Aratak evidently shared his doubts, for he heaved up the great ax and sheared through the juncture of upper body and abdomen. More blood poured out; slowed to a trickle; stopped.

"Hurry!" Dallith was shouting at them. "They're coming! This way, quick!" And indeed, figures were appearing over the far crest of the hill.

Dane, sheathing his sword, ran to Rianna's side. She gasped with pain as he lifted her, but threw her uninjured arm around his shoulder; he saw her bite down on her lip to keep from crying out as he heaved her up and ran with her in his arms for the stone cleft, Aratak close on his heels.

They ran up toward the cleft where Dallith stood waiting, her sling still whirling around her head, interrupted every moment or two for the fitting of another stone. Aratak stooped to retrieve his club and Dane saw he had also picked up the dead Hunter's spear.

"Where now?"

"The ruins. What other chance have we? We can't run far and carry Rianna," he said, gasping, "but we can hide there." Rianna was a small woman, but she seemed to weigh a ton; he suspected that in normal gravity he couldn't have carried her at all.

"Here." Aratak slung his club over his shoulder and bent to lift Rianna from Dane's arms. "Bring the spear," he said, and broke into a lumbering run with Rianna in his arms, Dane and Dallith hurrying behind. He looked back, briefly, as they came under the shadow of the city wall. Aratak had evidently been right. A group of Hunters—they must be Hunters—were climbing up the slope behind them. There was a catman of Mekhar type. There were one or two forms that looked human. And Dane's hair felt as if it were standing straight on end as he saw one of the spider-creatures.

My God, we killed that one, I was sure we killed it, or was there another one? I thought they were rare. . . .

The group of Prey were slowed by Rianna's weight, and behind them the Hunters were gaining. Aratak jogged along the ruined wall, looking for a gap. Rianna was limp in his arms—dead or unconscious, Dane could not even guess—and Dallith was stumbling.

"Here," Aratak said, his breath coming in great sobbing gasps. He set Rianna on the ground, and thrust against a fallen stone which blocked a gap in the wall. Dallith stumbled through. Dane picked up Rianna's apparently lifeless body and followed Dallith through into the semidarkness. Aratak, behind them, heaved the rock back into place. And behind them the sun sank and was gone.

Aratak dropped, panting, to the ground. "Sunset," he said grimly. "Look. They're going away."

"Talk about being saved by the bell," Dane agreed.

Dallith murmured, "I'm surprised. I thought they'd follow

us—so close—'' Now that it was all over, she was sobbing in reaction.

Dane, too, was surprised—it seemed that they were near enough that the Hunters would have finished them off, sunset or no sunset. He felt grim. He bent over Rianna, prepared to discover that she was dead.

But she was breathing, and he explored her injuries, Dallith kneeling at his side.

Her arm was limp and she moaned when he touched the shoulder; he suspected the arm was broken or at least dislocated. The blood on her tunic came from a long, angry gash which began high on her buttock and ran down her thigh; it had cut nearly to the bone, but when he examined it in the fading light it seemed mostly to be a flesh wound, for already the blood had clotted to an ooze.

Aratak tore several long strips from his tunic, saying quietly, ''I can spare them better. My hide needs less protection than yours.'' This was so obviously true that neither Dane nor Dallith protested; Aratak normally wore no clothing at all, and had put on the tunic only at Server's insistence. He bandaged Rianna's leg wound and explored the damaged arm. ''A tendon in the shoulder is torn,'' he said. ''She won't use it for a while. But better her arm than her leg. She can still walk if she has too.''

Dallith went off to look for water and returned saying that there was a stone pool, with running water which had evidently once been a fountain, not far away. They carried Rianna there by the last of the light, and laid her on her own cloak and Aratak's; then they sat on the rim of the stone pool, resting and eating some of their stored provisions.

''We're safe till midnight,'' Dane said, ''but after that there's nothing to keep them from breaking down that wall and coming in after us. I don't know why they didn't.''

Aratak said thoughtfully, ''I think I know. Remember what

high value they put on courage and skill? We're evidently something special and they'll play by the rules just because of that. Remember, too, they probably think they've killed Rianna.''

''We seem to have done some killing too,'' Dane said. ''If those things can be killed at all,'' he added. ''Do they come back to life again? I looked back and saw that same spider-thing, or his twin brother, following us.''

''We can't rule out the possibility,'' Aratak said. ''They are certainly no form of life I know.''

Dane was thinking it over. He had killed a Hunter who looked like a Mekhar, and the thing had run away with his throat torn out. They had had to cut the spider-man's head from his body to kill him. ''You said they were more than one species,'' he said. ''Have the Hunters simply learned how to give their recruits the power of regenerating lost parts?''

Aratak said grimly, ''Perhaps this is the Happy Hunting Ground; there is a legend in the folklore of the Salamanders—as in most warlike races that somewhere there is a great Hunting Ground where every good hunter goes after death, to live in eternal battle—to fight every day, and then every night to feast while his wounds heal again to fight the next day. Needless to say it is not *my* idea of heaven, but the Salamanders seemed content with it.''

Dane said, ''We have that legend too. We call it Valhalla.'' His skin prickled, but he said firmly, ''I refuse to believe that all the dead heros of the Galaxy come here after death to enjoy fighting through all eternity.''

''I didn't say I believe it,'' Aratak said. ''But we seem to be faced with an analogous situation. Perhaps it is hypnotism—the Hunters are all one form but can work on our minds to make us see them in any form we fear most.''

Dallith said, ''I don't think so. If they broadcast fear into our minds to make us see them one way or the other, why would we all see them in the same way? Cliff-Climber would have felt no fear of the Mekhar—in fact he rejoiced to meet him. *He took that form to trap Cliff!*"

Dane said, "Are you seriously telling me that you think those things change their shape?"

"I can't prove it," she said. She was chewing a piece of dried fruit; she finished, swallowed it, and discarded the stone. "But I believe it."

Aratak said, "It may be that they cannot be killed at all . . . that even at the end of the Hunt, the game is simply for us to keep killing them until the Eclipse frees us. If we are still alive, we have won the game."

"No, they can be killed," Dane said. "Remember the feast? *Nineteen have gone to join their illustrious ancestors.* . . . They're not easy to kill, but I'll bet that one we fought is dead."

Dallith said hesitantly, "When they were following us, I had the sense that some terrible catastrophe had been averted—for them, that is. That somehow they were terribly afraid of *something* we could do to them."

"Wish to hell I knew what it was," Dane said morosely. "I'd love to do it."

But before he could say more, Riana moaned slightly, opened her eyes, and tried to sit up. Dallith went quickly to her.

"Don't move," she said. "You'll be all right. But try to rest while you can."

Rianna's voice sounded low and dazed. "I was sure you were all dead," she said, "and I'd be waking up alone with your bodies all around me—what happened? Did you kill that thing?"

Among them they gave her a quick fill-in about the end of the battle. She looked around at the shadowy ruins, the brick-red Hunters' World just rising over them.

"Here I am in the city," she said. "I wanted to know more about it. And I'm not in any shape to go exploring, worse luck!" Carefully, she moved her arm and leg. "I seem to be reasonably well in one piece, but I'm half dead of thirst. I hear running water; can I have a drink?"

Chapter Fourteen

By midnight there was no chance of moving out of the city, for Rianna's wounded leg had swollen so that it would not bear her weight. Her face was hot and Dane wondered if she had developed a fever or the wound had become infected from the far-from-sanitary bandage which they had used for lack of a better one. There was no way to tell, but no matter what happened they could not move her just at this moment. They could, perhaps, carry her a little way, but they certainly could not carry her as far as one of the neutral zones. Nor, if they were attacked at the gates of the city—and it seemed likely, after last night, that they would be—could they fight off an attacker with Rianna, helpless, to protect.

"It looks pretty bad," Dane said to Aratak, moving out of earshot of the women—why, he didn't really know; Rianna was too weak to pay any attention; Dallith knew how he was feeling anyway.

The saurian nodded in agreement. He had washed the dried mud from his body and was glowing again in the dark, and

Dane realized that if there were Hunters around it would draw them. Well, if there were Hunters around they'd probably be found even without Aratak; there was no point in making him uncomfortable when all their lives might depend on his fighting trim.

They stayed in the open square near the pool and the ruined fountain until dawn. Dane slept little, though he made Aratak lie down and rest. Although Dallith wanted to watch with him, he said soberly that she should lie down by Rianna and try to keep her warm. It was the one thing they could do for Rianna now. He thought of changing the bandages from the partially mud-stiffened ones they had made from Aratak's tunic, but Dallith vetoed that. She said gravely that the one thing they *could* be sure of was that any bacteria, or fungi, which might be harbored in Aratak's clothing certainly would *not* get into Rianna's wounds to infect them. "Cross-infection almost never goes from biological stock to biological stock," she said. "And Aratak isn't even warm-blooded. Disease organisms harmful to him are probably completely innocuous in a proto-simian bloodstream; whereas anything we might be carrying could transfer quite happily from us to Rianna."

While his companions slept, Dane sat with his back to the ruined fountain, looking up at the strange world glowing high in the sky, seeming to obscure at least a quarter of it. Strange, strange, to think that three months ago he had been peacefully sailing in *Seadrift*, alone and content to be so; in fact, if you'd asked him he would have had to say he was not involved with another human being on Earth. Well, he wasn't on Earth, now, but he was certainly involved, with not one woman but two depending on him for care and support. And for the first time in his life he had a deeply loved friend of his own sex, and it wasn't a man but a proto-saurian ten feet tall!

He watched the red world sink when the sky was already flushing with dawn, and thought to himself that on Earth the moon wouldn't be more than a few days off full. And the

month was shorter here. But could they last even three or four
days? They had food enough, at a pinch—after the last hasty
visit, a few days ago, to a neutral zone—to last for the rest of
the Hunt; he'd gone without food for five or six days at a
time in the mountains on Earth, once or twice. They had
plenty of drinking water. Could they somehow manage to
hide in the ruins until Rianna was able to walk?

Could they, hell! Whether they could or not, they'd have
to.

So when dawn broke, he let the women sleep until the sun
was high—since all seemed quiet—then had Aratak carry
Rianna inside one of the larger buildings, with Dallith to look
after her. Toward sunset, when the chance of an attack was
maximum, maybe Dallith could get up on the roof and keep a
lookout, picking off any attackers with her sling. Meanwhile
he and Aratak would patrol by turns.

The building where they laid Rianna was huge enough to
have been an amphitheater, with enormous rows of columns
all built of an odd sun-dried reddish brick, and the remnants
of stone couches and platforms scattered at odd intervals.
They all had curious disk-shaped hollows in the stone, and
Dane found himself wondering what unimaginably strange
form had made them. Rianna might know, but she was in no
shape to be asked. That inevitably brought his mind back to
speculation about the Hunters; and that led nowhere, although
by now he'd had a damned severe object lesson: a Hunter
might turn up looking like *anything*.

If in doubt, it's probably a Hunter, so kill him. That would
have to be their motto if they wanted to survive, and damn
the ethics of maybe killing innocent Prey.

He slept during the morning for an hour or so, since Dallith
reported that the city was quiet, with no alien feel of anything
near. He hardly allowed himself to think that maybe they
were safe here, maybe this was a taboo place to the Hunters,

an unmarked safety spot in this odd game which might be Tag.

Later he went out to take a cautious look from the walls. If Hunters were approaching the city, he might be able to see them coming. He left the women with Aratak and cautiously skirted the square of the fountain, threading a long wide street between ruined, and partially fallen-in, buildings.

The strangest thing to him was how *little* strangeness there seemed in the city. It seemed no more alien, no more re-moved from him, than the time he'd walked through Stone-henge; or the night he'd spent in the Valley of the Kings before they flooded it for the great dam. Those were removed from him in time; this city only in space. But they were unmistakably houses, and what did it matter what kind of beings had built them? Proto-simian, proto-feline, proto-saurian, or whatever strange stock, they were people who had lived and suffered and rejoiced and then died, and not only human nature but what Aratak called Universal Sapience never changed—

He realized suddenly that without conscious thought he had his hand on his sword. What sound, outside the threshold of ordinary consciousness, had roused his alertness? Yes; now he heard it again. It was soft, like a cat rustling in the stones.

Something dark flashed across the outer edges of his vision and rushed him from behind; but Dane had the samurai sword ready. He whirled, slashed, and only then did he see the collapsing, convulsing body of a Mekhar, which fell, slashed half through, and lay still.

Dane looked at it with a certain amount of regret as he sheathed his sword. *Not a Hunter, then. They don't kill that easy.*

But evidently something was after the Mekhar, and if it was coming after him, it probably wouldn't mind a bit chang-ing direction and killing Dane instead. Or maybe they were hunting Dane and scared the Mekhar out of hiding.

Or maybe, even, the poor devil thought this was a good place to hide and, hearing Dane, thought he was a Hunter.

But if there are Hunters here, stalking either him or us, we'd better find a good safe place to make a stand. That building where I left the women isn't safe.

He turned to retrace his steps, and then, half expected, heard Dallith's shrill scream.

He broke into a run, pounding through the brick-paved street, jogging unevenly on its broken stones. His sword was out again; he burst out of the end of the street into the fountain square, and saw her; and, at the far edge of the fountain, where the running water still trickled from the broken lip, a man, dressed like himself in brick-red tunic, swayed and pitched to the ground, his face covered in blood. But Dane's first concern was for her.

She was standing with the sling hanging idle at her side, a look of utter horror on her face; but when she saw Dane she cried out in relief and threw herself, weeping, on his shoulder.

"It wasn't your body . . . oh, Dane, Dane, I was afraid I'd killed you too. . . ." He could hardly make out her words through her wild and uncontrollable sobbing.

"Tell me, darling," he ruged, holding her close. Then he let her go and whirled around, sword in hand again, thrusting her violently away at a sudden sound; but it was only Aratak coming warily into the square, his club raised, and Rianna, limping at his side, leaning on the spear they had taken from the spider-man Hunter.

He turned his attention to Dallith, holding her against him, dismayed.

If she's beginning to break up, he thought, *we're probably all as good as dead. She hasn't cried, but now—*

Her hysterical weeping finally began to calm a little and her sobs became coherent words. "I came here for water—to bathe Rianna's wound. She wanted to come with me but I said if there was any danger I had my sling and I could cope with it better than she could. I came out into the square here by the fountain, and I looked up, and I saw *you*, Dane. Only a minute, of course, and I knew it *wasn't* you, that it was—it was just that *thing* that killed Cliff-Climber. And that it meant to do the same thing to me. Only—only I wasn't afraid. *I felt the same way he did!* Do you understand? He stood there, trying to lure me away and kill me, and I was working out how I was going to trap him! Oh, I felt so clever—and so cruel!'' She shuddered with the memory. ''I waved and smiled, just as if I really thought it was you, and all the time I was turning so that I could load my sling without his seeing. And I gestured for him to come closer, and waited while he crossed the square, and I smiled at him sweetly—and then when he got just where I wanted him, when I had an absolutely clear shot, I let him have it right between the eyes!'' Her expression of horror deepened. ''He saw the sling, of course, at the last minute when it was too late. And that was the worst part. *I wanted him to see it!* I wanted him to know that I'd outdone him in craftiness, that I was cleverer than he was, more stealthy—that I'd won—I was *proud* of it!''

She strained herself to Dane and cried harder than ever. ''Oh, Dane, I don't *like* these people; I don't ever want to be part of anything like that again, to think like that or feel like that. It isn't just that they want to kill me. I can stand that. The Mekhars were fierce, they were savage, but it was—oh, how can I say it—it was clean compared to this! Cliff-Climber—I really got to like him, at the end; he fought everything so fairly and honestly. He would never, ever have done anything like that—he'd have called it cowardly and dishonorable—'' Once again, sobbing drowned out her words.

Through the sound of her sobs, Dane heard Aratak's voice.

''Dane,'' the big lizard-man said quietly, ''when you can, when she'll let you, come here for a minute. There's something over here that you should see—and that Dallith definitely should *not.''* And Dane heard, clearly, the sound of ripping cloth.

Dallith's sobs had lessened, and it was plain that she had heard what Aratak had said. Her own voice was low and stifled. "After the—the thing died, it all went away," she said. "I didn't feel like that anymore. That was when I screamed. Because I was afraid that some—some bodiless *thing* had got into *your* body, taken over *your* mind, and when I'd killed it, I'd killed *you*—I'd have died if that had happened." And Dane knew that she was speaking the literal truth.

"Here, I'll look after her, Dane," Rianna said gently, and unclasped Dallith's arms from his neck. Dallith, coming to herself a little, said, "I'm all right, Rianna; I ought to be looking after *you*—" but she let Rianna hold her. Dane left them and went to where Aratak was standing, leaning on his club and looking down at the dead body of the Hunter.

The thing had had the form of a man. Dane's own form. But now, looking down at what lay on the paving-stones, under the tunic which Aratak had ripped down, Dane, in one moment of astonishment and comprehension, saw the secret of the Hunters.

The thing which lay on the pavement was vaguely globular; only swiftly shrinking buds, like tentacles, showed where it had had arms, and legs, which were no longer even remotely human. The head was round, encased in a rounded skull, cracked open by Dallith's sling stone, and the horror was that hair, and Dane's features, still clung like a thin skin over the front of the gray spilling brain. As he watched they flattened and smoothed and there was only the round shattered skull with strange flat black eyeholes deadly staring at the sky. Attached by a thinning stalk to the head and shattered skull was a pulsing, slowing glob of almost transparent flesh, enclosing great blood vessels and oddly colored organs just visible through the membrane that surrounded the thing.

Dane whistled slowly. Aratak had apparently ripped off the tunic to observe the process as the dead Hunter reverted to what must have been its original form.

So they didn't use hypnotism. They didn't come back to life after they were killed, and they didn't reanimate the bodies of their fallen enemies. With that kind of organs they'd be hard to kill, but once they were really killed they were dead. But if you didn't hit a vital spot—the brain, the great pulsing internal system which must be the creature's heart and lungs—if you only sliced the budding organs which had differentiated out of the transparent flesh, then the *thing* could simply reconstitute its original form.

He should have known. The thing ran away with a severed arm and again with a torn throat. The spider-thing could handle cut off legs but when Dallith got his head he was dead, and only the arrival of reinforcements had kept them from seeing his body change back like this.

So they'd badly wounded one Hunter, and now they'd killed *at least* two. And knowing the creatures' vital spots meant they had a fair chance of killing more of them.

And yet—*the Hunter is never seen except by the Quarry he kills*. No rumors of this had come back then, that the Hunters were shape-changers. Perhaps the only survivors of most Hunts were those who never encountered true Hunters, but hid, or killed off other Prey?

And were the Hunters going to let them live to take the story back?

Oh, God. Suppose they had a group consciousness like the Servers? They'd programmed the Servers; maybe they had no sense of individuality. What one knew, maybe all knew, and, in that case, if one of them found out that they now knew the real shape—*We're going to be prime targets for every Hunter on the Red Moon,* he thought.

He said something of this to Aratak, but the great lizard only said, "Why borrow trouble? We don't *know* they have group consciousness. And if they did, how could they have such a fierce, individual sense of triumph in the Hunt? Remember what Dallith told you.''

That was true, yet Dane wasn't convinced. Wasps and bees could sting individually, even though there was ample evidence their consciousness was a group one.

But wasps and bees weren't sapient. Aratak seemed to think sapience depended on a sense of individuality, and who was to say he was wrong? And the Hunters were certainly sapient. *Aratak's right. Why borrow trouble? We have plenty to be going on with.*

"Rianna, can you walk? We've got to get out of the city before they all hit us at once. If they know we're here—and I'm sure they do, otherwise how could they take Dane's form?—it's going to be nothing but a trap.''

She said, "I can do anything I have to do.'' Her face was pale, but she looked resolute.

There was little to carry, except their weapons and a small residue of food, Aratak said, "We should reach a neutral zone tonight, and replenish our supplies.''

Dane said, "Well, we'll see.'' He tied his cloak over his shoulders. "I don't really trust the Servers—and they *do* have group consciousness, so anything one Server knows the whole gang knows. And who knows? Maybe they tell the Hunters where the game's moving.''

"Would that fit their concept of honor?'' Rianna asked.

"How the hell do I know?'' Dane yelled, startling her into a shocked silence. "Let's get moving.''

In silence they moved toward the gates. Dane said curtly, "Dallith, keep a lookout. You're the psychic. Tell us if any of those *things* are coming.''

She whirled toward him, her face drawn and rebellious. "No!'' she said harshly. "I won't, I can't. I can't bear it! I can't bear *touching* those—those things!''

Dane felt her anguish, but he dared not allow himself to

feel pity for the girl or he would come apart. He strode angrily toward her and looked down, his face hard as rock.

"You want to live, don't you?"

Her voice was a dreary monotone. "Not particularly. But I want *you* to—all of you. All right, Dane; I'll do what I can. But if I get too close to them, if I become *part* of them, I might lead you—not away from them, but *into* them."

Dane's face twisted spasmodically. He had never thought of that—that she might pick up not only the fear of the Hunted, but the craft of the Hunter. He touched her shoulder gently. "Do what's best," he said. "But try to give us a few seconds' warning before we're attacked." He turned away without touching her again. He didn't dare. "Let's go," he said, and strode away in the general direction of the city gates.

They had to cross the fountain square yet again, and Dane's skin prickled. He knew, he *knew* someone was watching them—

The attack, when it came, was sudden and so disorganized that to the day of his death Dane never could remember anything except dark forms—three or four of them—suddenly all around them, Dallith screaming wildly, Rianna stumbling backward, bracing herself on her spear and whipping out her knife with her good arm, Aratak's huge club crunching down. Dane was slashing with his sword, aiming at the belly of a great thing which could have been the Hound of the Baskervilles. It howled and spouted blood and fell; Dallith snatched up Rianna's fallen spear and thrust something through the chest; he saw Rianna flee into the darkness of a building. At one point during the fight Dane was lying on the ground and slashing up at something which blotted out the light.

Then there were dead dissolving forms all over the ground, cut to bits, and the Hunters were gone.

And so was Rianna.

Chapter Fifteen

They searched for her all through the ruined city, until darkness fell; disregarding caution and crying her name aloud, shouting for her, searching the nearest of the buildings and finding only blind passages and cul-de-sacs, with no sign of Rianna. Sunset fell; Dane remembered remotely that they had intended to be in a neutral zone by now, but it didn't seem to matter. They ate the last of their food as they searched, and rested for a few hours before moonrise, but Dane could not sleep, and his thoughts were bitter.

He had hoped to bring his group all through alive. *I've lost Cliff-Climber and now Rianna.* Dallith lay close to him, holding him in her arms; she was crying, too, and Dane knew that she shared his own agonized grief and sense of loss as if it were her own. He clung to the knowledge that they had not found her body, or so much as a drop of blood. *But where can she go, wounded, alone, without food or water, for all we know dying? Maybe dying alone, while we lie here waiting,* he thought. Finally, since he could not rest, as soon as Dallith and Aratak had rested a little, he got up and made them search the ruins by moonlight.

This would be a fine time for them to hit us. Who cares?

As the sun came up, bathing the ruins with clear light, Aratak finally called a halt. "Dane, my dear, my very dear friend," he said gently, "we cannot search every old building in this city. If she could have heard us, she would have answered. If she could move, she would have come back to us. Dallith says she does not feel Rianna's presence anywhere. I fear, my dear friend, we must bow to the inevitable. Rianna is dead, and the dead are beyond our pity or our help. We must save our strength now for ourselves."

"I can't give up like that," Dane said, despairing. "We should all live, or all die, together!"

Dallith was drowned in tears. Aratak came and embraced them both, a giant arm around each of their shoulders, as if they were little children clinging to an adult. He said in his deepest voice, "Believe me, I share your grief. But would Rianna want you to die?"

"No," Dallith said, wiping her face on a corner of her cloak. "Rianna would tell me to stay alive and look after both of you. I'm sorry, Aratak. We'll go."

Dane grimly summoned his strength. Rianna was gone—maybe. But Dallith was alive and she still needed his protection. "Let's not go back to the fountain square," he said. "Let's get through the ruined wall somewhere else."

"It will mean climbing down that long cliff—" Aratak demurred.

"So much the better," Dane said. "It's too steep for anything to come on us unawares. If they come at us from below, we can hold the slope. If they come at us from above, we can push them down."

But there was no need for either attack or defense. The sun shone brilliantly over the broken walls and abandoned buildings and on the slope below the city, but no living forms moved except their own.

We must have killed four of them last night. I wonder how many Prey ever bag six Hunters at a clip? Dane thought.

It's no price for Rianna. But it's better than nothing.

At the last Hunt there were forty-seven Hunters, and eighty or ninety Prey. And nineteen Hunters killed, and one surviving Prey.

We're not doing so badly. But then, they said they had a hard time getting dangerous ones. I guess they got their money's worth on us.

It occurred to Dane that possibly, in a day of Universal Sapience and the like, a barbarian from a world with a warlike history had a better chance. The Hunters wanted a fair fight, maybe, and not just mass slaughter. But a race which could take literally any form— Yes, they would have trouble finding Prey fierce enough to give them a good game. . . . Maybe a few hundred years ago there were more fighters in the Galaxy. Now there seemed to be the Mekhars, the spidermen, and not much else that was tough enough to fight. Without his help, Dallith and Rianna would probably have been killed off first thing. Dane had organized their defense. Hell—without his help maybe the others would all have gone peacefully enough to the Gorbahl slave mart—and Dallith would have peacefully died.

Maybe that would have been better. For all of us.

But what's done is done.

At the foot of the long hill, where the boulders lay strewn like vast tumbled giants' heads, Dane gave the signal for extra caution; this was all too good a place for an attack. He glanced quickly over his shoulder, taking a long last look at the city. Rianna had wanted to explore it; now she would lie there forever.

At the edge of his vision a solitary figure caught his eye; small, slight, sturdy, crowned with a cloud of curling red hair. Dane's grief and rage exploded in wild fury and he ran forward, sword whipped out, ready to run the Hunter through, the foul thing that had taken Rianna's shape as one of them had taken his own before Dallith. He ran, swinging his sword, until Dallith's shriek caught him.

"Dane! No, no, no, it's Rianna, it's Rianna, it's *really* Rianna—"

Momentum carried Dane on so that he could only turn aside, at the last moment, gasping. He lowered the sword and spun around, looking at Rianna in suspicious, disbelieving amazement.

"It's really me," Rianna said hoarsely. "Don't run me through, Dane."

Then he believed her. Never yet had he heard any Hunter utter any sound except the characteristic wailing scream when wounded. Dallith ran to clasp the other girl in her arms.

"I thought we'd lost you for good," she said shakily, and Rianna said, "I thought so too. I was sure you'd have gone away by midnight; I only hoped to find you at one of the neutral zones—"

"What happened? What happened?" Dane caught her close, in surprise and relief. *Too good to be true, too good . . . but don't question it, accept it, this fantastic gift of their luck.* It was really Rianna, returned to them beyond hope.

"I'll tell you, but let's move along," she said soberly. "I think perhaps there aren't many Hunters around. There's something very funny about this place—"

They clustered together, moving across the rock-strewn plain and beyond the cleft where they had fought the spider-man, Dallith keeping a defensive lookout to the rear; but none of them wanted to let Rianna out of reach.

"I ran into the building," she said. "I heard one of them behind me, I thought. I tried to turn around and make a stand, but I couldn't see anything; I'd come beyond daylight. I wandered in the dark, trying to find my way out, getting more and more lost in the darkness, and then they came."

"*They* came? Who are *they?*"

"I don't know. I never saw them clearly," she said, and she looked and sounded puzzled. "They couldn't have been Hunters. In the first place—I told you I've been taught non-verbal communication techniques for peoples without transla-tor disks—they made it clear to me that they meant me no harm. They gave me food—it wasn't good, some kind of fungus, but they evidently knew I could eat it without being harmed. And they rebandaged my wounds, cleaned them, set my elbow; it wasn't broken, just dislocated. Look." She showed them her arm, fixed in a careful sling of some dark-red fiber, quite unlike the terra-cotta tunic material. "But even at the best it was semidark—there are miles and miles of caves and tunnels under the city. There aren't many of them . . . the people, I mean; they must be the old inhabitants of the city. But I suspect that's why there are as many survivors of the Hunt as there are; evidently helping the Hunted is nothing new to them."

She was silent, puzzling it out. Finally she said, "In the morning they led me down, through the caves, and showed me an entrance—an exit, I should say—at the foot of the cliff below the city. But I never got a look at them."

They journeyed in silence for some time, each of them thinking over this new factor in the Hunt. If there were only some way to find out what they could do . . . but probably the Hunters came near enough to exterminating them, ages ago. . . .

Aratak said quietly, "On my own planet's satellite—our world's twin, as this one is the Hunters' World—we had a like civilization, and they came near to wiping us out. But in the end they learned enough of our philosophy to realize that one hand cannot clap alone; and now they are our brothers.

This tells me again what might have become of our world without that—"

They left the rock-strewn plain and began to traverse again the hilly land, cut through by streams and underbrush. Dane figured, roughly, that the nearest neutral zone lay about six miles away, now. If they weren't delayed by fighting they could reach it before sunset. Since the Hunters liked to attack at sunset it was very likely they'd use it as a salt lick— waiting here for the Prey to come for rest or refreshment—but that was a chance they had to take. Maybe they could stand them off until sunset again. When, when, *when* was that damned Eclipse? Dane tried to reckon up how many days they had come, but he found he had untraceably lost track of time. He kept trying to add up days and nights and coming up with different sums. *Let's see, was that the night we slept in the neutral zone? Did this happen before or after we lost Cliff-Climber? Was that the seventh or the ninth day we fought the spider-man?*

It's getting toward afternoon and the Hunters' World isn't in the sky yet. That means it's near full, and when it's full, the Eclipse comes; it's near, but God, how near? The Eclipse could be tomorrow night or even tonight—if it is, we might, we just might make it. . . .

Is it tonight? And again he began the obsessive counting up. *The first night when we slept here and the Hunt began at dawn and Dallith and I were together, and we spent one or was it two nights in the city. . . . The night we forded the stream . . .*

No use. His brain, half dazed by fatigue and stress and emotion, completely refused to focus on time. *The Hunt was all there was and he could not tie it to time at all.*

The last mile's always the hardest. Aboard the *Seadrift* the worst stage of the voyage had always been when he was actually within sight of land.

Dallith touched his arm. She said in an undertone, "Hunters. Along that rise and beyond—in the underbrush."

Damn, Dane thought. *I meant to go that way.* He nodded, tight-lipped, and said, "Right. Don't stay in contact any more than you have to," and beckoned to Aratak to change his course. It would mean a long detour, but they could still make the neutral zone by nightfall. *Better yet, just after. I'd hate to have to fight our way in.*

After a time Dallith nodded in agreement and Dane relaxed a little, knowing they were at least temporarily out of range.

God, when is that damned Eclipse?

Rianna was walking better. Evidently food and rest, and the tending of her wounds, had done her a lot of good. *I only wish Dallith looked as good, poor kid!* Rianna's arm was still in the bandage, but it wasn't her knife-arm.

The neutral zone shouldn't be more than a few miles, across that ridge—

"Hunters," Dallith said in a shaky whisper. "It's us they're hunting. Oh, Dane, Dane, they have a *picture* of us . . . I *saw* it—"

"Easy. Easy." He put his free arm around her. "Get out as fast as you can. Here. Hang onto me if you want to. Here, down this way. . . ."

Rianna said, low-voiced, "I think they're *herding* us, Dane. Trying to trap us down in the wedge of the hills here. Look—" She drew a quick diagram with the spear-point. "Hills to the right. Hills to the left. The neutral zone down here, off sunward, but they're driving us down away from it."

Dane considered that for a minute. By now the Hunters must surely know that they were traveling in a pack and sooner or later the Hunters were sure to gang up and attack them that way. "We'll avoid them while we can," he said, "but if we have to make a stand, better to do it before sunset than after midnight. I'm not eager to fight those critters in the dark—not even by moonlight.''

"The Divine Egg has told us; it is well to see one's enemy by daylight,'' Aratak said.

Dane said sourly, "I'll bet you'll quote the Divine Egg on your deathbed.''

"If I am fortunate enough to have one, what better place?'' Aratak retorted. And that was so incontrovertibly true that Dane only said, "Let's start looking for a place to make a stand.''

If the Hunters were herding them, they flushed out one or two other of the Prey; once Dane saw a fleeing form far away, another indescribably strange one pursuing it; a distant bellow of triumph or rage, a clash of swords as they turned and faced one another. Something died, and lay motionless, and since the survivor did not flee but quietly melted into the underbrush again, Dane surmised that another Hunter had his catch for the day.

"Dallith. Can you tell if they're still following us?''

She nodded wordlessly. He thought, *If they hit us, she's exhausted,* and finally made a decision.

They were finally coming out of the hills laden with underbrush that they had traveled all afternoon, and into the bottom of the valley. To the left lay a deep stream, or perhaps a shallow river; over it hung a dark cliff shadowed with caves.

"We don't want to get trapped between the cliff and the stream,'' Dane said. "Let's ford the stream before it gets any deeper, and make for the underbrush. The neutral zone is that way. If we can hold them off till dark—''

Rianna held him back, and pointed. On the far side of the stream stood a tall figure. Dane's instant reaction was, "Is that a bear, or a Russian, or what?'' Rianna, literal as always, said, "It's a Hunter. In proto-ursine shape—he probably killed the proto-ursine we saw on the ship.''

Dane had his sword out. Dallith said, uneasily, "Why

doesn't he attack?'' She had her sling out, but the Hunter was out of range. "He just doesn't want us to cross the stream—"

Dane said grimly, "Maybe he's already picked his own choice of fighting grounds. Or maybe he's waiting for reinforcements.'' He thought, *if it's as near the end as I think, there may be no other Prey left alive—and they're free to concentrate on us. One survivor last time, one survivor last time,* pounded in his head. *Prime targets, that's us. Good sport.*

Dane looked around. To the left the stream flowed; at their back the cliff was sheltered by an overhang, and to the right there was a flat place, hard and rock-strewn; Dane's mind, trained to crisis, thought, *Fighting room.*

"We'll wait here,'' he said briefly. "We're all tired from that forced march. If they keep driving us, we're playing right into their hands—tire us out, then pick us off. If we stand here until his reinforcements arrive, we get some rest.''

Rianna demurred. "I don't like it. We're boxed in.''

"We could be boxed in tighter,'' Dane said, "if we let him herd us into his own favorite fighting grounds.'' He didn't like the way the Hunter was regarding them; his skin prickled. *Is he measuring me for a spot on his wall? Does he have a grudge? Is he, maybe, the one I fought before and drove off, in pseudo-Mekhar shape, twice?* He did not need Dallith's half unconscious nod of agreement to know he had guessed right, and that this must be the leader, if there was a leader, to the Hunt.

At least the wait here was letting them get their breath back. Dane felt that he could do with a good dinner, but instead he knelt by the stream cupping up water, drinking. His skin prickled as if he were expecting a blow, or an arrow, but none came, and he thought, *Maybe they don't use bow and arrows. Maybe they like to feel the blade go in.* The water tasted cool and surprisingly good.

Tonight, if I get to the neutral zone, I'm going to ask old Server for that steak dinner, and see what he says.

He repeated this to Rianna, and she smiled faintly. "I was thinking about that myself. That victory feast, if we get that far, is going to taste awfully damned good."

Dallith was twisting her hands nervously. "Why don't they attack? He wants to attack, he wants—"

Aratak laid his huge paw on her shoulder. "Calm, my dear one, calm. Every moment they do not attack is a moment we have to regather our strength. I beg you to rest yourself as much as possible."

"Think I'll do the same," Rianna said in an undertone. "My leg could use it." She sat down, carefully keeping the spear at hand.

Dane looked at her bandaged leg, but it seemed not too swollen and she had no signs of fever. *It will be all over soon and we can rest. Wonder if they intend to polish us off for a final tidbit before the Eclipse?*

We probably can't stand them off. It's hope that hurts.

He rested, sword in hand, and alert but his body relaxed, between Dallith and Rianna. *Whatever happens to us now, I've loved them both.* His mind persisted in grinning behind his back at that. *Just like a proto-simian to be thinking about that now.* Once again his mind had the acid-etched, fatigue-sharpened, awareness of reality of the first morning of the Hunt. He thought, *What better time?*

I thought all my life I was looking for adventure, and now at the edge of death I've found out what I was really looking for. I was looking for reality—the two realities that are never found in twentieth-century civilization with its emphasis on sex, not love, and cruelty, not death.

And here I've found them—maybe too late, but I've found the two things which are the only things worth coming to terms with: love and death. Once you've come to terms with those, you know what life is. Everything else is just the trimmings.

Love—Rianna and Dallith by his side. And Aratak.

And Death—that Hunter across the hill, and all his little brothers in every shape and form. For an instant, half in a dream, he radiated a mad love toward the Hunter as well, the Hunter who had taught him about Death as Rianna and Dallith had taught him about Love. . . . He knew he was fey, and tried consciously to grasp reality, the physical situation. The cliff. The fighting ground. The rocks. The hilt of the sword in his hand. But some insane atom of his brain persisted in telling him that this *was* reality. *Each man kills the thing he loves.* . . .

Loves any man the thing he would not kill. . . .

Love thine enemies. . . .

Liebestod. . . .

Dallith suddenly flung her arms around him and kissed him. Her mouth was scalding hot and her face flushed, and he strained her tight in his arms, but he kept his voice low and calm, through the bursting excitement.

"Take it easy. It's going to be OK." But he kept wondering, *Is she fey too?*

Rianna's hand was hard on his. She was breathing deeply. "Dane—if anything happens—"

"No," he interrupted. "Don't say it! Don't say it! Say it afterward!"

And at that moment Dallith cried a wordless warning, and then the Hunters were on them.

There was no way to tell how many there were. They came in suddenly from all sides, bursting out from the underbrush so quickly that there was barely time to form their defensive line. Dallith dropped one and then another with her sling while she was running to take up her place, atop a small pile of stones that lay against the overhang. Aratak stepped toward the stream, his great club raised.

Dane came to his feet and even as his fingers found the sword hilt a Mekhar—*no! A Hunter in Mekhar form!*—came running at them through the rocks at their right, sword upraised; behind were three human shapes.

On impulse Dane waited until his enemy was almost upon him, then whipped his blade from the scabbard in a cut that brought it across his foeman's eyes. Before the cat-thing could recover he clapped his left hand to the hilt and, swinging the blade two-handed, brought it down in the "pear-splitting" stroke, cleaving the leonine head. It gouted blood and fell two ways. Freeing his blade, Dane stepped to meet the first of the human shapes—

And found himself staring into a face indisputably Japanese. A lean and hawk-nosed face, dark eyes alert and watchful, short whipcord body in the garb of a samurai of four centuries before. And his long curved blade was rising in the classic *Men* cut to the head, and Dane knew, in a flash, that this was the face of the man whose sword he bore.

For an instant the recognition froze him where he stood, and then the same face again, in perfect duplication, behind the other's shoulder, showed him that he faced no ghost, but a Hunter who, as a knight might wear the armor of a gallant, fallen foe, chose to wear the face of a man dead four centuries.

The pseudo-samurai's sword was raised above his head; as it fell Dane's old samurai blade—*the original?*—rose to meet it. The sides of the two blades brushed in passing, diverting the downward stroke so that it whistled harmlessly past Dane's elbow; then Dane's own blade snapped down sharply. For half a second he thought his stroke had missed, but then a thin red line appeared on the forehead where the razor-keen blade had bitten. Blood came pouring out, and the manlike form swayed and fell on its borrowed face.

Do they live that long? Dane wondered in a rush. *Or do they film the Hunts; do they somewhere have films four hundred years old showing how one brave, lost Earthman died?* Behind him he heard splahing sounds and Aratak's deep roaring bellow, but he was too hard-pressed to turn.

As his blade rose to meet the second ersatz samurai, he saw the flaws in the man's, the pseudo-man's, basic technique, the slight unsureness in stance and grip. *They're copying movements they've seen*, he thought, and only the simplest at that. With my training, I'm a better imitation samurai than they are.

The Hunter charged, blade brandished over his head, exactly as the other had. Dane sidestepped in a long lunge to the right, his sword dropping across his body in the classic *Doh* cut, the blade's razor-sharp tip shearing the other's body just below the ribs. Bright arterial blood spurted and hoarse breathing stopped with a choked gasp; the Hunter fell without a cry. *It would have taken a human hours to die from that cut, I must have hit whatever it uses for a heart.*

He felt a sudden, fierce exultation, an almost painful stab of hope. *They're vulnerable. God damn them, they're vulnerable after all, they're even easy to kill when you know how. But God! It's hard to learn how!*

Even as his blade snapped out to the end of the stroke he was already sizing up his fourth opponent and found himself, without surprise, looking into his own face. Whatever effect it might have had on him before, now it seemed only the natural thing, even obvious. *Maybe they thought while the samurai types polished me off, this one could get Rianna or Aratak. As the one that took Cliff-Climber off guard did.* But as this thought streamed through his head his body did not even pause in its flowing motion; a sharp snap of the wrists reversed the direction of his edge. The pseudo-Dane came in warily, his own blade at the center of the body approximating Dane's guard position; but the point was too low. Dane's blade lashed down in the *Priest's-robe* stroke, through the left shoulder and deep into the chest; and as the Hunter hit the ground, Dane turned on his heel and ran back toward the others. The Hunters he had killed were already regaining their original semblance, flesh flowing like water. *Does anyone ever live to tell about it?* he wondered. *Is that why they like to attack near dark?*

Aratak stood on the bank of the stream, spear and club both bloodied; there was blood on the slope and and already formless bodies were floating in the stream, showing where they had been at work. A few man-shaped and Mekhar-shaped bodies were in the water, weapons on guard, but for the moment they were keeping their distance. One of the dead bodies in the water was much bigger than the others; it was already dissolving, but Dane could see that it had been enormous and hairy. He wondered how they managed size.

On the opposite bank, dripping as if he had started to wade across and changed his mind, was a miniature copy of Aratak; only eight feet tall, but armed with club and ax almost as big as the real Aratak's and carrying a shield as well. Beside him, also dripping, stood the huge proto-ursine Dane had momentarily identified as the leader of the Hunt.

There were what looked like a dozen—perhaps more pseudo-men and perhaps as many more pseudo-Mekhars. Some of the cat-men, he noticed, had tails—and so did some of the humanoid types. Copies, he wondered, of slightly differing species? But men and Mekhars were still in the majority. There were a couple of things, he saw in a flash, that looked as if their ancestors had been wolves or raccoons, and a creature rather like a man-sized octopus, only it had ten limbs instead of eight and each brandished a different weapon. And at the back of the crowd of Hunters in all shapes, Dane saw a huge spider-man twirling its deadly spear. A chill touched him. That other spider-man had come so close to killing them all single-handed, and now they had all these to fight. But then he saw the spider-man fumble with his spear and drop it. The first imitation spider-man had been a natural, or maybe had practiced more, but even he had been slower than the real spider-man aboard the Mekhars' slave ship.

He and Aratak had killed everyone in the first wave and the

others had not yet crossed the stream. He spared an instant to look back at the girls. Bodies in the water showed where Dallith had been at work; Rianna stood leaning again on her spear, backed against the cliff. Two dissolving Hunter corpses were at her feet.

But no smell of blood. Their blood must evaporate as soon as it's shed, almost. . . . Dane stood, getting his breath, readying himself for the next attack. *Matter of time,* he thought, *but they've got to kill us. They can't let four survivors get back to spread rumors about their real shape—or lack of it.*

Not too far to sunset. Will even that stop them now? They're throwing everything at us.

He noticed that they had, as well as the pseudo-Aratak and the pseudo-Dane he'd killed, a false Dallith and an imitation Rianna. "Dallith" even bore a sling. Suddenly that frightened him, badly.

They must have been mimics, once, like some insects, hiding from—or trapping—their enemies by resembling them. Had he met one of those during the first wave of the battle, rather than the samurai, he might well have hesitated, unmanned, just long enough to be finished off. He tried to steel himself to the thought of slicing off "Dallith's" lovely head, or running his sword through "Rianna's" soft body—a body he'd held in his arms so often—but even while he reminded himself that they were just Hunters, his horror grew and he knew his nerve would break. *I'm no empath, I could never be sure it wasn't the real one—*

His agony and distress must have reached Dallith, and its cause; for an instant later he heard the whirring of her sling stone through the air; the false-Rianna crumpled, her face a mass of blood. The false-Dallith, maybe guessing what was happening, whirled her own sling, but the shot flew wide—so wide there was no way of knowing who she had aimed at, though Dane suspected it was himself. The real Dallith's answering stone took her in the temple, and Dane momentarily closed his eyes to avoid seeing her fall.

He opened them quickly, knowing that this would bring the others across the stream for the attack; and already they were splashing in the shallow water. One of the manlike ones (only it looked like a woman, with brick-red skin and long blue-black hair) came wriggling up the bank; Rianna's spear pierced the vital sac from the back and the thing gouted blood and lay still. One of the pseudo-Mekhars made it halfway up the bank before Aratak's club crunched down and crushed in his skull. Dane waited, sword raised, but no more of them climbed the bank. The huge proto-ursine called, with that wailing cry he had heard before, and they fell back and stood waiting, clustered in the center of the stream. Dallith's sling cracked an unprotected skull open, and they fell back a little.

Dane threw a puzzled glance at the great leader. *He's holding them back. Why? Surely he knows we couldn't hold the bank if they rushed it all at once—*

An arrow arched over the stream and sank quivering in the ground, followed by another; both flew wide. Dane picked out the archer, a tall gray-skinned creature with a prehensile tail that fitted the arrows while he held the bow two-handed. *That could be a mean one, but I guess they don't practice much with projectile weapons, or those pseudo-limbs can't handle them somehow. Maybe they lose interest when they don't get the kick of feeling the blade go in—*

One of Dallith's stones made a crater in the mud on the far bank; another splashed between the archer and another man. *What's wrong? She usually shoots better than that. . . .* Dane turned swiftly to look. Dallith's face was pasty white, and her eyes were blinded with tears; her lip bled where she had bitten it through. Her hands were shaking.

Oh, God. I knew it would come. She's breaking down, killing that thing with her own face must have been the last straw. . . . He started to run toward her, to comfort her, if only by taking a stand near her, when suddenly, along the stream to his left, he saw a flicker in the underbrush. *So that's what they're waiting for. . . .*

Swiftly he ran back toward Rianna. "Fall back by the Cliff," he ordered. "Aratak, hold the bank if you can, but don't wait too long; get back to the cliff if you have to. Dallith may not be able to help much—" He raised his voice, shouting with a cheerfulness he was far from feeling: "Dallith! Save your stones for the spider-man! We'll handle the rest of them!"

And at that moment the Hunt leader gave another of those strange wails. Dane saw them surge forward, and ran to meet the horde of Hunters who boiled toward them from the path along the stream.

If I'd stood there gawking another minute, they'd have cut us off from the cliff—and from Dallith.

Oh, God, Dallith. Poor, tortured darling. . . .

Two pseudo-Mekhars had bounded ahead of him; he dodged as one cut at him, jumped away from the other, his sword dipping for the *Doh* stroke and slicing through the Hunter's body. The falling corpse blocked the second cat-thing's stroke just long enough; Dane split its head open and ran on.

Even though he knew now, with absolute certainty, that they were all going to die, that nothing could save them now, Dane felt a wave of elation sweep through him, and a curious light-headed giddiness. *Is this the battle-joy they used to write about—Viking sagas?*

Then he saw the second spider-man. Pseudo-humans with long spears surrounded him and his own long lance flickered and twirled in the slanting sunlight. He loomed ominously huge among his man-shaped kindred.

As they burst out of the narrow way, Dane flung himself upon them, seeing no other course but headlong attack. There were still splashings from the stream and the crunch, crunch, crunch of Aratak's great club. He had no idea how long

Aratak could hold the stream; he knew he should retreat to the cliff so that he and Rianna could cover one another, but first he must kill some more. God, it was satisfying to attack instead of run; he was going to kill every one who came within reach of his sword.

Let the Hunters beware! Before they hung *his* head on the wall, he'd send as many as he could to tell their God damned illustrious ancestors that they could raise the price for humans these days, the Prey was getting rougher. And when he and the old samurai were hanging side by side on some Hunter's wall, he could tell his fellow Earthman that he'd kept his sword well-fed while it was in his keeping!

The two leading spearmen lunged at his chest; with a snap of his shoulders he drove one lance aside so that it fouled the other; his sword came flashing down on his foreman's spine, and as the blood spurted from the first one's severed neck Dane reached over the falling body to kill the other spearman with a slash to the head. And then the spider-thing was upon him, its shield pressed against his sword, and he saw the deadly lance whirling down.

Time seemed to have disappeared, to have stretched itself out into endless consecutive fragments. He threw himself slowly to the ground—but in his insane mood he seemed to move in slow motion—somehow managing to keep the razor-edge of his blade away from himself as he rolled. The spinning lance missed him twice by bare inches, striking sparks from the rock. Somewhere along there he became aware of Hunters in human form, with long spears stabbing at him; he curled his knees up over his belly and was amazed to find that he could fend off the spears easily with the sword from this position, snapping his blade across his body. Then one spearman came too close and Dane smashed his kneecap with a karate kick; the spearman fell across two of his own kind's spears and in the confusion—the Hunter with the smashed knee was impaled on his friend's spear—Dane rolled to his feet. He slashed one through the throat, remembered just in time he couldn't kill him that way, and brought the blade down on his head. *Nine, by God, nine, or is it ten? Who's counting?*

He swatted one spear aside a fraction late and the cloth of his tunic ripped; pain slashed along his arm and the sting of it cleared his head—*God in Heaven! What was happening to the others? The spider man had gone right past him.* He raised his sword and yelled, and as the remaining spearmen braced themselves for his new attack he turned and ran like hell for the cliff.

Aratak was falling back from the stream, his club pounding down again and again on the shield which sheltered the octopus-thing, which crawled along the bank slashing at Aratak's ankles with its various weapons; up the now unde-fended bank came a wave of the Hunters, led by the great proto-ursine and the pseudo-Aratak, and the larger of the spider-things.

The other spider-man stood poised between Aratak and the cliff; the long lance spun menacingly as the great red eyes moved from Aratak to the girls and back again. Arrogance was stamped in every line of the spindly gray body, so different from the stooped and crouching stance of the real spider-man he'd seen. A sling stone whirred past his head; he did not even turn. *Aratak's going to be trapped between the spider-man and that octopus-critter!* Dane opened his mouth to shout a warning, but his voice would not carry.

Another stone struck the spider-man where the upper body joined the abdomen; the Hunter whirled with lightning speed and scuttled toward Dallith and Rianna.

Dane ran, although he knew he could never match that thing's speed. He saw Rianna brace her spear to meet the thing and saw more clearly than anything else, sharp-edged as if etched in acid, Dallith's white, tear-drenched face as stone after stone flew from her sling without a pause. Out of the corner of his eye he saw Aratak sink back into a sudden crouch, then hurl his great bulk in the air, over the weapons slashing at his feet, to come down *on top* of the octopoid. One great paw gripped the shield; shield and tentacle went flying through the air, torn from the Hunter's body; the club smashed down and the octopoid squashed into a formless mass. The lizard-man turned and ran toward the cliff.

Dallith straightened, flung her sling away, and stared with horror, her hand clapped over her face. The spider-man had reached the cliff now; Rianna lunged for him with the spear, but the Hunter's shield brushed it aside and at the same instant two of his arms snapped his spear into a straight thrust that passed over Rianna's lunging head and pierced Dallith's slender body between the breasts.

Dane screamed her name; his one thought now was to kill that thing and throw away his sword and hold her in his arms.

But Aratak was there before him, and before the spider-thing could draw his lance back from Dallith's crumpling body Aratak's great paw gripped two of his spindly arms and heaved the creature over on his side. The terrible club crashed once and both vital spots splattered blood for yards around; the powerful lizard-man heaved the dead Hunter up in his arms and hurled the great body into the oncoming pack.

Dane's mind was numb. *Dallith! It wasn't true! Dallith*—He screamed her name again, without conscious thought; a cat-thing came lunging at him with a sword and Dane killed him. It was automatic. He wasn't thinking. He was just a killing machine, screaming. Aratak and Rianna were fighting desperately over Dallith's fallen body, and a little part of him stirred and woke.

Her body is mine. Not theirs to eat, or stuff, or hang on a wall. Dead or alive, she's mine; they won't get her even if I have to kill every Hunter on this accursed moon. . . .

With a tiny fragment of his brain he knew he was completely mad, but his body, undistracted by thought, exploded into a deadly ballet of death. The nearest spearman went down with his chest shorn open; a Mekhar-type swordsman lost his head. He was half conscious of Aratak fighting at his side, ax and club alternating in a deadly rhythm. Long spears were smashed aside or shattered and their owners died; swordsmen died before they came into reach. Rianna crouched behind them against the wall, her lance thrusting from the level of Aratak's knees. The man-sized Hunters clustered around Dane, getting in one another's way; he cut down a couple of them. It was automatic by now. Over Aratak's head he saw that the disk of the sun had touched the edge of the horizon. *Who cared, now? Kill them all or die trying!*

A bearded man-shape ran toward Dane, a round metal shield raised before his body, a straight heavy sword whirling over his head. A fleeting memory of the way the spider-man had trapped his sword made Dane lunge to the left, drawing his blade away from the shield, pivoting while his own sword flashed in a great circle that sheared through the man's right shoulder and into his chest.

The next few instants were confused, impossible to sort out. Aratak somehow sent the bearlike Hunt leader flying through the air, his blade broken by a blow from the lizard-man's club; stooping, he began to search for another weapon through the globular, dissolving bodies of his dead; Dane and Aratak rushed him together and the false lizard-man, rushing up to join battle, struck Aratak on the knee with a replica of his own great club. He went down with a grunt, but his ax whirled out and, as the Hunter's shield went out to intercept it, Rianna's lance drove in under his rim and the pseudo-Aratak went down. For a moment Dane thought it was his friend who had fallen; real Aratak and false one lay together on the ground. The great proto-ursine had picked up a lance like Rianna's and came rushing on, but stumbled over one of his own men, the gray-skinned archer. All around him, the Hunters were falling back, toward the stream, and Dane, looking around through a mist of blood over his eyes, realized that the last scrap of the sun had vanished.

Sunset. The battle was over. . . .

The Hunters who still lived—there could hardly be a dozen of them left, Dane thought in a dreamlike despair—were splashing back through the water. The great bear-thing shouted, as if to rally them, raised his club, as if to urge a final attack; one or two of the Hunters paused, fingering their weapons, but the others kept on going and, after a minute, dejected, the giant proto-ursine turned away, brandishing his weapons in a final menace, and retreated.

Aratak and I must have killed more than half of them. I'll bet every Hunter on this planet was here—there were only *forty-seven in the whole Hunt last time.*

But the price was too high. Even if they'd exterminated the whole breed, it would have been too high. . . .

He turned and ran to where Dallith lay among the rocks. Behind him he saw what he thought for a moment was the pseudo-Aratak rising to his feet, but at that moment he didn't care. Then he knew it was the real one, and he didn't care about that either.

Dallith lay on her back across the heap of rocks where she had made her final stand, her arms flung out to both sides, her great dark eyes—eyes of a wounded fawn—staring up blindly into the darkening sky.

Love and death. Love and death.

He cradled her cold body in his arms; then slipped down and lay unmoving, half unconscious, his head resting against her lifeless breast.

Chapter Sixteen

The Hunters' World was high in the sky, round and full and glowing brick-red, apparently obscuring most of the sky. Again Dane had that sense of claustrophobia, of moving under a lowering brightness that could come crashing down on him. *(Who cared? Let the sky fall; Chicken Little was right all along. . . .)*

He hadn't wanted to leave Dallith's body. Neither Aratak nor Rianna could help him carry her, and he finally had realized that it wasn't just that they didn't *want* to, as he'd screamed at them. ("You want to leave her here, for some damn Hunter to stuff for some kind of obscene trophy!") Then he'd realized that they were both wounded, Rianna's leg slash broken open again, Aratak's leg so badly twisted that he had to lean heavily on his club. Dazed and apathetic, Dane went along with them toward the neutral zone. He heard Rianna say something about battle fatigue and knew with some small fragment of himself that she was right, heard Aratak say that the Eclipse couldn't be far away now (but whenever it came it would be too late). But he walked in the dazed, dreamlike knowledge of Dallith's death and nothing else mattered.

Her braid of hair is still inside my tunic, he thought. He fumbled at it in an agony of grief, and only then realized that he was bleeding from a wound on the forearm and another slight one on the scalp.

He walked in a dark dream until Rianna gave a slight moan and collapsed, her wounded leg crumpling under her; then, forcing himself to care, to pick her up again, he tore a strip from his own tunic and bandaged it up with robotlike efficiency. He let her lean on his shoulder; he would have picked her up and carried her if she hadn't protested. He himself would have collapsed right there and slept, but remotely and without the slightest awareness that it had anything to do with him, he realized that the girl needed food and rest in safety. It could not have been more than a half hour that they walked before reaching the lights of the neutral zone, but to Dane it was a great amorphous stretch of time longer than the battle before it, longer than the Hunt, an abyss cleaving his life in two. He still had his life. For what that was worth.

Inside the neutral zone he smelled food, but the smell somehow made his stomach turn over. Rianna brought him a plateful, and he said, "I'm not hungry, I couldn't eat," but when she put it into his hand he began automatically shoveling it into his mouth without tasting it. He finished it all and she brought him some more, and suddenly his head cleared. The dark nightmare was gone but at the same time it was more real. Dallith was dead, and he sat here eating the steak dinner he'd planned to ask for—In sudden horror he put down the remnants of the second plateful. There wasn't much left. He wanted to vomit. He said in a sort of dazed wonder, "How I can sit here eating—"

Rianna didn't say anything. She simply laid her small hard hand over his without a word, and he saw that her own eyes were streaming with tears. She hadn't sobbed, she didn't wipe them away, she simply went on eating and crying at the same time, and Dane's mind and emotions awoke, aching. He took her plate away and put his arm around her. He wiped her face with his tunic and said, "Darling, if you keep on stuffing yourself, you'll be sick."

What a pig I am, he thought. *She's wounded and she had to look after me*. He looked with amazement at the amount of food they had devoured. Of course, after a hell of a fight like that. *How many did I kill, anyhow? I guess I'll never know, but I doubt if the old Samurai would be ashamed of me. He must have put up a damn good fight himself, if they still remember him well enough to wear his face after three hundred years*.

Again he wiped Rianna's wet face, tenderly. Dallith was gone, and nothing in the world seemed worth living for, but Rianna was alive and she still needed him.

She said, beginning to sob at last, "I loved her too, Dane. But she couldn't have gone on living, with the memory of that. The Hunt had destroyed her, had been worse than death for her—"

Aratak came close to them. He said in his gentle rumble, "She feared to go on living when her whole being had absorbed part of the Hunters. Rianna was right, Dane; empaths of Spica Four *always* die, away from their world alone. She began to die when she left her world, but she stayed with you while she could, because you needed her so terribly and she knew it. . . ."

Dane bowed his head. He had thought Dallith had lived because he had taught her to want to live. Maybe, for a little while, she had shared his own desire to live, as she had shared so much with him in that little while. But he realized that what Aratak said was true. He had saved Dallith's life not for her own sake but for his; while he fed her will to live he was holding at bay his own fear of coming too close to her death.

Love and death, love and death—I thought I understood them. But perhaps no one ever knows everything about them. . . .

They were the only ones in the neutral zone; probably, he thought, the only Prey left alive at all. The Servers, moving silently about the area and not speaking, nevertheless seemed to convey to them a certain sense of awe.

We're still the Sacred *Prey,* he thought.

He and Rianna lay down at last to rest, deathly weary, wrapped in a single cloak; desire stirred and flickered briefly in his body, but in the very thought exhaustion took him, and his weary body and exhausted mind fell down a bottomless cliff of deathlike sleep.

When he awoke the dawn had come and the sun was rising, and for an instant, realizing that they had all long overslept the time of safety, he wondered why they had not been slaughtered in their sleep. And then, seeing the Servers ranged around him, and a scant half dozen Hunters standing inside the neutral zone, he understood. After such a fight as this they respected the sleep of the gallant fighter. Rianna awoke at the same instant and shrank against him at the sight of the Hunters. Aratak reached for his club, wincing as he tried to put his weight on his foot.

And at the same moment Dane realized that above the sun the great brick-colored, crimson-glowing Hunters' World hung in the sky, a round and untouched disk, and the sun was rapidly rising to meet it. . . .

The great proto-ursine Hunt leader strode toward him. Dane rose to his feet, reaching instinctively for his sword.

The Hunt leader gestured to him to leave his weapon, but Dane grasped it anyway. He himself was weaponless, although his sword was in the hands of one of the metal Servers and the tall, featureless robot rolled quickly toward Dane.

The proto-ursine spoke. Dane could not understand him; but the Server's flat, expressionless voice rolled out.

"Our leader has a personal score to settle with you. You have killed five of his hive-brethren, but so gallant a Prey, who has made this Hunt greater sport than in the last seven-hundred-and-eighteen cycles, deserves some special attention to his end. The hour of the Eclipse is upon us. If you are willing, since your two companions are wounded and they too have fought with a truly Sacred bravery, we offer them their lives; had you not slain his five brethren of the hive, he would offer yours as well and see to your rewarding. As it is, he asks that you grant him a final bout in single combat. If you are the survivor, all of you shall be released; if you die, your companions will be freed in your memory."

"We fight to death?" Dane asked.

"Unless the Hour of the Eclipse frees us first," said the Server.

Dane looked around at Rianna and Aratak. Without consulting them, he said, "I'll do it."

"Dane—" Rianna protested, and Aratak said, "Don't be a fool. They've got to kill us. They won't let us live and tell their secret—how easy they are to kill."

But strangely Dane still trusted to their word. Maybe because he had no choice. He said to Server, "Tell him I accept."

Maybe the communication was telepathic, for Server said nothing he could hear, but the leader took his vast shield and sword, and Dane drew his own. The leader's left side was turned to him, vast shaggy chest almost hidden with the shield; the deep bend of the legs kept the lower body covered as well. The sword was hidden behind the body, probably straight back.

It's a fencing stance in reverse, Dane thought; *he can strike and guard at the same time. I can't.*

But he'll have to move the shield in order to cut. Go for his shoulder. . . .

Watch it, Marsh, he warned himself. *Don't get overconfident. Every time you've faced a shield, you've had friends to help. This is single combat.*

The Hunter advanced by cautious sliding steps that kept his body turned and covered by the shield. It looked like the Hunter wasn't too confident either and wasn't going to oblige Dane by rushing to trap his sword, so Dane could use the sidestep that had won the other fight. Dane ran forward, leaping into the air for a cut to the head. The Hunter lunged to meet the attack, shield snapping up to catch the sword and press it back, and as Dane jumped back he saw the tip of the broad blade as it arched across his thigh. The hack that would have taken his leg off only scratched the skin. The shield clung to his blade as if glued there, hindering Dane's movements; the broadsword was whistling toward Dane's temple and he sidestepped quickly.

Dane's long lunge back and to the left took him under his enemy's cut, though the wind of it stirred his hair, and at last he could free his sword from the shield. He spun to cut at the other's shoulder, but the bear-man pivoted to face him, shield rising to catch the blow. Dane's sword was pressed back against his left shoulder and the Hunter's blade was coming down at his head.

Like lightning Dane let his left knee crumple under him, managing to get his blade over his head; he took the shock in his wrists as the other's blade struck, the cold steel of his own sword striking him lightly and snapping back. He slashed out at the giant's thick shaggy knees.

There's no way to get at his head or chest with that shield. A leg blow won't kill him, but will weaken him—the pseudo-Mekhar howled and ran away when I lopped off an arm. If he traps my sword again, I'm dead. He's damned good—too good. But he knows a leg blow won't kill him, so he might be careless—

They circled one another slowly and deliberately for a minute. Then Dane shouted and leaped forward, his blade rising up over his head, drawn back until it rested between his shoulder blades. The ursine's shield lifted; Dane threw himself to the left, his blade falling away to the right in a great circling slash that sheared through the leg at the knee, came up without pausing to block the broadsword blow that Dane had half expected.

But it never came. He whirled, blade lifted, but the Hunter had rolled to a sitting position, balancing himself with the uninjured leg, shield raised over him and sword-arm raised to strike.

Good God! Now all he has to do is guard his head and chest; it's a draw; I can't hurt him but he can't attack. All I have to do is stay out of his reach, until—

Rianna shouted and Dane, flicking a glance upward, realized that the shadow was sweeping over the land; the disk of the sun, seeming tiny, was already half gone behind the huge mass of the Hunters' World. Below his astonished glance the leader was crumpling, collapsing; the severed leg flowed into shapelessness; the sword fell from a paw which could no longer grasp it. As the light lessened and was darkened, a wind sprang up and the shield crumpled down on the Hunter's body, fast liquefying.

Of course, Dane thought. *That's the secret. They turn back to their own shape when they die—or in darkness. But by bright moonlight they can attack. But the Eclipse ends the Hunt.*

They all go back to globblies. . . .

Two servers rolled up, trundling a third between them, and, while Dane and Rianna watched in the dying light, they gently lifted, on their extensible arms, the globular and transparent form of the Hunter. They packed it tenderly into the metal shell, and closed down the lid, and at once the strange metal voice of a Server spoke from it.

"My most gallant foe. In these last moments before I return to the hive-knowledge of my resting-life I pledge to you that you shall go free, whatever the cost. If I live another thousand cycles I shall know no such Hunt. Now I must spend another half year in the dormant stage, with no individual knowledge of self, before I emerge again, but I pledge myself to fight only in your shape for a hundred cycles in your memory. . . ."

Oh, God. They spent half their time in those metal cans, as Servers. Not robots at all, no wonder the Servers tended and cherished the Sacred Prey . . . they represented the only individual life and awareness the Hunters knew. . . . Only during the Hunt were they alive as individuals, and at no other time were they, perhaps, truly sapient. Was a hive-consciousness sapience? Dane wondered.

"Again I salute you—in my last moments while I am self, I—we—"

The Hunt leader's voice vanished; from another of the metal Servers came, without interruption, the unbroken breath.

"We honor you. And yet you may have ended our Hunt for all time, if we release you, as honor demands, to tell our secret throughout the Galaxy."

"Not a bit of it," Dane said, sheathing his sword. "Remember the Mekhars kept running away to volunteer? Once it's openly known that you do exist, that it's not a meaningless slaughter but a duel, and that you reward the survivors richly—the tougher citizens of the Galaxy will be lining up on your doorstep; you can pick and choose your own Prey, instead of buying or stealing them! Do you wonder a lot of them have no will to live, facing only formless fear? But give them a chance—and you'll have so many volunteers that you'll have to put them on a waiting list!"

Server's flat voice somehow managed to convey joy. "Perhaps it will be so. In any case, Honorable and Sacred Survivors, let us now serve and refresh you. The next Prey await your victory banquet to give them courage and hope, and our brethren who have spent the last moon readying for the oncoming Hunt are even now boarding the ship to come here and make all ready."

The Servers couldn't do enough for them. They were conducted to baths and fed again lavishly, and clothed in fresh clothes and garlands of flowers. Rianna clung to Dane and it seemed like a dream to him.

"Riches," she murmured, "enough to start a scientific foundation—maybe to come back here and explore the old city and find out about the old race that saved my life—"

Aratak said quietly, "The Divine Egg has seen fit to preserve my life; he must have work for me somewhere in the Unity. But before I go and do it, I will journey to Spica Four and tell Dallith's people how she died—and Cliff-Climber's. I have no other use for wealth."

Dane stroked the scabbard of the samurai sword. Had the old Samurai been the only survivor ever to commit suppuku when he realized he must give up his sword to his victors? *I'd like to keep it, but probably I'll never use a sword seriously again.*

Rianna said, "Dane, you can go home!"

"What—and spend the rest of my life sounding like a flying saucer contactee?" he demanded, and drew her tightly into his arms.

First—Dallith's world, with Aratak, to tell her people how she died. And then—well, it was a big Galaxy, and he had a lot of the rest of his life to live, and this was going to be the biggest adventure of all.

He hugged Rianna exultantly to him, and laughed aloud.

Love and Death. For the rest of his life he would carry

Dallith in the innermost core of his heart as he carried her braid of hair next to his skin; but he had no longer any fear either of love or death.

He had mastered them both and come out alive, and he would keep learning about them until he mastered his own death someday.

Attention:

DAW COLLECTORS

Many readers of DAW Books have written requesting information on early titles and book numbers to assist in the collection of DAW editions since the first of our titles appeared in April 1972.

We have prepared a several-pages-long list of all DAW titles, giving their sequence numbers, original and current order numbers, and ISBN numbers. And of course the authors and book titles as well as reissues.

If you think that this list will be of help, you may have a copy by writing to the address below and enclosing one dollar to cover the handling and postage costs.

DAW BOOKS, INC. Dept. C
1633 Broadway
New York, N.Y. 10019

DAW

A GALAXY OF SCIENCE FICTION STARS!

DAW

Presenting C. J. CHERRYH

Two Hugos so far—and more sure to come!

The Morgaine Novels
GATE OF IVREL   (#UE1956—$2.50)
WELL OF SHIUAN   (#UE1986—$2.95)
FIRES OF AZEROTH   (#UE1925—$2.50)

The Faded Sun Novels
THE FADED SUN: KESRITH   (#UE1960—$3.50)
THE FADED SUN: SHON'JIR   (#UE1889—$2.95)
THE FADED SUN: KUTATH   (#UE1856—$2.75)

DOWNBELOW STATION   (#UE1987—$3.50)
MERCHANTER'S LUCK   (#UE1745—$2.95)
PORT ETERNITY   (#UE1769—$2.50)
WAVE WITHOUT A SHORE   (#UE1957—$2.95)
SUNFALL   (#UE1881—$2.50)
BROTHERS OF EARTH   (#UE1869—$2.95)
THE PRIDE OF CHANUR   (#UE1694—$2.95)
SERPENT'S REACH   (#UE1682—$2.50)
HUNTER OF WORLDS   (#UE1872—$2.95)
HESTIA   (#UE1680—$2.25)
VOYAGER IN NIGHT   (#UE1920—$2.95)
THE DREAMSTONE   (#UE2013—$2.95)
TREE OF SWORDS AND JEWELS   (#UE1850—$2.95)